FALL OF A SPARROW

S.J. Hamilton

Dancing with Dilemmas (DWD) Publications
Flat 1 Hillsborough
Hillesdon Road
Torquay, Devon TQ1 1QF
www.torquaysharon.wordpress.com

Copyright © 2013 by Sharon Jean Hamilton

The moral right of the author is hereby asserted in accordance with the Copyright, Designs and Patent Act 1988.

All characters and events in this publication, other than those clearly in the public domain, are fictitious and any resemblance to any persons living or dead is purely coincidental.

The story is set in the fictional village of Coombe Gilbert within the landscape of South Devon. Churston Manor and Churston Grove are real places as are the other locations outside of Coombe Gilbert mentioned in the novel.

All rights reserved. No part of this publication may be reproduced, stored in a retrieval system or transmitted by any means or form without prior permission of the publisher.

Cover design by Spiffing Covers.

Typeset in 11/14/16 Calibri by DWD Publications

Printed and bound by Short Run Printers, Newton Abbott.

For Deejay

One for sorrow, two for mirth
Three for a wedding, four for a birth
Five for silver, six for gold
Seven for a secret not to be told
Eight for heaven, nine for hell
And ten for the devil's own sel'

Traditional Country Proverb

ONE: SATURDAY

Impossible angles state their stark truth. Four minds hover between guilt and fear.

"We should call the police."

"No. Let's think this through."

"He's really dead, isn't he?"

"Could we make it look like an accident? Like he just fell down the stairs?"

"Never. Not the way he looks."

"We have to get to the wedding. We'll be late."

"What'll we do?"

"I'm so sorry. This wasn't meant to happen. I didn't..."

"Leave it to me. I'll work something out and let you know after the ceremony."

One by one they leave. One turns back.

***

"A wedding symbolises an extraordinary faith in the future," mused Karen Lawrence as she struggled with her hat, a whimsical concoction in blue purchased especially for the occasion. She loved the idea of hats but could never quite make one work. She could say the same about marriage. That thought plunged her back forty-six years to her tussles with her bridal veil immediately prior to her own wedding. It had been a bitterly cold January day, with all of her family and much of the rest of the world watching the televised state procession of Winston Churchill's coffin. "I'll never forget the day we were married," her husband had stated later that evening, too patiently undoing the lengthy row of buttons along the back of her bridal gown, "because it's the same day Churchill was buried." She shuddered back into the present, trying in vain to recall whether faith in the future had been as much on her mind when she was a twenty year old bride as it was now.

"I suppose all rituals do," responded her friend Mary Kemp, whose hat, also new but much more dashing in purple and silver, perched perfectly on her mass of graying curls. "They exemplify, you could even say they venerate, tradition while at the same time pointing to a future substantially different from the past." She paused to slip on a ring, amethyst, to resonate with the purple in her hat. "A connection between the known and the unknowable. A true mystery." She stood momentarily motionless, gathering her thoughts. "Possibly that mysterious connection between the known past and the unknowable future in rituals offers people something they need."

"Like what?" asked Karen, tidying up the bits left over from wrapping the gift for Betty and Rob, the young bride and groom at the centre of all these preparations.

"Like," she deliberated as she checked her ensemble critically in the full length hall mirror, "like hope, obviously, hope for the future and possibly some form of comfort, some solace for the past, and perhaps for the future as well." She paused to consider this idea. "Yes," she said more firmly, content for the moment with her tentative sculpture of the idea of ritual, "a combination of hope and solace."

"Solace?" Karen grimaced doubtfully. "They won't need solace yet, will they?" A stab of clarity pierced the soothing veil of forgetfulness, rendering all too vividly her concerns for the future on her wedding day almost a half century ago. Hope and solace. She had needed huge doses of both. She was unsure whether she had experienced either during the ritual of being married. She had been too much in the moment.

Mary chuckled at Karen's flippancy. "I was speaking generally, not just about weddings but about all rituals -- such as those associated with coming of age, graduation, retirement, birth and death -- any major transition from one stage of life to another. Rituals take people beyond their own individual concerns and worries and help them to see their circumstances in a larger perspective. That more universal view helps them to make personal sense of their own hopes and fears, especially at weddings – and at funerals, for that matter."

"Hmmm," replied Karen, "let's hope no deaths are imminent but I do suspect a birth will be occurring in a few months, judging from Betty's slightly bulging tummy." Indulging in a last-minute glance in the hall mirror, she lightly patted her abdomen, recalling her own small bulge the day of her wedding. She noticed an errant wisp of hair which she quickly tucked away into the brim of her hat. "There now! That's the best I can do with this wretched headgear. We're off. Do we look properly attired for our first English wedding?"

Karen and Mary, both retired professors and both recent immigrants to England, were learning to navigate the eddied waters of cultural difference between North America and the United Kingdom. Having grown up in Canada, both in families that revered their British heritage, they had anticipated a smooth transition and had been surprised – or gobsmacked as many of their new friends and neighbours might say -- by the plethora of differences in language, customs and expectations. Their acquisition of British driving licenses, for example, had been particularly harrowing. With many years of experience driving in Canada, they had anticipated an easy exchange of licenses in the UK. But because their most recent licenses were from the US, they had been required to take the full test. In preparation, they had learned unfamiliar terms such as 'chicanes' and 'toucan crossings', encountered signs at roundabouts so complex they sometimes had to go two or three times around in order to take in all the information, relearned basic procedures such as steering, braking and overtaking, all of which were quite different from what they were accustomed to, and memorised seemingly bizarre medical expectations for the theory test, including how many times per minute to compress an unconscious person's chest in the unlikely event of needing to apply that knowledge. It had been a similarly unexpected but much more pleasant cultural surprise to be presented with a wedding invitation while purchasing a litre of milk and some freshly laid eggs.

Betty Barton, who worked part time at the village grocery and who had recently joined their walking group, the South Devon Ramblers, had included the invitation with their receipt. "Saves on postage," she had smiled. "We hope you can come. Rob and I both enjoy our walks with the ramblers so much when we can manage to get away from our other responsibilities. We want you to help us celebrate. It won't be fancy," she almost whispered, "we have to be careful with our finances, but we want to have a great party with all our family and friends and fellow ramblers in the village."

Mary had answered for both of them. "Of course we'll come. We look forward to it."

The first thing Karen had thought of was hats. Bemused by the brouhaha over the hats of the Princesses Beatrice and Eugenie and the hatless Samantha Cameron, wife of Prime Minister David Cameron, at the wedding of Prince William and Kate Middleton and incapable of wearing a hat with any kind of panache, she had wondered whether one would be required. At the question, Betty's mouth had dropped in astonished dismay. "But it's a wedding," she had almost stammered. "Yes, of course you'll need a hat." To cover Karen's sartorial faux pas, Mary had quickly explained the bumpy process of acculturation they were experiencing. "In Canada, we don't generally wear hats to weddings. Nor is it common in the United States, where we've both worked for several years. We just want to be certain we get it right."

While initially unsure of the need for a hat, they had both been completely confident that their Tilley hats for rambling would not suffice. Consequently they had spent an unaccustomed afternoon of fun and foolishness at Debenhams and House of Fraser in nearby Exeter trying on sundry hats before settling on the ones that now adorned their heads.

"We're fine with what we're wearing. I'm more worried about the appropriateness of our gift," said Mary. "I always feel uncomfortable giving people any of my artwork. Art is so personal. It's difficult to gauge what someone I don't know very well would like."

"But we do know that she was as excited as we had been on that walk through the Sacred Grove in Churston Woods, where we saw those masks in the trees gazing down at us. They were so serenely passive and yet, at the same time, gruesomely horrific." Karen's spine still trembled slightly at the memory. "What was her comment again?" She chuckled as she mimicked Betty's outburst of astonishment and pleasure. "'Those masks are amazing! They're magical! To think I've lived here all my life and have never been to this fabulous Grove.' So I think your miniature copies will be well appreciated. Not to mention they're beautifully executed."

Mary gazed at the wrapped gift in her hands, almost as though she could see through the wrappings to the contents. "Strange, though, that she grew up less than two miles from the Grove and had never before visited it. She didn't even seem to know much about it."

"That's true. I had wondered about that also. And, when you think about it, it's also strange that we were invited to the wedding in the first place. I'm delighted that we were but, as you pointed out, we don't really know either Betty or Rob very well, except to see Betty working at the grocer's from time to time, and, of course, on the rare times that she can come out walking with the group." Karen paused to check that all the lights and appliances had been turned off prior to leaving for the wedding, bearing in mind that another cultural surprise had been the high cost of electricity in England. "I wonder if everyone in the village has been invited. Possibly even our mysterious neighbour, James Anderson."

"Our very own recluse! I can't imagine him going to a wedding. He's lived next door for several months now, almost as long as we've been here, and I've rarely seen him out of his hermitage."

Karen's face took on her mischievous look as she finished her final check of the cottage. "I'm tempted to knock on his door and ask if he'd like to walk to the church with us but that could be embarrassing if he hasn't been invited."

"That's a temptation best resisted," responded Mary. With her usual tendency to attempt several activities concurrently, she was struggling with the large brass key in their Victorian-era lock with one hand while balancing the wedding gift in her other.

"Here, let me help," said Karen, taking the key and more deftly negotiating the lock's stubborn triggers. "I will never understand how your hands can create such brilliant art and play such beautiful music and yet have difficulty with simple mechanical tasks."

"In a word," began Mary and they completed the sentence together, simultaneously laughing outwardly and sighing inwardly at the ignominies of their ageing bodies, "arthritis." "Although," continued Mary, "I must say that lock is unusually sticky – has been for about a week now. We'll need to get Tommy over again to fix it."

Leaving Kestrel Cottage securely locked, Karen scrutinised the adjacent Sparrow Cottage for any indications of their neighbour's imminent or likely departure for the wedding. "I thought I saw Tommy there earlier today. He seems to be over there as often as he is at our place. Something always needs fixing in these old cottages."

"Rather a bit more than I had anticipated," agreed Mary. "No sooner do we have one thing repaired than something else breaks down. If Tommy weren't so hard working and conscientious, I'd be tempted to think he was deliberately creating the next problem while he repairs each current one."

"You know," responded Karen, fiddling with yet another wayward strand of hair, "I was thinking the same thing about the car the last time we took it in. And yet I doubt we could find a better mechanic than Dan at the village garage."

"Even so, it's frustrating to be needing repairs on both our home and our car almost constantly. And we don't even drive the darn beast very often."

"Well, I don't see any signs of life at Sparrow Cottage at the moment." Karen stretched her neck trying to peer into the windows. They set off for the Churston Court Church, passing Lark Cottage, the third and tiniest of the three connected stone cottages that, in the eighteenth century, had formed the village school. Possibly because of its diminutive size, it was the one remaining house for sale in the entire village.

"There's been some activity at Lark Cottage recently. Have you noticed?" asked Mary. "And look, the front door's been recently painted, possibly even this morning, because I'm pretty sure it was not so shiny and white yesterday when we walked past it. It looks quite smart, almost as though ready to welcome new inhabitants."

"Gosh, you're right. I must confess I haven't really noticed much in the past two weeks or so. When I'm not distracted by the perpetual repairs or buying fancy hats," Karen smiled ruefully, stroking the small feathery plume fluttering just over her left ear, "I've been mulling over how to begin my novel, now that I've finally decided to try to write one." Not receiving any response from Mary, who rolled her eyes and said nothing, she returned to the original point of discussion. "Do you think perhaps the cottage has a buyer?"

"It seems to be local trades people in and out of the cottage, including our Tommy. Possibly they're doing some refurbishment in preparation for a buyer. It certainly would be good to have another neighbour. We're somewhat set apart from the rest of the village on this little lane, much as I love it. The villagers are very kind, but most of them know each other so well. It's difficult to feel part of them even after having lived here for several months now. Perhaps that will change with time." Mary glanced briefly back at Sparrow Cottage. "And our neighbour James seems even more isolated, possibly because, from something I overheard at the bank, he intends to live here only part of each year and spend his winters in Florida. I wonder if he has family there. Other than having Tommy over there for occasional repairs, I've never seen him with anyone from around here except at the local shops."

"I have," said Karen. "I had intended to mention it to you at the time but I forgot. One very hot day about three weeks ago, when you were in your studio and I'd gone for a walk, I popped into the Trout and Salmon, not so much for a drink but just for a spot of cool shade. And there was James Anderson chatting up Mabel, the butcher. Well, possibly it was Mabel chatting up James. Difficult to know. They were both engaged in very intense conversation with each other. James had his back to me, but I could see Mabel's face and she had the oddest expression, almost as though she had been transported to another time and another place. She seemed both intent on what James was saying and transfixed on something within herself. I realised I had been staring at her for several seconds and so looked away but I doubt she was even aware I had come into the pub. Oh, and I wasn't the only person to see them. Mabel's brother Willie was there also, in his usual place in that little nook, sitting behind them reading the paper but so close he could probably hear them."

"What? I didn't realize that Willie and Mabel were brother and sister. Mind you, I rarely see Willie except when he walks down our little lane, which, in the past couple of weeks, now that I think of it, he seems to have been doing more frequently. When did you learn that he was Mabel's brother?"

"Let me think. It was a few weeks ago, when I was at her butcher shop and Willie popped in to purchase something. It was obvious from their conversation that they were brother and sister. I must have neglected to mention it to you. Getting back to Mabel and James, they were so engrossed in each other that I don't think they even noticed him. And he was so involved with his paper that I'm not sure he even knew they were there. But I've not seen them together since. Maybe Willie did notice and told his little sister not to flirt with the newcomers." Since Mabel at roughly twelve stone and forty-five years of age was little in neither size nor years, Karen chuckled to herself at her little joke, which Mary, as was her custom when Karen was being frivolous, simply ignored.

"I'm beginning to think people are treated as newcomers until they've lived here for a decade or more. Beneath their surface of polite kindness, the born-and-bred-in-Devon villagers seem to bear a level of resentment against recent arrivals."

"Actually, I can understand that. It's likely because we newcomers have purchased all the available homes and have paid prices that local salaries will simply not support. Betty mentioned to me just the other day, when I was purchasing flour for our Wednesday evening chicken pie, that she and Rob would dearly love to live here after their wedding but they've been forced to rent a small flat several miles away, somewhere near the centre of Torquay, because affordable housing is not available in the village. And even if it were, they'd never be able to qualify for a mortgage under the new regulations."

"Yes," Mary agreed with a sigh. "It's the same all over the country."

Walking on in silence, and despite her feelings of guilt about purchasing a cottage that many of the locals could not afford, Karen revelled yet again in the decision to make their home in Coombe Gilbert. The small village nestled on the outskirts of Brixham, close to the celebrated coastline of the English Riviera, and enjoyed easy boating access to the River Dart through the nearby hamlet of Galmpton. Karen had fallen in love with the scenery and culture of England more than twenty years earlier, when she had been studying for her doctorate in language and literature in London and making frequent forays into the English countryside to explore the literary landscapes of favourite authors. After earning her PhD in England, she had accepted a position at a university in the American mid-west and had frequently brought small groups of post-graduate students overseas to research the rich literary heritage of Wordsworth, Shakespeare, Hardy, Austen, the Bronte sisters and others. Over the years, the idea of retiring in England gradually took root and grew. The catalyst she had needed to finalise her decision occurred during her sabbatical in the Lake District. Her stay in Rydal Hall, formerly the elegant Georgian home of Lady Le Fleming, William Wordsworth's landlady, had ignited a desire to live in Cumbria. Her British friends had dissuaded her from choosing the Lake District, with the highest annual rainfall in the country and heavy influx of summer tourists. Instead, they had directed her south-westerly, to the gentle hills of Devon, with luxuriant palm trees flourishing in the warmth of the gulf stream and the wildness of Dartmoor looming over the coved and cliffed coastline carved by centuries of Atlantic tides. Her friend and colleague, Mary, had agreed to help her find a place to live. When they discovered Kestrel Cottage with its bright and airy aspect on the edge of this lovely village close to larger towns and transportation to London, Mary had decided that she would like to join Karen in her retirement adventure. Karen would have time and space to write and Mary would have a spacious studio for her art as well as room for her piano, a concert grand she had cherished since childhood. And they both could participate in their mutual enjoyment of walking and going to concerts, movies and the theatre.

Passing the hewn stone outbuildings of the 13th century Gilbert Farm across the lane, Karen was enchanted by the riotous flowers in the hedgerows, the names of which she was working hard to learn: brightly scarlet poor man's weather glass and flurries of white yarrow and cow parsley, all reclaiming their natural right of colourful existence since the banning of toxic pesticides twenty years earlier. Blackberries twisted their thorny way through the hedge, offering only the potential for scratched fingers at the moment but promising delicious summer pudding in a few weeks. As usual, the names of the three attached cottages in their lane were proven apt, with sparrows flitting in balletic arcs to the larks' mid-afternoon melodies. And today there was even a kestrel in implausible defiance of gravity hovering over a space on the large green behind their cottages, no doubt a tiny trembling rodent its intended victim.

"I wonder how difficult it would be to change the name of our cottage," Karen pondered. "Why would anyone name a home after a predator that does not even build its own nest but instead uses nests built and abandoned by other birds?"

"From a villager's perspective, the name might be perceived as appropriate for us," responded Mary drily. "Just be glad we don't live in a place called Magpie Cottage," she added, noticing a tendentious battle between two male magpies on the green while an apparently bored female calmly awaited the outcome. "Then we'd have larceny, aggression, and the eating of road kill added to our list of foreigners' sins."

Where the lane joined the main road through the village, the hedgerows became more domesticated, blossoming with deep pink hydrangeas replacing the scarlet blooms of the rhododendrons that so brilliantly had announced the coming of spring. They passed by the recent development of several large and expensive homes clustered in elegant cul de sacs sweeping up the hill on the right, seemingly out of place amongst the older, more modestly gracious homes of the central part of the village, and then came to the little parade of village shops which supplied almost all of their daily necessities. "I so enjoy being able to walk to the grocer, the butcher, the bank, the post office and newsagent. And, of course, our cosy 16th century Trout and Salmon, with its seafood fresh every day from Brixham. So much better than having to take a car everywhere," said Karen for at least the hundredth time.

"Yes. I hope we can keep all these village services. Development is inevitable but if that Tesco application is approved I'm not sure the grocer or the butcher will be able to survive."

"Oh look, speaking of the devil, there comes Mabel now, just locking up the shop. She's carrying a huge package. Surely it can't be a wedding gift wrapped up in butcher's paper."

"Well, that would be a practical as well as creative idea," replied Mary. She called over, "Hi, Mabel, we're walking to the church. Would you like to join us?"

Looking unusually flustered, Mabel nodded to 'the ladies' as Karen and Mary were called by many of the locals. Either 'the ladies' or 'the Canadian ladies.' "Oh. Yes, of course. It's lovely weather for a wedding, isn't it? I've just closed the shop for the occasion. Although..." she glanced at the heavy and bulky parcel in her arms.

"Hey, Mom. Like a lift to the church?" Tommy, their handyman, with his wife, Sue, and their son Little Tommy appeared with felicitous timing. He stopped his van, an early nineties derelict model but well-tuned and spotlessly clean. "And you ladies as well?"

"Thanks for the offer, Tommy, but the day is so lovely we'd prefer to walk," replied Karen.

"I'll join the ladies," said Mabel, surprising both herself and Tommy, who had been certain his mother would prefer to ride. "I'd enjoy the walk," she explained, observing the puzzled and somewhat dismayed look on his face. "I've been rushing around like mad all day, it seems, and the walk will be calming." Inwardly, she was still heaving with the scene that had occurred less than an hour earlier at Sparrow Cottage. She was not yet ready to make small talk with Tommy while the image of James Anderson sprawled at the foot of the stairs, her son pale and frightened beside him, still dominated her mind. "But Sue, would you kindly take this package in the van? It will need to go into the fridge in the Churston Court kitchen as soon as you get there. Cold cuts for the wedding buffet," she said over her shoulder to Karen and Mary. "And Little Tommy, my love, you look so handsome for the wedding. Gran is going to give you a great big hug at the church." Tommy, whose lips stretched to a publicly acceptable smile while his eyes battled with some kind of inner distraction, started up the van and the ladies waved to Little Tommy who was blowing kisses to his Gran.

"Mabel, I have a question for you," said Karen as the three women headed toward the Church at Churston Lodge. "Every time we walk along this stretch of the road, I notice those little gates in front of the doors of this row of cottages. They are so close to the front door of each cottage that it seems impossible for anyone to get in or out. Do you know what their purpose might be?"

"Oh, indeed, yes," replied Mabel, gratefully diverting her mind from the gruesome scene at Sparrow Cottage to her limited but practical knowledge of local history. "That was Lady Churston's doing, that was. Time was, whenever she'd pass by in her fancy carriage with her fancy clothes, the people living in those cottages would dash outdoors onto the streets to look at her. She didn't like that, did she now, commoners staring at her, so she had Lord Churston order those gates put up, so the people in the cottages couldn't get out their front door. They'd have to go out the back and around the cottages and by that time she'd be up the road already, wouldn't she, and wouldn't have had her passage sullied by the gawking presence of common folk. High and mighty, she was."

"But does that mean that even today the owners of those cottages cannot use their front doors?"

"Indeed it does. Grade II listed these cottages are, or at least the gates are, and you can't change anything that's Grade II listed. Every time there's a new owner, Tommy gets a call asking him to remove the gates and he has to tell them the story, although I'm sure it must be in the paperwork they signed before they moved in." She shook her head as she recounted the behaviour of newcomers who should have known better. "The owners would be heavily fined if they had the gates removed and then they'd have to pay to put them up again anyway. The last one who ignored the regulation paid a £3000 fine in addition to the cost of the new gate. The silly sod had sold the old one and so he had Tommy construct a new one. To do it right, Tommy needed to find the same grade of metal used in the 19th century and the same formulation of paint. It took him a considerable amount of time, didn't it just." Mabel agitated her head even more violently in an effort to hold back the comment about the stupidity of necomers with which she usually completed her recounting of that story.

Mary nodded her head in accord. "I can imagine what a challenge that would have been. We're learning that living in a listed building may seem romantic and charming initially but it comes with quite a set of obligations. We're so grateful to have Tommy as our handyman. He understands all these requirements set out by English Heritage. Your Tommy has done a considerable amount of work in our cottage," added Mary, "and it is always completed to perfection. We'd be lost without him."

"Yes," agreed Karen. "In fact our entire little lane seems to be benefitting from his work these days. He was at our place just last week for a couple of days, and next door at Sparrow Cottage earlier today, just a little over an hour ago, I think, and Mary thinks she saw him coming out of Lark Cottage yesterday."

Mabel stiffened. Unbidden and unwanted, the image of James Anderson twisted at the foot of the stairs and Tommy shaking with fear crammed itself once again inside her head as she considered what to say. Walking with the ladies instead of riding in the van with Tommy, she had not escaped after all from having to negotiate the conflicting paths forking through her mind. She had hoped that Tommy had not been seen coming out of either Lark or Sparrow Cottage in the past day or two, for entirely different reasons. After the announcement this evening, his presence in Lark would not present a problem, but Sparrow...the body...she shuddered, lost in consideration of possible – even probable -- repercussions. She stumbled and almost tripped in a pothole that was entirely familiar to her. "How silly of me." She recovered herself and deftly used the lapse to change the topic. "I guess I was day dreaming about the wedding. My niece is so happy. She's been head over heels for Rob since she was just a little tadpole in polka-dotted wellies splashing around with him in mud puddles."

"Betty is your niece?" queried Mary, smiling at the vision of the wedding couple as kids mucking about in puddles. "Oh, of course. Karen told me earlier today that Willie was your brother. And only last week I learned that Betty was Willie's daughter. For some reason, I just hadn't yet put it all together. I've met each of you in such different contexts and none of you together at the same time. In fact, I haven't actually met Willie yet. I've only seen him walking past our cottage on occasion and asked Karen if she knew who that gentleman was. I usually do the banking and Karen usually does the food shopping, so we each see different people from the village."

"Well, between both those places you will meet my two brothers. I claim both Michael Barton at the bank and Willie, who likes to walk to the grocers when Betty is working. I was a Barton before I married Tommy Ambrose. He was actually Tommy Ambrose Junior, since his father, also Tommy, was still alive when we married. Our first and only son has maintained the family naming tradition, and took his turn as Little Tommy while his father and grandfather were still alive. Now there's just my son Tommy and my first grandson, the current Little Tommy. I don't think he'll like being called 'Little Tommy' when he gets a bit older, but for now it keeps everyone straight."

Mary nodded and smiled but was perplexed. Mabel was babbling. Mabel had impressed her from the first time she had met her as being a tersely articulate woman, speaking her mind clearly and directly. She began to wonder whether Mabel's flood of words, which seemed unusually distracted, might possibly have been intentionally distractive, away from any conversation about Tommy's presence at Sparrow Cottage. Or might it have been his presence at Lark Cottage? But why?

Walking as a threesome, each woman nonetheless walked alone, brows furrowed in thought and speculation. Karen was wondering how many more familial relationships she would enjoy discovering among the villagers at the wedding; Mary was wondering why Mabel had so obviously, literally clumsily, changed the topic of conversation; and Mabel was becoming increasingly concerned at the likelihood of her son being placed at the scene of a murder. Murder? Surely not. Scene of a death. That sounded better and really was more accurate but, in the eyes of the law, who could predict how it might all be perceived? They would have to put the body somewhere else and quickly.

Losing all awareness of Karen and Mary walking beside her, Mabel focused on the problem not only of how to keep Tommy from being apprehended but also of how to keep the secret behind their wedding surprise planned for tonight from being discovered by the authorities. Her entire family was at risk. Progeny of her desperation and fear, the idea of what they might do burst into life with such gruesome force that she shivered with the sheer horror of it despite the warm sunlight. She would talk to Michael as soon as she reasonably and discreetly could.

***

While the villagers were making their way to the church at Churston Court, Betty, with the help of Adele, Rob's aunt, was attending to all the final little touches to her ensemble that would make her as pretty a bride as possible for her new husband. Adele, with her large, rough hands, almost as large as those of her bricklayer husband, Sam, was amazingly delicate in her arranging of the veil and the skirt. Betty had few women friends her age in the village, possibly because of having dedicated much of her life to her father's welfare since the death of her mother five years earlier. Her husband-to-be had been her best mate for many years, and his aunt, Adele, who had hired her part time at the grocery, had in some ways replaced the kind of companionship she might have enjoyed with her mother. Her bridesmaid, Sarah, was the twelve-year old daughter of a distant cousin, chosen because she had implored, "I really, really want to be a bridesmaid, please, please Betty." How could Betty have said no? But it was not quite the same as having someone her own age or with more experience to help with these last minute preparations. Adele, with no children of her own, had happily offered to fill in as needed.

The annexe to Michael's home that Betty shared with her father was too tiny to accommodate both Betty and Sarah dressing for the ceremony in addition to Willie's needing a short nap and then getting himself ready. At least that was the excuse Betty had given to her father. The real reason for wanting to use her Uncle Michael's home rather than the annexe was to maintain the secret she had managed to keep from her father ever since she had begun to plan the wedding. With Adele's help, she had reworked the full-skirted white lace bridal gown her mother had worn so that it would fit her slightly larger frame and accommodate the little life just starting to affect her otherwise trim waistline. Consequently, Michael's comfortably masculine furnishings were arrayed with lace and satin and flowers which the women had moved into his house for their preparations. On the pretext of having to attend to something at the bank, Michael had left the excited hubbub which had invaded his quiet sanctuary. When they were ready, Adele's husband Sam would drive Betty and Sarah to the church, while Adele would wait for Michael, who would return as soon as his business had been concluded.

Willie, who did not drive, would either come with Michael and Adele or walk there on his own, depending upon timing and how he felt after his nap. Before she had left to get ready in Michael's home, Betty had been concerned about getting her father into his formal clothes and having him feeling refreshed and looking his best for the wedding. Willie had put his arms around his solicitous daughter. "My darling, I am going to take a little walk now, just as I usually do at this time of day, and then rest briefly, get dressed – you've laid everything out beautifully for me -- and I assure you I will be all ready and on time. Please do not worry. I will be there. I promise you."

Betty had looked at him, a little puzzled. Well, of course he would be there. The thought had never occurred to her that he would not.

"Smile those wrinkles away, dear girl. You don't want to be a frowning bride. Come dance with me," he had twinkled, taking both her hands and swinging their arms together, a game they used to play when Betty was very small and angry or worried. "Now go with Adele and get yourself ready for what will be one of the happiest days of your life. I know it was the happiest day in my life when I married your mother, well, next to the day you were born, of course. I want the same for you. Be off with you. I'll see you at the church."

As soon as she had left, Willie had opened the top drawer of his wardrobe and had taken out a photograph of his own wedding day. He had gazed at it and then closed his eyes, as though to see more than any photo could project. He had then picked up a miniature of a larger photo of Amanda with a two-year old Betty. This he had put in the breast pocket of his jacket laid out on the bed. He next took out a sheaf of papers and rifled through them, searching for a detail. He switched on his computer and located what he was looking for. Then he had left for his daily constitutional. It would have to be a quick one in order for him to be ready on time but he had one stop he needed to make.

***

Deep in thought, Karen, Mary, and Mabel turned into the narrow lane leading to the enchanting stone edifice of Churston Court Inn and its adjacent Churston Church. Karen caught her breath. "This is amazing," she said. "I can't believe we've lived here all these months and haven't visited this place before now."

Mabel, her grim thoughts interrupted by Karen's enthusiastic burst, appreciated the easy neutrality of this topic of conversation. She happily explained. "Yes, it's an impressive building, isn't it? Betty was thrilled to be able to have her wedding here. It's really a dream come true for her. Of course, they could not afford to have the regular wedding supper in the restaurant or the banqueting rooms, and the church is no longer in regular use, but the owner, Melvyn Ambrose, a cousin of my late husband Tommy, arranged for us to use the church and to set up a marquee on the grounds. He even offered to provide some preliminary nibbles if the two families would bring our own cooking and baking for the buffet and arrange the music for the dancing. Earlier, I brought over a haunch of beef and a leg of lamb and started them roasting. I would have roasted them at home but my oven's not working. Tommy was going to fix it this morning but," she paused and her eyes narrowed as she struggled for words, "he had to complete something he'd started yesterday and couldn't get to it. And Sue's oven is too small."

"Oh gosh, we could have helped. We didn't realise it was a pitch-in." Seeing the blank look on Mabel's face, Karen explained that was the North American word for people contributing to a shared meal, everyone 'pitching in' to make a good feast. "Kind of like the story of the loaves and fishes in the Bible," she concluded lamely, as Mabel's countenance did not soften. It took awhile for it to dawn on Karen that contributing food for a wedding supper was a family and close friend responsibility, not one to be shared with newcomers.

"What a marvellous site for a wedding. Do you know much about the history of the place?" inquired Mary, who was developing proficiency in rescuing Karen from her frequent foot-in-mouth disease.

"Never was much of a one for history," replied Mable, "Michael's the reader in our family. But I do know that it was built sometime in the 12th century, originally as a coaching inn. It's gorgeous inside, with Inglenook fireplaces, lovely tapestries and real knight's armour displayed as though the knight is still standing in it. There are also some lovely gold-leaf mirrors and several original portraits of people who lived there after the inn became a manor house. Because of its age and its importance to the history of the community, it's Grade I listed, but that's where my knowledge stops. However, I'm sure you'll find many of the others at the wedding more than happy to tell you stories about the place. The only story I know is that the ghost of some monk who used to live here still haunts the kitchen. In fact, speaking of the kitchen, I think I'd better check on the beef and the lamb before the service begins. I promised to have them out of the ovens before the chef needed them for the restaurant meals." With that, she was hastily off, almost in relief it seemed to both Mary and Karen.

They entered the ancient church and right away noticed a glorious stained glass window. As a consequence of their jaunts to several cathedrals since moving to England, they were beginning to recognise the different hues and design elements of original and more contemporary leaded windows in churches and cathedrals and could tell almost immediately that this was fairly recent. "You like that?" said a familiar voice which turned out to belong to Dan, their local auto mechanic. "It was donated by Agatha Christie in the 60s. She frequently dined at Churston Court and set her Poirot mystery *Murder on the Links* here. Well, more or less hereabouts, on what is now the Churston Golf Course. With creative license, of course. As you can tell, I'm an Agatha Christie fan."

"Fanatic is more like it," chuckled his girlfriend, Linda. "He's read every one of her novels at least twice.

He even quotes from them on some of our dates. And I'm sure we've seen every Poirot and Miss Marple film and TV show ever made." Arm hooked in his, she looked as though she didn't mind one bit.

Guided to the bride's section of the pews, probably because they knew Betty slightly better than they knew Rob, Karen and Mary were able through this simple traditional sorting method to figure out who was a member or friend of the Barton family and who was a member or friend of the Masons. They both enjoyed the general hubbub and bustle of clan gatherings, especially when they were able to be on the outside looking in. Both found human nature fascinating and enjoyed watching the hugs and greetings of people who, for the most part, they had hitherto seen only at the local village shops. Knowing so few, they chose a place next to Tommy, Sue and Little Tommy, making sure to leave space for Mabel, who presumably was still in the kitchen checking out the roasts and ensuring the cold cuts were in the fridge. Tommy leaned over to ask if either Mary or Karen knew who Bruce Reynolds was.

"I don't think so," replied Karen, "but the name seems vaguely familiar."

"You've no doubt heard of the Great Train Robbery in 1963 – over two million pounds stolen?" At their affirmative nod, he continued. "Well, Reynolds was the mastermind behind it. He was the last person captured – there were well over a dozen involved in the robbery – and for part of the time he hid out in Churston Court and in this church. Even though the police searched while he was hiding here, they couldn't find him. There are just so many nooks and crannies and hidden corridors in the two buildings, especially in the Court. Some people swear there is an underground tunnel connecting the Church to the Court but nobody I know has been able to locate it."

"Was he ever caught?" asked Karen.

"Oh yes. He lived quite lavishly for awhile, spent all of his share of the loot trying to avoid being captured, and then, when it was all spent, he was caught after all, did some time, was released, reoffended, and did time again. Then he turned his life around. Nowadays he even gives talks and writes about his former life as a criminal. I guess sometimes crime does pay after all." He paused for a moment and the light in his eyes dimmed. He continued, "He's written the post script or afterword in the two most recent books related to the robbery, *Signal Red* last year, and *The Great Train Robbery – History of ...we*ll, something about history – I can't just now recall the full title – this year. I'm pretty keen on everything to do with the Great Train Robbery. I've read all the books written about it, over a dozen. The guys involved were all so different and have travelled such different paths in their lives. I find discovering what can turn an ordinary bloke into a criminal fascinating. Even more intriguing is how some can turn themselves back into living fairly normal lives." Once again his eyes faded for a moment and then resumed their normal sparkle. "But anyway, that's our local claim to fame with that notorious crime, right here in Churston Court and the Church."

Mabel entered the nave and took her saved place between Tommy and Karen.

"Roasts coming along all right?" asked Karen.

"Hmm? Oh, yes. Just fine," responded Mabel, her attention diverted by some movement among the guests, her eyes darting from pew to pew, as though in search of someone. Gradually the conversations quieted. The clock sounded the hour and then ticked on past the hour, ten minutes past, and the rustling began and people began to wonder whether there might be a problem. Rob and his best man were waiting to take their place at the front of the church and someone mentioned that Betty and her young bridesmaid, Sarah, had arrived with Sam just a few minutes before 4:00. So what was the holdup?

Mabel cast her eyes around the nave. She couldn't see Adele or Michael, had in fact been looking for Michael for a frantic ten minutes after she had quickly inspected the roasts and, finding them done, taking them out of the ovens so as not to inconvenience the chef. She didn't recall seeing Willie, either, when she had dashed into the church right as the clock was striking the hour, stopping only momentarily to admire Betty's and Sarah's dresses and wish them well as they hovered in the front entrance, waiting for Willie's arrival. Had something happened to Willie? Was he with Michael? The buzz went around the nave. Had anyone seen Betty's father? One of the ushers went outside to discover Michael racing his car up the lane, stopping in front of the church to spill out Adele and Willie, then spinning into the small parking lot to seek a space.

In the fluid burst of a single motion, Adele adjusted Betty's veil, gave her an affirming nod accompanied with a huge smile and streamed into the church. Willie, on the other hand, as though in shock, stood stock still and took in the sight of Betty in her mother's bridal gown. "My lord, girl, you've taken me back a quarter of a century. You look just like your mother did on our wedding day." Beaming the fullest smile imaginable, while quieting all the turmoil within himself, he took the miniature photo of Amanda and Betty from his pocket, showed it to Betty and then slipped it into her bouquet. Then he put his hands on her shoulders, looked her intently in the eye, and clasped her close to him, as though wanting to keep her beside himself forever. Slowly he released her and took his place beside her, nodding to the usher to cue the organist.

Thrilled that her secret had worked, Betty tucked her arm firmly into her father's, the organist began to play and the ceremony began.

***

All weddings are fundamentally the same. Rarely are the actual vows remembered by the family and friends who witness the joining of two hitherto independent lives into one shared life. Instead, the quirks and quiddities are what make every ceremony unique. In this case, the quirkiest aspect was the vicar himself,

Reverend Nicholas Potts, a youthful-looking ginger-haired version of Rowan Atkinson. His arched eyebrows lifted heavenward after every sentence and his head bobbed distractingly as he spoke of the delights of the wedding day and the hardships as well as joys the new couple will face as they "walk through the hills and valleys of a shared life." With a dramatic sweep of his hands, he exhorted Betty and Rob. "There will be the large challenges of mortgages, babies, illnesses, and ultimately death. Those you will probably be able to cope with, drawing upon each other's strengths." His head bobbed and eyebrows pumped up and down distractingly in anticipation of the remarks to follow. "But it will be the day-to-day challenges that will try you both the most, from toothpaste in the sink to taking out the rubbish to washing up after tea to burned dinners to over-indulgent nights at the pub, parts of everybody's marital experiences." Here several guests, familiar with the vicar's unconventional ways, chuckled, while Karen and Mary looked at each other in astonishment. "These are the hardest, because they are grounded in your individual weaknesses and vulnerabilities and in your daily habits. Rather than drawing upon your mutual strengths, you may need to change your expectations for each other or else change your own behaviour in order to resolve these problems when they arise. Neither is easy. It's how you deal with these trivial day-to-day issues that will stamp the character of your marriage. And now I must test your character right at the start. Before you sign the register and take your first steps down the aisle as man and wife to exit the church, followed by your family and friends, I have a few practicalities I must attend to attend to for the comfort of your guests. I beg your patience for the next couple of minutes."

Nic the Vic, as he was referred to by some of his parishioners, bobbed his head and raised his brows several times in quick succession before re-commencing. "My friends, as you know, the Church is focused on our spiritual lives but has to attend to our physical needs as well. I understand you will all be staying to enjoy the wedding supper in the marquee. I have been asked by the Churston Court manager to let you know that he has a fully booked restaurant tonight and therefore requests — very adamantly requests -- you not to use the toilets in the main building. For your comfort, he has arranged the installation of four portaloos behind the marquee. On your behalf, he and I have tested these portaloos," a little chuckle from the nave, "and have found them to be somewhat whimsical." Another chuckle. "If the thought of a whimsical loo concerns you, there is one loo in the church and I can personally vouch for its reliability." Some outright laughter from a few of the guests. "You will need to make your decision soon because in precisely thirty minutes the function room of the church, near where the loo is located, will be used by the yoga lady for her bi-weekly class and she has assured me most vehemently that she will devour anyone who passes through the area while her class is going on. To reinforce this threat, she will lock the door to the function room as soon as the class is ready to begin. So be warned. Look to your bodies and your souls will be comforted." Another gentle chuckle filled the nave, this one including the rather bemused bride and groom.

Register signed, Betty and Rob, now officially Mr. and Mrs. Mason, left to the joyous strains of the Triumphal March from Aida and joined the happy crowd of friends and family waiting in the courtyard. No confetti, as this tradition had been recently abolished in favour of more environmentally friendly alternatives, but a pastel rainbow of the petals of June flowers swirled around them, lightly floating down to create a soft carpet leading them to the marquee.

Mabel and Adele dashed across the courtyard to the inn to organise the buffet so that the kitchen would be clear in time for the Churston Court staff to prepare for restaurant diners. "Pity that Amanda couldn't be here to see Betty looking so beautiful in the wedding gown from her own marriage," said Adele, turning to Mabel, whose face had suddenly turned to stone. "Oh, I'm so sorry, I probably shouldn't have mentioned that. You lost your Tommy as well then. A terrible time that was."

Karen and Mary, who were lingering at the back of the well wishers so as not to impede the view of family and other friends of the bride and groom, overheard the comment but neither of them could hear Mabel's response as the women strode with purpose to the kitchen. Karen was about to say something to Mary when Michael came toward them. "I'm so glad to see you

Canadian ladies here. Did you know that there is a tie between Churston Court and Canada?"

"No. Not at all," replied Mary. "But I look forward to your telling us what it might be."

"Does the name Humphrey Gilbert ring a bell with either of you?"

Karen frowned, trying to wrench up a memory and failing. Michael continued, "Well, Sir Humphrey Gilbert, whose family at one time owned Gilbert Farm across the lane from you, just one small part of their considerable land holdings in the area, lived at Greenway, which, as you will surely know, later became the favourite holiday home of Agatha Christie. Sir Humphrey visited Churston Court frequently, with his half-brother Sir Walter Raleigh. Yes," he smiled, "I see you've heard of him. Well, Sir Walter was not the only one in the family to navigate into new territories. In fact, Winston Churchill once described Sir Humphrey Gilbert of South Devon as 'the first great pioneer of the West.' He sailed across the Atlantic in 1583 and landed in what is now called Newfoundland. He claimed the island as England's first overseas colony under Royal Charter of Queen Elizabeth I of England, officially establishing the British Empire. Newfoundland still proudly considers itself to be England's oldest colony, with over half the population claiming British ancestry."

"Oh yes, I recollect now," interrupted Karen. "Remember we read that book about the colonisation of Newfoundland -- I can't for the life of me recall the title just now – soon after we had read *The Shipping News*. Now I realise why the name Humphrey Gilbert sounded so familiar. Thanks, Michael. It's good to know of yet another connection between the country of our birth and the lovely village we've chosen for our retirement. Somehow it makes me feel more rooted here." At this point, Sam joined them, delivered his greetings heartily, and indicated, apologetically, that he needed a moment with Michael. They walked off together and Mary and Karen proceeded to locate a table so that they would have a good view of the wedding party and be able to hear the speeches.

They watched as Mabel, Adele, Sue and several other ladies brought out dishes for the buffet. While Mabel carved her roast and her lamb, Sue arranged the cold meats and vegetables into a magnificent salmagundi. The aroma of the hot dishes was tantalizing: duck and peach casserole; lamb casserole; pineapple curry with prawn and mussels, Dorset jugged steak, Cornish caudle chicken pie. The mingling whiffs heightened everyone's appetite and before long every man, woman and child, each with a bounteous plateful of food, had taken a seat at one or other of the picnic tables in the marquee. Karen and Mary were joined at their table by Teresa and Marvyn Fergusen, both of whom they knew from the ramblers. "I'm delirious over this food," declared Karen. "This chicken pie is unlike any I've even tasted."

"Oh, it's much more than just a chicken pie," explained Teresa. "It's called a Cornish caudle."

"What's a caudle?"

"It's put together quite similarly to an ordinary chicken pie, but when you make the pastry for the top, you punch out a hole in the centre. Then, just a few minutes before the pie finishes baking, you take it out of the oven and pour a mixture of egg and cream through the hole. Then you sort of jiggle it or caudle it for about a half minute or so, pop it back in the oven for a few minutes and that's your caudle."

"Kind of like a gastronomic Cornish cuddle," observed Karen. Mary started to roll her eyes, anticipating yet another verbal blunder from Karen, but Teresa and Marvyn both laughed and they all relaxed into enjoying their food. Eve and Rowan Bell, another couple from Coombe Gilbert who walked with the ramblers, approached their table. "Would you mind if we joined you?"

"Not at all," said Mary. "It feels good to be with people we know. Most of these wedding guests we haven't met yet, although I'm looking forward to getting acquainted with some tonight. You'd think in a village this size everybody would know everyone else but I guess we just haven't been here long enough yet. Are you originally from this area?"

"No, I'm from Buckinghamshire and Marvyn's from Watford. We moved here almost four years ago," replied Teresa, "and we still feel very much like newcomers. We bought one of those newer homes on the hill. But Eve and Rowan, you've lived here most of your lives, haven't you?"

"Oh yes, born and bred in Devon, Eve right here in Coombe Gilbert and me in Paignton. We wouldn't move anywhere else."

"Oh, there's Tommy," interrupted Marvyn. "Excuse me a moment. I've something I need to ask him to do."

"You'd think with a fairly new house, we'd not have very much work for a handyman," explained Teresa, "but for the past year, it seems, or close to it, we've had to have something fixed almost every week. Tommy's very responsible and efficient," she hastened to add, "but we certainly do see a lot of him."

"Same with us," said Karen, "although we somewhat expected it with the old cottage we live in. And he's very reasonable at eleven pounds an hour."

"That's odd," said Rowan. "I'm sure he's been charging us only ten pounds an hour. We called him to do some painting last month, and I thought it was ten pounds an hour. Isn't that right, Eve?"

Eve, a longtime acquaintance of Tommy and a good friend of Linda and Dan, the auto mechanic, suspected that she might know the reason behind the cost differential. On the night of Betty's and Rob's engagement party, she had overheard a discussion about the couple's inability to find affordable housing in the village. Somebody had made a suggestion about how people in the village might use their jobs and talents to try to raise funds to help the bride and groom financially but she had just been passing by on her way to to join another group and had not heard what eventually transpired. She was disinclined to speculate in this public and festive environment and so formulated a blandly neutral response to her husband's question. "I'm not sure, Ro. It was ten pounds a few years ago. Perhaps he's increased it recently. He's always been so trustworthy that I just pay what he asks."

"That must be it," said Teresa. "We used to pay ten pounds an hour the first three years we were here, and then sometime last year, oh about nine or ten months ago now, he raised it to eleven pounds an hour. I remember now."

"Well, that was odd," said Marvyn as he rejoined the table. "When I explained to Tommy that our door had begun squeaking about a week ago, almost right after he had just finished his last job with us, he got all flustered and said he'd be out to fix it as soon as he could, no charge, almost as though he thought it was his fault. Then he just put his head down and almost ran away from me. I guess I shouldn't have bothered him about it during the party."

Karen and Mary exchanged glances but said nothing. Indeed, they couldn't have said anything because the evening's speeches were about to begin.

Wedding supper speeches are similar to wedding ceremonies. One remembers only the unexpected. And it came, right as Willie was finishing his father-of-the-bride speech.

"And so, in conclusion, since I have to lose my Elizabeth, my little Betty, I cannot think of anyone finer to love her and care for her than Rob Mason. If her mother Amanda were here beside me, she would be saying the same thing. Almost everyone here has known these two since they were born. We all would prefer to have them stay here to work and raise their family among us." Willie's voice began to tremble. He consulted the notes he had written the previous day for tonight's speech, written before his shocking discovery earlier this afternoon. He decided to stick to his written script. "Regrettably, they cannot and so, with pride and happiness in their union, but sadness," Willie paused and looked at his daughter, "such sadness I can barely speak it, that they will be leaving our village, I ask you to raise your glasses to Mr. And Mrs. Robert Gilbert Mason."

Willie Barton lifted his glass and, with a supreme act of will, managed a beaming smile for his daughter and her new husband.

Michael Barton stood in response to his older brother's toast. Amongst the "cheers" and "God blesses" for his niece and her new husband, his head was reeling, not with the third Guinness he'd pretended to drink that evening, nor with the champagne in his toasting glass, but with the storm of thoughts raging for his attention. The announcement he was about to make was certain to please everyone in the marquee but the body in Sparrow Cottage and Mabel's abhorrent idea for disposing of it clamoured for attention, sweeping away too much of his pleasure in what he and Sam together with their families and friends had accomplished for this wedding. The irony brooded, loss for gain, death for life, the mess to be sorted out in Sparrow Cottage just as they had finally clinched the deal for its adjoining Lark Cottage. Fingering the key in his pocket, considering possibilities, computing potential consequences, his contrived smile gradually became real as the paradoxes of the situation finally managed to rearrange themselves into a possible solution building on Mabel's bizarre but practical suggestion. Palpable relief blended easily with his genuine enthusiasm.

"Willie, you've outdone yourself," he said quietly as he took the stage, astonished at how effectively his unrelentingly honest brother had surmounted the ethical quagmire he had sunk into earlier that day. "A fine speech for a joyous occasion," he continued, speaking into the microphone. "And I hope what I have to say will offer some further joy." He turned to face the wedding guests. "As Willie mentioned, tonight is bittersweet. We rejoice in Betty and Rob's marriage, but in the knowledge that they have planned to move several miles away to the centre of Torquay. However, and this is a big however, you all know about plans. Nobody puts it better than Robbie Burns: 'The best-laid schemes o' mice an 'men gang aft agley, An' lea'e us nought but grief an' pain, for promis'd joy!' Well my two lovebirds, your plans have 'gang agley', or at least are about to go astray, because we have come up with a new plan for you. We hope this arrangement will bring you neither grief nor pain but as much joy as possible. Sam, c'mon over here and help me talk about the Barton-Mason family scheme for Betty and Rob, will you."

Sam Mason, Rob's uncle and Michael's mate since infant school, joined Michael on the platform, enveloping Rob's and Betty's hands in his giant paws. Mindful that their own scheme had 'gang aft agley' and could potentially cause considerable grief and pain, had, in fact, already done so, Sam and Michael forced themselves to focus on the 'promis'd joy' for the moment. Sam began the narrative. "Ten months ago, these two celebrated their engagement at our beloved Trout and Salmon. Many of us here today were there that evening and drank to their good health and happy future, just as we are doing again tonight. Many of you will remember hearing them tell about their difficulty trying to find a house in the village that they could afford and also trying to secure a mortgage as first-time buyers. Even with the bride's uncle and the groom's godfather managing the local bank," Sam nudged Michael who obligingly winked at the wedding guests, "they could not satisfy the stringent new banking rules for a mortgage on any home in Coombe Gilbert. They were devastated but held out hope that the affordable housing in the proposed development for Churston would be approved and they could still live nearby."

Subdued murmurs buzzed amongst the villagers. Almost everyone in the village had taken a stand on the Churston Golf Course proposal that, in its original format, would have enabled the development of a hundred twenty new homes, many of them intended to be affordable for first-time buyers. Several villagers were members or else strong supporters of the Churston RAGS (Residents Against Golf Club Sell-Off) and families and friends had divided over the controversial issue, in some cases almost as fiercely as the neighbourhood and family divisions that occurred up north during the 80s miners' strike. RAGS had succeeded in delaying the approval of the proposal for over a year and was currently staging a legal appeal over the recent decision of the Council to proceed with the development of just ninety new homes, with far fewer to be set aside as affordable. But the delays had already been too long for Betty's and Rob's hopes.

"C'mon, Sam, let's steer away from that thorny issue tonight," said Michael, who had been finding it difficult the past few months to speak out in favour of the proposed development when so many of his neighbours, including his best mate, Sam, were against it. He understood their argument that the proposed development would lead to population congestion, increased traffic, the loss of some lovely green space and a diversion from part of the right-of-way to Churston Woods. On the other hand, he also sympathised with the rights of the Golf Club members to sell some of their land for much needed revenue while providing reasonably priced homes for young people like Betty and Rob, who wanted to live and raise their children in the village where they had been born and bred. And, not to be overlooked, the local bank, and he, as manager of the bank, would also reap benefits from the proposed development.

"Long story short," continued Sam, acceding to Michael's request, "Michael and I and the rest of our two families and some of our friends in the village hatched a little plan to try to put together a deposit for a lovely little cottage in the village so that the monthly mortgage payment would not be any more than the rental fees that Betty and Rob are intending to pay in Torquay. Well, hallelujah, we did it! Just three days ago the documentation was completed." With his hand Sam quickly silenced the delighted burst of applause. "It is our pleasure on behalf of the Mason and Barton family and our friends in Coombe Gilbert, all of whom are here tonight," another short burst of applause accompanied by cheers, "to present you with this key to Lark Cottage. May it provide you comfort and security as you begin your life together."

The applause crescendoed to a roar, while the jaws of those unaware of the scheme dropped in stunned amazement. Betty and Rob turned and clutched each other close and hard, as though they could not believe what they had just heard, while Willie stood cemented in place, his face inscrutable. Sam quieted the room and then Michael took over. "So, Willie, you won't be losing your daughter after all. You can now enjoy the rest of the evening in the comfort of knowing that Betty will still be right here in the village." He gently hugged the frail shoulders of his brother, then turned again to Betty and Rob, frozen motionless in each other's arms. He tapped Betty on the shoulder, as though to unfreeze her. The audience laughed as the couple reluctantly unclasped themselves, looked at each other and then at all of their friends and neighbours, faces alight with pleasure and good wishes, while they were still just beginning to comprehend the implications of this gift. Michael, moving directly to logistics, concluded the speech portion of the wedding. "Sam and I will organise transporting your wedding gifts to Lark Cottage tonight so that when you newlyweds return from your honeymoon weekend here at Churston Court, you'll find Lark all ready for you, with your gifts inside." Another burst of applause approved these arrangements and Michael signalled for the music to begin.

Waving off the astonished thanks of the newlyweds and nudging them and the rest of the head table toward the dance floor, Michael turned and quietly spoke to his brother. His manner was discreet but his intentions were entirely strategic for the benefit of anyone who might be observing or passing by. "Willie, I realise this is a shock, and that you would much prefer to have provided for Betty yourself. But you and I both know that with Amanda's death, God rest her sweet soul, and the loss of Gilbert Farm, that just couldn't happen. Sam and I figured you would not accept this gift if you'd known about our plan, which is why we had to keep it secret. But we hope you will accept our good will and good wishes for Rob and Betty, and our sincerest love and respect for you and forgive us our secrecy."

Willie stood as tall as his weary frame would allow. He physically grasped his brother's hand even as he intellectually grasped the reasons for the tactically staged apology. The real shock and surprise had occurred not just two minutes ago but almost three hours earlier. Of course he was delighted that Betty would continue to live in the village but the horror of how this had been achieved, the compromises with his own conscience that he had been required to make, would not be easily erased. Might never be erased. Michael was trying to ensure that the role he had forced upon Willie would not be discovered. Willie appreciated that, despite his immense rage at the circumstances of the day. He replied within the stratagem. "Michael, I don't know how you did it, and I strongly suspect I probably don't want to know. I have my daughter still in the village. Tonight I can forgive anything for that." He paused, and allowed, for a brief moment, his eyes to reflect his troubled soul. "And who among us does not need forgiveness?" His eyes resumed their intensity, his face some cheer. Noticing someone passing by, he grasped Michael's hands in his once again. "I thank you, little brother."

***

Music blared, dancers swayed, and the freely flowing beer and wine stimulated lively and occasionally raucous conversations. The ginger hair of the jaunty Reverend Potts bounced rhythmically as he joined the dancing crowd. He whirled with the village matrons when a waltz or fox trot was played, led one of the line dances, and even hip hopped at the centre of the younger crowd. In the darkness at the edge of the heaving throng, Michael conferred briefly with Sam, who nodded his agreement. They then separated and with apparent jovial abandon, drinks in hand but only minimally imbibed, they moved through the crowd, joking with some, dancing a few steps from time to time and discreetly informing those who had been at Sparrow Cottage earlier in the afternoon what now needed to be done.

Sam took charge of organising the gifts to be taken to Lark Cottage.

"Tommy, you take the first load of gifts to Lark. While you're doing that, take one of your dust sheets and leave it there. No, make it two, just in case we need a second. Do not go back into Sparrow, not for any reason. Your Uncle Michael wants me to make sure you understand that. Not for any reason! Then come straight back to the party and give your Sue a turn on the dance floor before she has to take Little Tommy home. "

"Is that all I have to do? But it was my fault..."

"Hsst. No talk of fault. No talk of anything. Less talking less explaining. "

For the briefest of moments Tommy felt the burden lift, a split second of relief. Sam and his Uncle Michael were looking after things, looking out for him, protecting him. The burden then thumped right back down onto his shoulders, heavier than before. Protecting? From what? Arrest? Prison? Surely he deserved both. But if he were in prison, how then could he protect his own family? Continually amazed at the young life he and Sue had created, watching Little Tommy already developing a sense of right and wrong, how could he ever justify being protected from the consequences of his own behaviour? He'd taken a life. Not deliberately. A moment of fear, a rash response. So quickly a man was dead. He could never unlive that moment. Going to prison could not bring back that life. And going to prison would not help Sue or Little Tommy or the other little one soon to be born. But how could he ever look his son in the eye if he managed to escape punishment? There seemed no way out of this mess. These warring clashes of horror, fear, and guilt were wearing him down. Best just to keep busy and follow the instructions of those with clearer minds.

He carried several loads of gifts to his van, packing them in carefully so as not to separate cards from the gifts nor disturb the elaborate bows. But he could not banish his memory of James Anderson's final moments, falling to his death, the look in his eyes as he realised what was happening. Nor could he stop thinking of Sue, expecting their second child in a few months, and their Little Tommy, just starting to toddle. His mouth, sour with rising gorge, twisted with the effort of holding back tears. He knew his Uncle Michael and his mother and Sam and the others would try their best but he also knew the police would find him, probably sooner than later. He watched CSI -- they all did. He knew that no matter how careful everyone was, something was always left behind at every scene of crime. At least he still had his dust sheets in the boot from last minute touch-ups at Lark, not having had time to clear out his van prior to the wedding, and he was relieved to be able to leave them at Lark Cottage. He definitely never again wanted to enter Sparrow Cottage. There was no problem acceding to that request – or rather command – from Uncle Michael. And then he remembered. "Oh damn, is my wrench in the boot? No it's not. I dropped it after...bloody hell, what did I do with it?"

***

Away from the boisterous drinking and dancing and general gaiety, Tommy's mother, Mabel, was conferring with her brother, Michael, in a conversation she would never have thought possible just a few hours earlier. "It's better if I do it on the table in the shop. Fewer traces of blood." Her pragmatism belied her revulsion at the course she was committing herself to. Tommy was trying so hard to support his pregnant Sue and Little Tommy. She couldn't stand by and allow him to be arrested for a death he hadn't intended. But still, there was dignity to human life and death. Having taken over as the local butcher when her husband Tommy died, she held no romantic illusions about the killing of animals and the cutting of dead meat. But a human being? She felt her brother's supportive hand on her shoulder and she knew, without his speaking, that he understood her torment, her decision, and her ability to carry it through. "I'll take the leftover meats from the party to the shop to keep in the cooler. That'll provide an excuse to be in the shop to prepare for...to prepare." Perhaps if she didn't actually speak the words of the act she could retain some distance from it but she doubted it. "You'll need to bring him to me as soon as you can. He'll need a good twenty-four hours in the fridge to congeal the blood before I can cut cleanly and effectively."

***

Andy Mason, father of the groom, approached his brother Sam just as Tommy was finishing with the first load of gifts to be taken to Lark. "Anything you need from me?" While Betty's father Willie had deliberately been kept ignorant of the Mason and Barton family plan to obtain Lark Cottage for the newlyweds, partly to protect his frail health but primarily to protect their plan from his implacable sense of right and wrong, Rob's father Andy had been included from the start. For many generations, back to the sixteenth century, his Mason forbears had been master thatchers, living and working, for the most part, within a twenty-mile radius of coombe Gilbert. For the past two decades, his honoured craft had enabled him to support his family and to put a little extra aside and even to engage his son as an apprentice thatcher. The disastrous economic climate of the past three years, however, had taken its toll. People were now waiting longer before having their roofs rethatched and new builds were steering away from the more expensive thatched roofs. The resultant dearth of business had cut deeply into his income and had eroded his savings. Despite the five new homes he had thatched in the ten months since the engagement party, when Sam and Michael had hatched their plan for Lark Cottage, he had not been able to contribute as much as he would have liked. The plan concocted by Sam and Michael had seemed so simple, just charging newcomers an additional ten per cent for any goods and services, with the trickiest element being to keep Rob from finding out. But now, just as it had come to fruition, this stupid accident, with its disastrous consequences, threatened everything. "Might a fishing trip help?"

"You know, a fishing trip might be just the thing. Let me talk with Michael."

TWO: SUNDAY

"Oh, darn." Karen bounded out of bed to greet the new day as sunlight poured into her window. "I've overslept. It's too late now for our walk to Churston Grove." She could hear the middle section of her favourite Chopin Ballade, just before the brilliant crescendo about three quarters of the way through and so realised that Mary was already up and playing the piano. She quickly showered, threw on some jeans and a yellow jumper to echo the joyous morning sun and padded downstairs to find the kitchen table set for breakfast and Mary, coffee cup in hand, dressed for their walk.

"It's too late now for our walk," Karen complained. "Why didn't you wake me?"

"I popped into your room and you looked so peacefully asleep that I thought I'd leave you there. I wasn't sure whether you would just as soon do the walk later today. Or, if you really have to see the sunrise in the Grove, we could leave it until tomorrow."

"Hmmm. Let's just have breakfast, work for a couple of hours and then walk to the shops to get the Times. We can do the walk to the Grove tomorrow. That's actually better. It's the day before the summer solstice. I really do want to catch the first rays of sunlight piercing through the trees at the Grove." Karen flipped on the kettle switch for her morning cup of tea. "How late did we get in last night? I was so exhausted I didn't even look at the clock."

"It was well after midnight and the party was still going strong when we left. Small wonder you slept in." Mary started preparing their usual breakfast of fruit salad and poached eggs. They had established a ritual of taking turns on a weekly basis to prepare breakfast and this was the start of her week.

"I never expected we would stay that long. It was much more interesting than I had thought it would be. I hadn't realised before that most of the people we know and do business with in the village are part of either the Mason family or the Barton family, either directly or through marriage. It was kind of fun sorting out who was related to whom during the wedding speeches."

"Yes, I had known that Mabel was Tommy's mother, but until she mentioned it when we walked together to the church, I hadn't realised that she was also Michael's and Willie's sister."

"Or that our mechanic, Dan, is Michael's son! Neither ever mentioned the other to us but of course they would have no reason to. That Barton family must have their fingers in almost every business in Coombe Gilbert."

"And what a surprise to learn that Betty's father and several generations of Bartons before him had been tenant farmers on Gilbert Farm, right across from us. How sad that his wife died right while he was struggling with three years in a row of drought and then bovine TB in his herd. I can't imagine how difficult it must have been for him -- and Betty too -- to have to deal with all of that. Do you remember what Betty's mother died of?"

"No. People seemed to assume everyone knew the cause of her death and it didn't seem polite to ask straight out. Also, did you notice that Michael did not have a wife or companion at the wedding? I wonder what happened to his wife?"

"I did notice that. And remember we overheard Adele and Mabel talking about Willie's wife Amanda and Mabel's husband Tommy dying right around the same time. Or at least that's what I thought I heard."

"Yes, I overheard that as well. Maybe something terrible happened in the village. Maybe there was a terrible flu or even some kind of scandalous ménage a trois or desperate housewives or something," chuckled Karen as she selected a particularly luscious raspberry from her fruit salad and spooned it into her mouth. "Just kidding, of course. I can't imagine anything like that among these people. They all seem very straightforward and straight living."

"What seems and what is are two entirely different things," countered Mary. "But back to Willie. How dreadful for him to lose his wife and his farm in the same year. You would think that whoever owns the freehold on the farm would have cut him some slack. No wonder he looks so much older than his brother. I think I heard someone say there's only two years between them. Looks more like ten or even more. Life's dealt him some nasty blows."

"At least he won't have to contend with Betty moving away from the village. Did you know that she and her father have been living in that small cottage annexed to Michael's house ever since Willie lost the farm? I understand from what people were saying last night that she's been caring for him since her mother's death and intends to visit him every day to make sure he's eating well and to look after some of his domestic needs. I find that a bit strange, actually. It's as though they've become co-dependent upon each other. I don't think he's even fifty years old yet, although I agree with you, he certainly looks much older. I wonder if there's more to his frailty than meets the eye. He might be clinically depressed and unable to fend for himself. No wonder he was terrified at the thought of her going away." Karen paused to enjoy a long sip of tea. She had chosen Assam this morning, light and delicate to match the fresh and bright day. "What a fabulous gift both families arranged for them. And now they will be our new neighbours. That will be fun."

"Yes,' Mary replied, "it will be lovely to have them as neighbours of course, but..."

"But what? Surely it will be better not to have Lark Cottage sit there empty."

"That's not the problem. Not at all! It's just that I've been thinking about that gift of a mortgage deposit for the cottage that Michael and Sam announced last night and I've been wondering how they managed to put together a sufficient amount of money. It must be selling for at least a hundred and fifty thousand pounds, possibly even closer to two hundred thousand. And what do first-time buyers need now for a mortgage deposit — thirty per cent? That would be forty-five to fifty thousand pounds. Even if it's just twenty percent, which it might be if Michael, as a banker, could obtain the most favourable rate for Betty, that still makes the deposit thirty thousand pounds or more. That's a lot of cash to raise. Michael and Sam mentioned there was some sort of plan that involved both family and friends but they all were quite tight-lipped about it. Of course it's none of our business and they may have access to money that is not immediately obvious in how they live their lives. And we don't even really know how they live their lives or how well off they are. But something about the whole affair is bothering me. I can understand the secrecy for the most part but it was quite evident that Betty's father, Michael's own brother, had no idea of what was happening. Why make him suffer anxiety about losing Betty longer than he had to? Unless maybe they feared they would not actually be able to purchase the property in time for the wedding and didn't want to build his hopes up and then have them crash down. I just think there is something deeper going on here." Mary paused in order to enjoy her poached eggs before they became too cold to eat.

Karen, who had hungrily devoured her eggs while Mary was speaking, slowly sipped her tea, mulling over what Mary had said. "I can see your point, although I must admit I haven't thought much about it except to be happy for Betty and Rob and excited about having more neighbours. Well, having any neighbours. Invited or not, James Anderson didn't show up last night and he isn't really much of a neighbour. We see him so rarely we would hardly know whether he lived next door or not. Although last night I thought I heard his front door open and close a couple of times soon after I had gone to bed and turned out my light. You know how his front door has developed that annoying little squeak over the past couple of weeks. We don't see him come and go, but we do hear him, or at least I can from my bedroom when the window's open. But it's such a tiny squeak -- it may have been something else I heard."

"I didn't hear anything from my room. Are you sure the noise was from Sparrow Cottage and not simply more gifts being delivered to Lark?"

"Possibly that's what it was. I have no idea whether that door also squeaks or not or whether we'd hear it if it did. It's farther from my window. And perhaps I was just overtired and didn't know what I was hearing. I know I fell asleep almost immediately."

"Something else I noticed last evening," said Mary, "was that neither Michael nor Sam drank very much. They always had drinks in their hand and they appeared to quaff them frequently but the level in their glasses rarely changed."

"My goodness, you're observant. Like a detective. However did you think to pay attention to something like that?"

"Their behaviour last night was dramatically inconsistent. They both strike me as very responsible people. I was intrigued by their take charge attitude throughout the wedding, as though the responsibility for the success of the evening rested on their shoulders. In that role, they were masters of control, acting like convivial hosts, chatting with everyone, smiling and ensuring everyone was having a good time. But underneath that facade was an undercurrent of agitation. They seemed almost conspiratorial. I saw them in a long huddle with Mable after which none of them looked very happy. Then Sam's brother Andy, father of the groom, went to join them and left after a few minutes looking completely wretched. Within moments, however, they all resumed their jovial aspects as they blended into the party. Despite everything going so well at the wedding, they seemed to me to be worried and to be trying to hide that worry. So, whenever I could without being too obvious, I observed them."

"Gosh, I didn't notice any of that. Of course, I was sitting right across from you and so couldn't possibly see what was happening in your line of vision. But you certainly didn't give anything away in your expression." Karen stood to refill her teapot, struggling to recall any visual anomalies from the previous evening. "I did see them speaking quite earnestly with Willie. Do you think he might be even more ill than we thought? He looks so weak and frail."

"Perhaps. But there's also that strange interaction that Marvyn had with Tommy. I had actually caught it out of the corner of my eye but didn't have an opportunity to distract you from your food."

"But it was such fabulous food," sighed Karen, breathing deeply through her nose as though trying to capture an olfactory memory of the culinary delights of the evening.

"Anyway, from my perspective, Tommy looked guilty or ashamed or something. He certainly was stressed by the conversation and Marvyn's right. He really did almost run away."

"And there was that peculiar conversation about how much he charges. Unless it's just that he's known Eve and Rowan for years and so charges them less. But then he raised his rate for Teresa and Marvyn right about the time we moved here." Karen paused to allow a slowly forming connection to seep into her consciousness. "Which was right about the time Betty and Rob were engaged. Of course, we didn't know them at the time, but I do remember some excited conversation about the engagement the first time I went to the grocer's. So possibly right around the engagement he raised his rates. Do you think raising his rates might have something to do with the money for the deposit?"

"Ah well, it's not our concern. Tommy told us his charges up front and we hired him on that basis, so I don't see anything to worry about there. I'm going to work in my studio for awhile. Why don't you start actually writing that novel you keep talking about and we'll meet again in two hours for elevenses."

"I will and, Mary Kemp, since you are so observant, I think I'll use you as the model for my detective! Oh, just one more thing."

"Stop that. You're just delaying."

"Possibly, but I'm still very curious about what happened to Willie's wife. And Mabel's husband. I'll bet I can look it up online in the archives of the Torbay Express. I know, I know – I should begin my writing, but I won't be able to concentrate so long as this is on my mind. I'm going to check that out right now on the computer. If I discover anything interesting, I'll come to your studio. If not, I promise to begin my writing."

Yet again, her writing was put on the back burner, as Karen burst into Mary's studio less than twenty minutes later. "You'll never guess what I found!"

"So tell me," said Mary, putting down her knife and the piece of wood she was shaping.

"They all died at the same time, Willie's wife Amanda, Michael's wife Margaret, and Mabel's husband,

Tommy. A car crash. Between here and Dartmouth. They had been celebrating Mabel's birthday on the Resnova, you know that boat restaurant on the Dart?" Mary nodded impatiently and Karen continued. "Tommy was driving. He crashed head on with a rental car driven by an American man, a Gilbert Anderson, who was visiting the area. Mabel was the only person in the car who survived, but she was hospitalised for concussion. Tommy was found to be considerably over the limit for alcohol and therefore judged legally responsible for the accident. The other driver, Gilbert Anderson, suffered very few injuries and was allowed to return to his home in Florida without any charges filed against him."

"How awful for Mabel. No wonder she's a bit rough around the edges. She's had to be tough to cope with all of that. And poor Michael. He's so sympathetic with Willie because he must completely understand what he's going through. Although Michael seems to be coping so much better with his own loss."

"But what about the other bit? Gilbert Anderson. From Florida. Ring any bells?"

"What bells?" Mary was puzzled for a moment, seeing from Karen's expression that she should be making some connection. "What? Oh no. You can't think that some tourist might be related in some way to James Anderson next door, simply because they share the same last name and come from the same state?"

"He wasn't just a tourist. The news story states that the purpose of Gilbert Anderson's visit to the area was to research his ancestry, to try to identify connections to the Gilbert family. And here we have James Anderson, five years later, moving to Coombe Gilbert, choosing a cottage on Gilbert Lane, across from Gilbert Farm. Don't you think that's a lot of coincidence?"

"Actually, I do find it very interesting. Perhaps we should invite Mr. Anderson over for tea and ask him."

"You're being sarcastic, aren't you? I'm never quite sure with you."

"Here's one thing you can be sure of. I'm going to work in my studio for the next hour and a half and you are going to your study and begin to write. Aren't you intending to write a mystery? Here's your mystery. A car accident, multiple deaths, a reclusive neighbour, a wedding, a secret plan and...and what? See if you can make a good story out of it."

THREE: MONDAY

This fishing trip would be vastly different from any he had done before. Preparing the boat in the darkest hour of early morning, Michael tried to use memories of his youthful jaunts to block images of Mabel's gruesome task from his mind. He even managed a slight smile as he recalled some of his crazy adventures and the tricks he had played on Willie in order to sneak away.

Michael's primary intellectual strength was mathematics coupled with an enthusiasm for economics. This combination had proven ideal for his chosen career in banking. Even so, he had also been an avid reader from the day he had started school. He had especially enjoyed drama, *The Importance of Being Earnest* one of his all-time favourites. Oscar Wilde's concept of Bunburying had resonated with his adolescent need for privacy from grown-ups while cavorting with his mates. There lay the basis for dozens of so-called fishing trips throughout his teenage years. A few of them had even involved actual fishing. For his sixteenth birthday, his father had given him a wooden twelve-footer with a small outboard motor. Fascinated by Joseph Conrad's *Heart of Darkness,* which he had been studying in his fifth form English class at the time, Michael had christened the boat *Nellie,* the name of the cruising yawl moored in the Thames near Gravesend in which Charlie Marlow narrates his apocalyptic story to four friends. Most of Michael's youthful escapades had consisted of using *Nellie,* moored handily at nearby Galmpton Pier, to get from Coombe Gilbert over to one of the several appealing coves, villages or towns along the Dart, usually accompanied by his best mate Sam. On very calm days, he and Sam would occasionally venture along the south coast but the tidal currents were unpredictable and risky and so mostly they had drifted alongside the banks of the river. From time to time, Michael had invited a girlfriend for an exploratory sightseeing cruise but these romantic interludes had been anomalies. A fishing trip in *Nellie* was primarily a blokes' day out.

Anyone can have a bad day fishing and neither of his parents had seemed to notice or at least had never mentioned his paucity of actual catches as long as his homework and chores had been completed first. His brother Willie and sister Mabel had been another story. Mabel was younger than Michael but keenly observant and equally mischievous. She could be bribed or, if necessary, threatened and occasionally, but very rarely, even included. But Willie had always taken his position as eldest child very seriously, as he did everything in life, and had considered it his duty to know the whereabouts of his two younger siblings. He could be neither bribed nor bullied and so including him in these 'fishing trips' had been unthinkable. Evading his wary eye had been the greatest challenge of their childhood adventures.

As the night air curled around him, he recalled the first time he and Sam had crept out of their homes near midnight and had taken *Nellie* to a forbidden beach party, really an alcohol-fuelled melee at Stoke Gabriel on the Dart. Just as his mind was settling into a good reminiscence of that party, Sam and Andy arrived with the packages from Mabel's shop, some stowed in their fishing kit and others bulging inside the huge rucksacks on their backs.

"You got the lighter task of tonight's work," moaned Andy at Michael as he hefted his share of the burden into the open boat, looking relieved to be rid of more than just the weight. "I think I've become too accustomed to Rob doing the heavy part of the labour the past couple of years."

"Ah, it's not so bad," said the burlier and stronger Sam, placing his packages carefully to balance the weight in the boat and then, as if to contradict his insouciant attitude, wiping his hands on his vest as though they were irredeemably sullied. "And," he continued, in a voice as burly and strong as his arms, "we can divide these parcels among all three of us when we take them ashore and up to the Grove." He looked Michael straight in the eye.

Michael, accustomed to Sam's voice, which tended to become louder the more a situation required it to be softer, spoke with quiet authority. "No more talking except about fishing. Voices carry." He pulled the cord, the motor revved almost soothingly in response and the three men began the most bizarre escapade of their lives.

The journey was a long one, both literally and figuratively. In measurable terms, it would have been much quicker to drive one of their cars to Fishcombe Cove and then walk roughly four hundred metres along the path through Churston Woods to the Grove, their intended destination. Alternatively, they could simply have walked directly from Coombe Gilbert to the Grove, a distance of less than two miles. But, in addition to the brightly lit parking lot at Fishcombe Cove where they could be easily seen with their bulky packages, the first path involved one very steep hill, difficult to negotiate carrying their heavy burden. The alternative way would have required them to walk through almost the entire length of their village where they would have been highly visible for most of the first mile. Even more important, however, was the fact that they were not known to be walkers, particularly at night. They were, on the other hand, well known for their nocturnal fishing trips, which had continued from their childhood into their adulthood, now with more actual fishing than had occurred during their youth. If seen, they wanted to be seen doing something familiar. While the likelihood of being noticed walking through their sleeping village with overloaded rucksacks in the small hours of morning was slight, it was nonetheless possible, especially so close to the summer solstice, which often brought out many more early walkers to catch the dawning light.

Consequently, they had chosen to navigate Michael's small fishing boat down the Dart through the Kingswear-Dartmouth passage and around the headland at the mouth of the Dart into the sea. They would then turn back east along the jagged coastline, push through the rough winds and tricky tides of Berry Head and then complete the comparatively easy last section around to Churston Grove. It would take a good two and a half hours each way in their small craft, possibly longer, depending on the wind and tide. There was an inlet, not really a cove, quite close to a reasonably level path leading directly to the Grove. It would be a scramble, especially in the dark, but it would leave neither the boat at shore nor the men in the woods for very long. Unfortunately, the tide would be at its lowest ebb right about the time they would most likely arrive and so they would not be able to manoeuvre *Nellie* over the rocky base of the inlet and close to the shore, sheltering her under the trees and thereby making her almost invisible from land or sea. Instead, they would have to locate a more exposed sandy bit for their anchor in the predominantly rocky base of the inlet and hope they did not have far to clamber over the slippery rocks. If the wind turned and the sea became too choppy to land, Michael had brought an inflatable dinghy they could use as a tender.

Figuratively, the journey was much longer. All three men had committed the usual misdemeanours of youth, shoplifting, being drunk and disorderly, speeding, and enjoying wacky baccy every now and then. Like most mischievous adolescents, however, they had grown up to be solid citizens, respected in their community for both their work ethic and their conventional values. The engagement of Michael's much loved niece Betty to Andy's son Rob, both of whom wanted desperately to remain in Coombe Gilbert with their friends and families but who could not afford to purchase even a modest cottage there, had spurred these men to the edge of their principles. The idea had seemed harmless at the time in comparison to the good they could accomplish by helping Betty and Rob to remain in the village where their families had lived for generations. Michael had masterminded the scheme to overcharge newcomers to the village by ten percent for goods and services whenever possible. Sam and Andy had immediately signed up to this plan as had most of the other members of the Barton and Mason families.

When it all went pear-shaped in James Anderson's cottage just an hour before the wedding, they had known they had options. They could have called the police when they realised that James Anderson was dead. However, their presence at Sparrow Cottage would have been questioned and as soon as their involvement in the plan for the mortgage deposit for Lark Cottage was discovered, they would all have been arrested and charged. None of them wanted a criminal record or possible prison time. The mortgage for Lark Cottage would be withdrawn, as the deposit had been obtained through fraudulent means, and Betty and Rob, despite not having been involved in the plan, would lose their home and end up having to leave Coombe Gilbert after all. They could have left Tommy alone in the cottage to call an ambulance in vain hope that Anderson was still alive but that also would have led to questions and probable exposure of the plan. They could simply have left the body in the cottage and let somebody else discover it. But they considered that someone may have seen Tommy there and, as Mabel learned less than an hour later, the Canadian ladies next door had indeed seen him. They had also weighed up the likelihood that even though everyone except Tommy had arrived through the back way, virtually invisible between the high hedges, it was always possible that someone had been walking behind them or that one of the ladies in the neighbouring cottage had been looking out an upstairs window at just the wrong moment. Even Michael, the master strategist, had been at a quandary about how best to proceed.

When Mabel had articulated her horrific idea of how to dispose of the body, they initially had all been repulsed, including Mabel herself. But not one of them could think of an alternative which would avoid having the plan for Lark Cottage exposed. Eventually they had all agreed it was the best of a sorry lot of choices but it had been a huge ethical leap for each one of them. This journey, with its source in their familiar world of life and morality in Coombe Gilbert, would thrust them into a different relationship with themselves, each other, and the world around them. This trip down the gentle moonlit Dart into the black wilderness of the sea and then into the dark secrets of the Sacred Grove mirrored the path of their roughly thirty-six hour journey from a conventional existence to their unanticipated and unwanted discovery of just how much capacity for iniquity existed untapped within them.

Nellie is proving to be a portentous name for this little boat that is carrying us into such darkness, thought Michael, as he steered his trusted companions down the narrow Galmpton Creek into the Dart. "Great night for fishing," he said, in as normal a voice as he could muster, unable to avoid looking at the packages brought by Sam and Andy and unable to avoid visualising Mabel cutting up a man as though he were a carcass of beef and wrapping up the parts neatly in butcher's paper as though preparing them for customers to take home. While he would never have described himself as a righteous man like Reverend Potts or an honourable man like his brother Willie, he generally thought of himself as an honest broker with, of course, an eye for an opportunity should one present itself.

He could readily rationalise, in his role as a banker, overcharging the new residents who had purchased expensive homes in the area with hidden and unnecessary extras such as invented fees and mortgage insurance with kickbacks. These sources of income, nudging only just a little beyond the boundaries of propriety in Michael's perspective, had provided the bulk of the deposit for Lark Cottage. Without them, the scheme would never have reached its funding objective. Besides, these newcomers, many of them foreign owners of second homes in the village, often used as holiday homes, were wealthy by village standards. Moreover, because they did most of their shopping and business in Exeter, Plymouth, or even London, they often contributed little to the support and maintenance of village amenities. They were justifiable targets. But he could not rationalise the desecration of a body, the sin, yes, sin, not a word he used lightly or even very often, the sin of what they were about to do with the body and most particularly what Mabel had already done. His kid sister. What was inside the two of them that made them capable of these gross violations of the most basic aspects of decent human behaviour?

"Hey, portside," yelled out Sam, as Michael jumped, suddenly aware of the ghostly shape of an anchored sloop just ahead and slightly to the left. Swerving starboard, he muttered his usual "bloody hell" expletive and refocused on the task of steering the boat, slowing to the six knot speed limit imposed on all vessels navigating the Dart. Nearing Dartmouth, the channel narrowed and the sailing craft moored in the river multiplied, although at least there were no ferry crossings to complicate their progress this early in the morning and the night lights of Dartmouth and Kingswear helped to illuminate the boats. The easiest part of the journey was almost done. As soon as they were through the mouth of the harbour, past the castle and around the headland, the ride would become much more difficult. So far, the outgoing tide had been their friend. But when the outflow of the Dart rammed into the churning tides of the sea at the headland, they would encounter tiny overfalls and turbulent waves. It would be a challenge to steer their small craft around the cliff and head east but one that he could handle as long as he remained focused.

Andy, not having the work of negotiating the cross tides of the narrow channel, became mired in his own thoughts about what they had done and what they were about to do. "I did not kill him," he kept muttering silently to himself. *I did not kill him. What is done after death does not hurt him in any way. And if it will save Tommy from having a prison sentence and a criminal record, it's worth it. But Anderson will be easily identified and connected with the village and then it won't take long before he's connected with us. I don't want to go to prison. And if – when – we're discovered, Rob will never be able to live in that cottage knowing what his father did to get it for him. What an appalling mess. A truly appalling mess. I wish I'd never become involved. How do Michael and Sam stay so calm about it all? We should have just left the body there. It was an accident. Not murder. All of our actions have been to distract people from discovering the Lark Cottage deposit plan so that we won't be arrested for fraud. I just don't see how it can work. Making it look like some sort of ritual murder done by fanatics or weirdoes in the middle of the woods. That's just crazy. We'll be caught for certain. This is only making it worse. But these are my mates and I can't see any way out.* "Why don't we simply throw these body parts into the sea right now?" He spoke the words as he thought them, reaching for one of the packages.

"What the hell are you doing?" Sam grabbed his arm,

"We should just throw these into the sea. They'll sink, be eaten by fish, be taken away on the tide."

"Yes, and be brought back to shore on the tide, some shore somewhere, and quite possibly not that far away," snapped Michael. "You'd be surprised. It's much more difficult to hide a body in the sea than you imagine. That's why we decided to hide it in the open, making certain it would be found with identification. It's more confusing for the police because it's unexpected."

"It's senseless is what it is," muttered Andy.

They were plunged into blackness. As soon as they turned east the lights of Kingswear and Dartmouth had disappeared, hidden behind the massive cliff of the headland. In a gigantic ebony bowl, moonlight obliterated by thick cloud, the boat tossed on the uncontained waves of the open sea. It was so dark they couldn't even see the huge Mews Stone just a hundred or so metres away, shrouded with sleeping cormorants. While steering the boat through the heaving waters, Michael took advantage of the brief absence of all light to pull Tommy's wrench from the pocket of his fishing mac and drop it into the water, the barely discernible splash covered by the sound of wind and wave. It took fewer than five seconds and the slight lurch and correction of the boat were unnoticeable in the general sweep of the small craft from wave to wave. Gradually everyone's eyes became accustomed to the blackness and they could make out, in the distance, the dim lights of two or three and then a half dozen commercial fishing boats trawling for their morning catch. They had a light on the boat but were hoping not to have to use it until they neared the inlet and needed to locate the precise landing spot.

At this point, Sam came to life, brandishing his decoy fishing rod like a sword. "It's like the smugglers of old," he uttered in a strange kind of boyish glee, almost as though he'd forgotten the seriousness of the night's work. "Beware the coastguards," he almost chuckled, as they passed by the row of tiny coastguard cottages, now holiday lets, used in a previous century by customs officials to catch the pirates and smugglers trying to get their contraband ashore. Then he settled down as the rough waters of the approach to Berry Head swept their boat into the heights and valleys of the waves. From the depths of every trough, each wave towered above them, ready, it seemed, to collapse right into the boat. Then, momentarily, they would feel on top of the world as the crest of the next wave lifted them skyward, only to plunge them down into the next trough. Everyone tensed as Michael struggled with the ferocious tides around Berry Head. Then Sam pointed. "There's Fishcombe Cove. I can tell by the lights. I don't see any boats setting out for an early morning fishing trip. We're out of sight of those distant trawlers. We might make it safely to the Grove without being seen after all."

"It's time to put on the beam," said Michael, "so that I can make out the shoreline better. The rocks are treacherous. Get your fishing rods and use them like rods, not like swords," with a glance and a wink toward Sam, the humour and the authority unseeable but audible in his tone, "just in case we do encounter someone. Does anyone have the time?"

"It's almost half three," replied Andy.

Reality struck. The sea had calmed sufficiently for them to navigate the boat safely to shore. In a couple of minutes they were going to land. Then they were going to carry the remains of James Anderson to the Sacred Grove, unwrap them from the butcher's paper which they would cram into a bin bag for later disposal, and scatter them around the intricately carved stumps. Crime after horrific and punishable crime. Could they really do this? While nobody uttered these thoughts, each man saw in the eyes of the others that they were all thinking the same thing. Andy said it first. "Can we really do this? Really go through with it?"

"We're on a course," said Michael. "What we've begun we need to finish. It's not right. It's not good. But it's the best damned thing I can think of at the moment. No more talking."

***

Karen handed a mug of hot coffee to an early-morning-grumpy Mary. "Thanks for agreeing to do today's walk at this beastly hour. I've wanted for so long to see the first light of the morning sun penetrate the Sacred Grove. I think it will be enchanting."

"It might well be," agreed Mary, peering out into the pre-dawn blackness, "but I'd still rather be snugly asleep in my bed."

"I know," said Karen, "and I really appreciate your getting up so early." She savoured a final sip of tea and then rinsed her cup and put it into the dishwasher. "This will probably sound strange but ever since we first saw that Grove I've been thinking it would be a perfect place for a murder. Remember P.D. James at the Dartington Literary Festival -- yes, of course you do -- saying that her most effective way to begin writing a crime novel is to discover a place that she thinks would make a perfect site for a murder and then to work everything else out from there. That's exactly how I felt when I first saw the Grove. I just want to check out a few things I've been thinking about and then I can really get going on this novel I'm having so much difficulty getting started." Karen stuffed some cranberry muffins and a couple of apples into their rucksacks, added a flask of coffee for Mary, the flask of tea for herself, two bottles of water and waited impatiently.

"You're not having difficulty with the novel," countered Mary, finishing her coffee much more quickly than she would have preferred. "It's just that you keep talking about it instead of sitting down and actually writing it. But I agree. The Grove in Churston Wood seems appropriately creepy. So does walking to it at three o'clock in the morning."

Karen and Mary had first encountered the Grove on a walk with the Ramblers. Initially it had seemed magical, an unexpected opening in the midst of the woods, almost a perfect circle guarded by sentinel trees, tall and lean of trunk and limb, with leaves spreading out far above their heads. The four stumps in the middle, elaborately carved to represent each of the four seasons, had drawn their eyes to the center of the Grove, where they had discerned a much more simply carved bowl providing an intriguingly plain counterpoint to the complex forms on the stumps. While they were absorbing the visual intricacies and contrasting simplicities of the carvings, Annie, the walk leader of the group that day, had directed their eyes upward, below the leaf lines of the encircling trees, to make out among the branches nine carved wooden masks equally spaced around the circle of the Grove, grimacing horribly like gargoyles to keep out unwelcome spirits. Whereas others in the group, many already familiar with the Grove, had found them fascinating, particularly Betty and Mary, Karen had suddenly felt immensely uneasy and unwelcome. The hairs on the back of her neck had prickled and her soul had recoiled, even as her mind was shouting, "This is the spot. This is where you set your murder."

Setting off in the still black hours of early morning, they were amazed by the powerful illumination of the moon as it abruptly broke out of the heavy cloud cover.

Everything seemed moving shadows, palpable shapes, like ghosts, rather than the pitch dark they had expected. They didn't even need to use their torches until they entered the woods. And then, under the heavy cloak of overhanging trees, they really did enter the dark. On went their torches, two intense little spots exposing almost nothing in the blackness. Hushed into silence by their surroundings, they barely heard their own footfalls on the soft path. They tried switching off their torches when they thought they were nearing the Grove but no moonlight penetrated the thick canopy of leaves. Just as they switched them on again, an owl burst in front of them, wings at full spread, completely filling the width of the narrow path before settling down again a few yards up the trail. Startled, Karen tripped over a root and fell crashing to the ground. "No harm done," she whispered, brushing away the leaves and dirt. Her crash seemed to echo in a fractured sort of way, as the sound of scrambling through leaves and what seemed like harsh sudden reverberations of her whisper shot through the night. "Probably frightened some poor animal. Are there deer in these woods?"

"I don't know," Mary whispered back. "Badgers, more likely. Shhh, let's listen." But the rustling sounds had quickly faded to nothingness as they approached the Grove. "Look, the sky is beginning to brighten. Turn off your torch."

As they entered the Grove, the soft dawn warmed the cool moonlight, creating a shimmery glow like the cooling embers of a dying fire. They saw what they had hoped for and anticipated, the magical opening to the sky bathed in a golden halo. How many seconds before they saw what was actually there? They were never able to remember.

The horror, the nasty, foul, evil horror hit like a punch in the gut.

Their eyes saw the lumps, eerily blanched by the dawning sun, before their brains realised what they were. Scattered randomly throughout the Grove were parts of a body. No, not at random. Mary discerned the pattern first, pointing it out to a stunned Karen. A foot, a calf and knee, and a thigh and hip formed a rough triangle at the base of the spring stump. Another foot, calf and knee, and thigh and hip formed another triangle at the base of autumn. Summer and winter each towered over a smaller triangle comprised of a hand, forearm, and upper arm. The head was balanced in the central bowl, overlooking the torso lying on the ground. And if the entire scene were not completely incongruous in itself, placed neatly on top of the torso was a wallet and on top of that, catching the first beams of sunlight to penetrate the Grove, something giving off a burst of gold. It took a moment to realise it was a shiny brass key, very similar in style to their own cottage key.

"We should call the police," said Karen.

"Already on it," replied Mary, pulling her mobile from her rucksack. "Damn, the battery's dead."

"I have mine." Karen punched in 999, heart pounding, her back to the grisly sight.

They had wanted to wait for the police at the Fishcombe Cove parking lot, the nearest a car could get to the Grove, but the officer on call had insisted they stay where they were.

"'I need to sit down,' said Karen, "but somehow it doesn't seem right."

"I know. I can't bear to look."

A thunderous flapping of wings forced them both to turn again toward the Grove. "Omigod, those bloody scavenger magpies have already descended. I'll shoo them away."

"Don't touch anything," cautioned Mary.

"Don't worry. I'm not even looking. I'm just waving and jumping up and down as close as I dare to get." Mary stood transfixed as Karen, her eyes two slits to minimse what she could see, jumped around the stumps and body parts, alternately flapping her arms and clapping her hands at the aggressive birds. The atavistic primitivism of Karen's movements seemed so appropriate to the horror of the scene that Mary wanted to scream. She had to stop this terrible dance of woman and bird around the desecrated body. She opened her mouth, but nothing came out except the scratching sound of a hollow croak. And then, with a unified whoosh, the birds swooped into the air. "There. They've gone," a breathless Karen managed to utter, " but they'll be back. I can feel them hovering."

Huddled together, Karen and Mary took a few steps onto the path leading toward Fishcombe Cove so that they could greet the police when they arrived and not have to look back at the gruesome sight. Every couple of minutes Karen stomped noisily into the Grove to shoo away the marauding magpies, relentlessly interested in the head in particular, surrounding it like a flapping shroud, picking, picking, picking until Karen screamed in anger and disgust at the birds. And then she screamed again in sheer terror at the enveloping mantle that seemed to be settling on her shoulders. She shook and shook, trying to rid herself of the weight of the darkness, but it held her fast. Held her still. Held her gaze on the head. Held her until the features took shape in her eyes, in her skull, her brain, her memory. The words were like cotton bunting in her mouth; she could barely speak them aloud. "It's James Anderson, I think. No, I'm sure of it. It really is. James Anderson. And there's a dead sparrow stuck in his mouth."

***

DI Cora Bodkin was in her twentieth year of policing with ten years at the rank of detective inspector at Scotland Yard. She was just beginning her first year with the Devon and Cornwall Constabulary. "Working backward and downhill," the less kind among her colleagues had described her career path. Others respected her steady and committed work ethic and acceptable, but far from stellar, arrest rate. All were shocked but few dismayed when she requested and received her transfer from the hothouse of the Met to the hotbed of drunken surfers and stag and hen parties in the Southwest. None asked "Why?" Not because they weren't curious but because Cora Bodkin did not explain herself to anybody.

Shortly before 5.am on Monday morning, two weeks after she had been assigned to the Torbay area of South Devon, the call came in reporting a suspected homicide in Churston Grove. A quick glance at Google maps on her iPad and out she drove to Fishcombe Cove, parking her red and black Smart car at the edge of the lot closest to the footpath to Churston Grove. Anticipating the walk through the woods, she had worn thick-soled comfortable shoes. Beige. Her bright red hair, now dyed to more than match the ginger hair of her youth, was covered with a broad-rimmed beige cotton hat to protect her from the myriad of spider webs spun between trees to trap the early morning insects. A beige tweed jacket and skirt obscured any feminine curves in her wiry frame and sturdy beige tights encased her legs, dully detracting from any inherent shapeliness. Cora Bodkin did not wear trousers. Ever. Two bright green slashes of eye shadow, one above each green eye, and a green scarf around her neck provided the only colour in her trimly official sandstorm presentation of self. She moved more deliberately than speedily yet quickly covered the distance to the Grove. Greeted with relief by Karen and Mary, she requested that they step aside and wait quietly while she inspected the scene and called on her mobile for the forensic team.

"Tell me again what you heard after you fell," she interrupted Karen, after she finally got around to listening to their story.

"Well, I'm not sure," replied Karen. "At first I thought it was an echo so it must have sounded similar to my crashing down onto the ground. But then I thought I heard sharp whispers, but not words, just whispered sounds, quick and hard, not whistly like a breeze through the trees. And then I thought I heard a deer or other largish kind of animal running, possibly more than one, cracking on twigs and leaves, and then silence."

"Could it have been a person, or more than one person?" asked Cora.

"That didn't occur to me at the time. Did it occur to you, Mary, that it might be a person?"

"I'll ask the questions," stated Cora. Firmly. Then, turning to Mary, she said, "But I would like to hear your answer to that question."

"I've been thinking about that," said Mary, "and trying to recall the exact nature of the sound. We didn't think it was a person at the time because we had no reason to expect anyone else here so early. We did expect nocturnal animals might be about, or early rising animals. Most of the time what you expect is what you see or hear so we immediately thought of animals." She paused. "In retrospect, thinking of the apparent echo of

Karen's falling, the harsh whispered sounds, the crashing through the woods, and then no discernible sound, it could have been a person or persons startled by the noise of Karen's fall moving quickly away, possibly whispering to alert others, and then disappearing down one of the paths, which might not give off very much noise at all once they were on it."

"The magpies," interrupted Karen."There were no magpies when we first entered the grove. They didn't arrive until after we had left the centre, where the body is," she shuddered and continued. "But then they swooped in as though they were already in the vicinity just waiting for it to be clear."

"I see what you're suggesting," said Mary. "You think we might have scared off the actual killers just as they had finished with the body. Then we arrived almost right away, giving no time for the magpies to attack the remains."

"Ladies, please. I ask the questions. You answer the questions. That's all you do. I analyse the answers. And I speculate about the possibilities. That's my job and I'm good at it. Got that?"

Karen, chastened, and Mary, miffed, both nodded.

"I'd like an answer please."

"Yes, Ma'm," seemed the only appropriate response but both Karen and Mary recoiled from the whiplash of her words.

"You," Cora Bodkin pointed with her nose at Karen Lawrence, "mentioned a brass key on top of the wallet. There is no key there now."

Carefully choosing her words to avoid another rebuke, Karen replied, "I'm sure that's what I saw. It looks very similar to ours." She fished the bulky Victorian-era key out of her pocket, startled to notice DI Bodkin stiffen and move her hand toward her truncheon as she pulled it out. "Could the birds have knocked it into the grass?" As she asked the question, remembering too late her earlier reprimand, she realised there were no more magpies hovering around the body, almost as though Cora Bodkin's formidable presence had frightened them away.

"The forensic team will be here momentarily and will check the site thoroughly. You can go now but I or one of my officers will need to speak with you again. Here is my card if you recall any further details."

Like children freed from an oppressive school classroom, Karen and Mary almost fled down the path out of the wood and back to sanity. Only when they were into full daylight on the edge of the woods did Karen turn to Mary with her anger. "What an irritating person that DI Bodkin is. How on earth would she ever gain the trust of any witness? I certainly will not be calling her if I think of anything. Although I'm pretty sure we told her everything that happened from our perspective."

Mary's brow scrunched in thought, certain that something crucial had not been said. Not able to ascertain what it was, she shook her head and focused on Karen's words. "Yes, she intentionally irritated us. I'm sure it was a ploy, a strategy, but to what end? I can't see that it was in any way helpful."

"Do you think she intended to frighten us into revealing something we might have held back? She'll learn first that we don't frighten easily and second that we have no reason to hold anything back. Hmmm. That missing key. Do you suppose she thinks we took it?"

"I doubt it. The forensic team will likely find it. The birds must have knocked it off somehow."

"We had our backs to the grove for more than a half hour, except for my intermittent forays with the magpies. Could someone have come back for it?" Suddenly the image of the magpies around James Anderson's head seared her mind. "Oh no! I can't believe it." Karen thumped her forehead. "Neither of us said anything about knowing James Anderson, that he's – that he was our next door neighbour. Bodkin never allowed us to finish our story."

"Well, just as Barry Manilow writes the songs, DI Cora Bodkin asks the questions. She made that perfectly clear. If she doesn't ask the question, we can't provide the answer."

"So you don't think we should go back to tell her?"

"Frankly, my dear, no!"

FOUR: TUESDAY

Torbay Express, Tuesday, June 21, 2011
MUTILATED MURDERED MAN MAGPIE-MAULED

Churston Grove was the site of a grisly find early Monday morning as two local walkers discovered the mutilated remains of a man as yet not formally identified, although there is speculation that he resided in the village of Coombe Gilbert. Few details have been released by DI Cora Bodkin who is in charge of the investigative team. Ritual murder is suspected because of the unusual disposition of the remains and the timing, the day before the summer solstice. All paths through Churston Woods to the Grove have been closed and the entire area within the Woods has been declared a crime scene. Our reporters are forbidden to take photos until the forensic investigation has been declared complete. We will provide more details as we are informed by the Devon and Cornwall Constabulary.

"Did you see this?" queried a surprised Karen, bursting into Mary's studio. "The paper says the body is as yet unidentified. How can that be? We saw his wallet!"

"Calm down. Let me read it." Carefully putting down her small but very sharp carving knife, Mary took a sip from her morning coffee before reading the news story. "We just assumed it was his wallet. Perhaps it wasn't his. Or perhaps the identification had been removed."

"Or might it be pending notification of next of kin? But don't they normally write that when the police are trying to locate family?"

"Possibly the protocol works differently if the person is from another country and it's difficult to identify next of kin."

"The story refers to the police suspecting a ritual murder. I never really thought about that phrase before, 'ritual murder'. I'm thinking of our discussion the day of the wedding. Rituals are ceremonies following traditions that are honoured because they offer hope and solace to participants. I think that's what you said and at the time I agreed with you. Still do. But how does ritual murder fit with that?"

"I'm not sure it does. There's the obvious difference that rituals are grounded in tradition whereas murder, at least in the legal sense, involves aberrant behaviour."

"So a ritual murder would be an oxymoron? An aberrant custom – or rather a traditional aberration? And is all murder aberrant? What about war? And don't societies that use capital punishment for murderers exercise a form of ritual murder? The taking of life to provide solace to the survivors of the victims of the criminal while providing hope to the general populace that the streets have one less murderer prowling for victims? Would capital punishment be aberrant murder or ritual murder?"

"I suspect that those who believe in capital punishment don't consider it to be any kind of murder. Don't be so quick with those devilish false dichotomies. I don't think it's an either-or situation and I definitely do not want us to bog down in a debate on capital punishment, particularly when we both believe it's abhorrent." Observing Karen's mouth open ready to speak, she quickly went on. "And don't start playing around with 'abhorrent aberrations'," warned Mary, attempting to avoid Karen's penchant for wordsmithery, often with ridiculous results. "On the other hand, you've given me an idea. Someone who does not feel that a person has received an appropriate punishment from society for a crime might kill that person and try to validate that killing by setting it up as a kind of ritual murder."

"A sort of vigilante application of ritual murder as a punishment for some kind of abhorrent crime committed by Anderson?" Karen shook her head, trying to imagine the quietly reclusive and seemingly gentle, from what little they had seen of him, James Anderson committing an abhorrent crime.

"Possibly," replied Mary, picking up her carving knife and continuing to work on her wood sculpture. "But ritual implies repetition. I hope I'm correct in my assumption that this set-up seems more personal, or rather more idiosyncratically individual, more like a one-off. But now that I've said that, I'm not sure why I think that. We don't know anything about James Anderson, much less who would murder him and for what reason."

"Maybe it's the wallet and the key and the sparrow in the mouth. That set-up definitely seems more personal and idiosyncratic to me, certainly unlike anything I've ever read about, but then, on the other hand, neither of us really knows anything at all about ritual murder, or any kind of murder for that matter."

"Set-up," repeated Mary, with a sharp flourish of her knife. "That's exactly what it is, like a set-up for a play or a film. The key, wallet, and swallow are props. My best guess at this point is that this was not a ritual murder but rather a murder disguised to look like a ritual murder by someone who also does not know much about ritual murders."

"Why would a person do that?"

"The main reason I can think of is distraction, to distract the police away from the motive of the real killer by trying to put them on the wrong path."

"That works for me. Deliciously devious. No, I take that back. It's appallingly unfeeling of me considering what's happened to our next door neighbour. It's just that I feel so unconnected to James Anderson as a warm, breathing human being. It's almost as though he were a prop himself, a prop neighbour. Even so, I cannot believe he deserved this abominable treatment. And I cannot imagine what kind of person would commit this sort of atrocity." Karen picked up the newspaper again. "Look, here's a follow up article on the Sacred Grove. It's quite interesting. I didn't know all this about it."

CHURSTON GROVE: SACRED OR CURSED?

While Churston Grove is known to many residents of Torbay, few know of its origins and evolution. As part of an art project implemented by Brixham Community College in the 1970s, the area was cleared, leaving four large stumps in the centre. Students carved elaborate designs on these stumps to symbolise the four seasons, the four directions and the four suits in a deck of cards. In the centre of the area marked out by the stumps sits a chalice carved with ancient runes. The Brixham art students also designed and carved a set of nine masks which they situated high on the trees encircling the Grove. The Grove was well used for the following ten years, not only by families for picnics and students for small dramas, but also by people camping overnight. Earth ceremonies were carried out on a regular basis. Gradually over the years it has fallen into disuse and is rarely visited except by the occasional picnickers or hikers passing through. In the 90s some stories circulated about aliens and green monsters but were never verified. Rumours abound concerning sexual misconduct during some of the earth ceremonies but these rumours have never been substantiated and no arrests have been recorded for legal violations in this area. Last night's mutilation in such a symbolically evocative location and at such a symbolically evocative time, the day preceding the summer solstice, conjures up the possibility of a ritual murder. The police are remaining silent on this point, offering no conjectures as yet.

"That article is simply speculative journalism at its worst. Aliens and green monsters! How can that sort of garbage be published? On the other hand, what a fascinating art project for the Brixham students," remarked Mary. "And their creations continue in my work," she smiled, pointing to her latest miniature reproduction of one of the wooden masks in the Grove. "I wonder if the Brixham College Art Program has retained its vibrancy. I'll have to check that out. I'd love to see if I could become involved in some project that creates public art in and for the community."

A strident ring interrupted their discussion. "Hey, the doorbell's working again. That's terrific. Tommy must have come by yesterday to fix it while we were out. Strange, though, he didn't pop an invoice through the letter box."

"Oh dear, it's that detective. I feel guilty just looking at her."

"Good morning," pronounced DI Cora Bodkin, making it seem anything but good as she strode through the door opened for her and headed, with some internal radar, straight into the sitting room. "Please sit down," she continued, reversing the roles of host and guest.

Karen smiled, with effort, and asked, "Would you like some tea?"

"Later, perhaps, thank you. For now, I need to know why you deliberately withheld information yesterday. Please sit." Bodkin indicated the two chairs she wished Karen and Mary to place themselves into and took a third, the least comfortable, for herself. She perched straight-backed on the seat, her beige summer suit impeccably pressed, white shirt collar crisp, with only a small green scarf around her neck to provide any relief of colour to her outfit.

Karen and Mary were aghast. All their ire from the previous day's interview returned, enhanced by this further charge. Mary internalised her anger and sat, hands folded in her lap, fingers interlaced, not saying a word. Karen's anger erupted. "We did not intentionally withhold any information. You requested clarification of what we saw and heard and then dismissed us before we could complete our narrative of events." With audible force, she thumped herself down into the indicated chair.

Was it actually the flicker of a smile that crossed Bodkin's face for a nanosecond? Mary quietly observed and wondered.

Coolly, DI Bodkin replied, "Then would you like to complete it for me now?"

Karen tried to visualise the scene exactly as she had experienced it. Over the past twenty-eight hours she had been encountering considerable difficulty trying to wipe it out of her mind. It seemed almost an affront to these efforts to have to relive it all over again. Having opened the floodgates of her emotions with her anger, she was unexpectedly overwhelmed by the mantle of darkness that descended upon her, just as it had in the Grove, imprisoning her will, opening her eyes once more to that horrible scene, forcing her eyes to observe the attack of the magpies on that severed head. With the same feeling of cotton bunting filling her mouth, she almost whispered how she had come to realise that the head belonged to their next door neighbour, James Anderson, and how difficult it had been, in the dim light, to discern that the brownish blob protruding from his mouth was a small sparrow.

"Quite an important piece of information to have left unsaid," Bodkin spoke softly, then waited.

For what seemed several minutes, but was barely more than one, no one spoke. Karen was trying to untwist the short history of spoken and unspoken between her and DI Bodkin. Mary was pondering how coincidence can swiftly shift to a perception of evidence, how perception can quickly disguise itself as knowledge and how evidence and knowledge can precipitate judgements which may be used to identify and potentially to charge suspects. Being first on the crime scene was high on the list. Withholding information was also high. And having some relationship, such as being close neighbours, added weight to the other two. Three strikes, and oh my gosh, was Bodkin actually thinking of them as suspects?

Astonished and feeling oddly guilty for something but not knowing what, Karen was asking herself the same question. Mary calmed her breathing and steadied herself. Bodkin simply observed and continued to wait, her expression inscrutable, like a snake before it strikes.

***

Sue Ambrose opened the door to the detective inspector's knock. DI Cora Bodkin flashed her credentials while introducing herself and asked to speak with Tommy Ambrose. Without having been specifically told anything about the scheme to raise the deposit for Lark Cottage, Sue had worked out that something not quite right was going on, that something very bad had occurred and that Tommy was involved, possibly deeply involved. Despite her best efforts, all this awareness, not quite knowledge but nonetheless resident in her mind, betrayed itself in her aspect, her forced smile, her formal politeness, and most of all her inability to look DI Cora Bodkin in the eye. "Tommy is not in right now," she began, but was quickly interrupted.

"Yes I am," stated Little Tommy matter of factly. "I right hind you."

Happy relief momentarily banished the worry lines from her forehead as she smiled at her son. "Of course you are, Little Tommy, my lover. Right here with Mummy." Turning to DI Bodkin, she relaxed a bit and finally smiled a real smile. "This is our Little Tommy. His father is Tommy." She sighed. "Little Tommy is indeed here, as you can see, but Tommy is working. I can reach him on his mobile if you would like."

"I'd like that very much, thank you," replied DI Bodkin. "And, if it would not be too inconvenient, I'd like to wait here and talk with you until he arrives." The nod to convenience was taken as politeness only and the implicit request to have Tommy return as quickly as possible was taken as a command. Sue's anxiety returned.

"Your wife has been most helpful," said DI Bodkin to Tommy as he burst through the front door fifteen minutes later, immediately annihilating the false courage he had managed to muster on the drive home, making him wonder what Sue had said, and what, in her innocence of the plan and resultant death, she might have inadvertently given away. In actual fact, all Sue had done was to make some tea and her conversation with Bodkin had centred primarily on Little Tommy. "I understand that you have been doing some work at the home of James Anderson?"

Tommy blanched, so quickly had the pigeons come home to roost. "Yes, something is always going wrong at these old cottages in town. I've been at all three of those cottages on Gilbert Lane repeatedly over the past few months, doing odds and ends, painting, fixing the electrics, repairing tiles, a bit of plumbing, the usual sort of thing," Tommy elaborated, forgetting in his unease Sam's advice to say as little as possible.

"When was the last time you were in Sparrow Cottage?" asked Bodkin.

Having already been alerted by his mother that the ladies had spoken of his presence in Sparrow the day of the wedding, the day of the murder, no, not murder, the accidental killing, Tommy darted his eyes from side to side just once before deciding that only the truth would suffice. "It was Saturday. I was repairing a clog in the upstairs loo."

"Was James Anderson present?"

How should he answer that? One would assume that he would be present if his loo were being repaired, so he should say 'yes'. However, James Anderson had not been present most of the time. He had been at the bank, having an argument with his Uncle Michael about some extra charges on the mortgage but had stormed out earlier than expected. He'd returned home to discover Tommy repairing the loo he had deliberately clogged up two days earlier, before he had been told that all the needed monies for the deposit on Lark had finally been collected and the plan was no longer in operation. How ironic to have successfully caused and repaired problems at least a dozen times at Sparrow over the past months and then be caught trying to put it right by secretly fixing free of charge the last problem he'd created.

He briefly allowed himself to smile inwardly at that thought. At least, thanks to Miss Halstead, who had brought English suddenly to life for him in the fifth form, he was able to recognise the irony of his situation. However, knowledge of irony as an abstract concept seemed far more useful in school than awareness of irony in a real situation in his life. Instead, his natural canniness took over as he realised that James Anderson could hardly contradict anything he might say at this point. He decided that honesty was the best policy for this question as well. "No and yes," he finally replied, looking DI Bodkin straight in the eyes, anticipating her resultant, "Would you care to explain that?"

Now he really was going to have to lie, a direct face-to face lie, never one of his strengths and definitely a challenge in this particular situation, facing this intimidating detective. Grateful that Sue had taken Little Tommy into the kitchen, he took a deep breath, spread both hands on his knees, and shifted his eyes downwards, suddenly noticing Little Tommy's favourite truck on the floor beside his chair, a red wooden fire truck discovered at a recent car boot sale. He recalled the time in his youth when he'd wanted to be a fireman. OK, so he did not have the courage of a fireman, the courage to face up to what he had done and take his punishment like a man, as his father would have said, but he did have the courage to lie to protect his family.

To protect yourself an inner voice said but he put that aside. If it were just himself involved, he would gladly, well perhaps not gladly but at least dutifully, pay the price for causing the death of a fellow human being. He knew that much about himself. *To thine own self be true* he recalled from his English class, *it follows as the night follows the day thou canst not then be false to any man* -- or woman, he supposed, thinking of the indomitable DI Cora Bodkin. He was about to discover more than he ever wanted to about his ability to be false to others.

And was the corollary true – if he were false to others, was he then false also to himself? Or did his self change in some irrevocable way to match the falseness of his lies? When he had lied in the past, he had never thought to ask himself this question because the safety of his family and the essence of who he was had never before seemed to be in jeopardy. In comparison with this situation, those misrepresentations of the truth seemed almost innocent, the stuff of childhood. Even the more or less indirect lies involved in the plan for Lark Cottage had not been as difficult as he had originally feared. Overcharging newcomers, retired foreigners, and wealthy summer residents from London and from the

North was acceptable, primarily because he saw the goal, to contribute to the deposit for Lark Cottage for his friends, Betty and Rob, as honourable. He had tried to make up for the additional charges by doing the best work he could on every job he undertook.

He noticed DI Bodkin's toe tapping. OK, she's waiting. I'm ready. Ready to lie. *The readiness is all* leapt into his mind. Deep breath.

"On Saturday morning James Anderson saw me painting the front door at Lark Cottage, right next door to where he lives at Sparrow Cottage. *Good. I remembered to use the present tense. As far as anyone knows, certainly as I far as I am supposed to know, James Anderson is still alive.* He told me about a problem with his upstairs loo, wanting it fixed as quickly as possible. *That's pretty good. Nobody can check on the truth of that.* He has another loo on the main floor, but the upstairs loo is more convenient for him at night, as he's afraid he might trip and fall down the stairs. *Ah, that's a good bit; shows it's possible that he could fall down the stairs, even that he was concerned about the possibility of falling down the stairs.* Because of a family wedding Saturday afternoon, the timing was difficult. I had to finish painting the door at Lark Cottage, which was to be a gift to the bride and groom, and then I had to clean up and be ready for the wedding. James said he had an appointment at the bank around the time I told him I would be finished the painting and able to start on his loo. He brought me an extra key to his home, telling me to let myself in and then shove the key through his letterbox after I had finished and locked up. *OK, that explains how I could get into his home.* Why are you asking about James Anderson anyway? *That's good. Since I should not know about his death, it's right that I should be wondering why the police are asking me about him.* Has he complained to the police about my work?" *Bloody hell! What a stupid thing to say. The more I talk the more I give myself away. The only thing he could possibly complain about would be suspicions about my deliberately causing problems that needed repair. Damn, damn, damn.*

"Now why might he complain about your work?" Bodkin sat perfectly still, not giving any indication of her awareness that Tommy was layering lie upon lie, blended with just enough truth to make the tale seem plausible.

"I can't think of any reason but then I can't think of why you are here talking with me about James Anderson when the only thing that connects the two of us is the work I do at his home. Is anything wrong? Has something happened?"

"I'm afraid I cannot share that information with you at this time," responded Bodkin in a tone neither friendly nor threatening. "However, I would like you to think very carefully about all of your actions on Saturday. If you can provide me any additional information concerning your interactions with James Anderson, I would very much appreciate it." She handed Tommy her card, called good-bye to Sue and Little Tommy in the kitchen, and let herself out, thinking that, despite not having discovered one solitary bit of real evidence about the killing of James Anderson, she had learned quite a lot from the misinformation she'd been given. Between her chat with Karen and Mary and her questioning of Tommy, it had been a good day so far.

***

Two young detectives, DC Dave Kendal, with just under two years of experience at the rank of detective constable and DC Jenny Johnson, who had been promoted to detective only three months earlier, were busily awaiting DI Cora Bodkin's arrival, setting up information in the incident room assigned to the James Anderson inquiry. Both had suffered under the acerbic reign of Cora Bodkin in the two weeks since her arrival but, eager and ambitious, they were both still trying to please her and were gradually learning to respect her. They had worked hard since the discovery of the remains of James Anderson in Churston Grove, keeping in close contact with the forensic team and checking out the leads and avenues of inquiry relegated to them by their mercurial boss. They both had understood that it would take some time for her to settle into her new position but were not yet certain of her expectations for them. Sometimes she would appreciate their hard work even when it harvested few results but at other times results were all she was interested in. In the short time that they had been assigned to her, their team of three had made eight arrests for serious assault crimes, all eight resulting in charges being assigned, a solid and respectable record bordering on outstanding. It could potentially position them well for future promotion if the team continued at this rate. During the same period, however, two impending arrests had been scuppered at the last minute as Bodkin had quickly and unceremoniously moved the team on to other cases, leaving questions in their minds about the basis upon which their DI made her decisions.

DI Bodkin scanned the evidence chart being developed by Jenny and Dave. She had quickly seen through the crude attempt to create a scene of ritual murder but nonetheless retained that possibility on a back burner, for reasons she kept to herself. The forensic pathologist, Keith McKenzie, had confirmed her hunch that the death of James Anderson had occurred in a different place and several hours before the discovery of the body. He had estimated death to have occurred at least a day earlier than the placement of the body parts in Churston Grove, basing his supposition on his observation that the body parts had obviously been kept chilled but not frozen. He had also noted, in addition to some bruises and contusions on the legs and arms, three discrete blows to the head, each blow apparently made with the same blunt instrument in roughly the same place, just above and slightly forward of the ear, but distinctly divergent in force, angle and depth. At least two were made post mortem, the third right around the time of death. He was uncertain, however, about the actual cause of death and was awaiting test results on internal organs. She turned to face her two detectives. "So, what do we know for certain?"

"Tommy Ambrose was the last known person to see the victim," replied Jenny quickly, certain at least of that fact.

"The vic argued vehemently with Michael Barton, manager of the bank in Coombe Gilbert, shortly before his death," added Dave. "The vic held a mortgage with said bank. He was up to date with his payments."

"The vic was a person, DC Kendal. I'd prefer that you use his name. Do you know what the argument was about?" asked Cora.

Dave continued, Bodkin's point taken with equanimity because he actually agreed with her. He had fallen too easily into the form of verbal shorthand used by many of his fellow officers to distance their work from human feeling. It helped him to avoid becoming emotionally involved with the terrible atrocities he dealt with on a regular basis but it also had begun gradually to dehumanise him. He welcomed Bodkin's call back to humanity. "They were yelling at each other quite loudly and Anderson continued to shout as he left Barton's office and walked through the bank. According to the clerks who overheard the argument, it had something to do with fees and mortgage insurance and financially-related delays on a land purchase. Apparently, Anderson had gathered some information suggesting that these additional charges for the mortgage were unnecessary and he wanted a refund. And he wanted quicker results on the fund transfer for the land purchase."

"Doesn't seem quite enough to kill for," Bodkin observed. "Do you have anything more about the land purchase?"

"No, I was about to follow that up this afternoon."

"Anything else?"

Jenny eagerly responded. "The body was cut up professionally by someone who knew how to dismember a corpse or a carcass. Possibly a doctor? However, according to Keith McKenzie, the person did not use a knife specifically designed to cut through flesh and bone. The cuts, while cleanly carried out, were nonetheless cruder than one would expect if it had been a doctor. Possibly the person did not have an appropriate instrument to hand." She held her breath, knowing how Bodkin hated speculation from anyone other than herself.

"Anything on the local doctor?"

Relief. No caustic comment from Bodkin. Yet. "There is no evidence that Anderson ever visited a doctor while in residence in Coombe Gilbert. We checked all surgeries and hospitals within a thirty mile radius."

"Good work."

Astonished at Bodkin's uncharacteristic reception of their information, Jenny hazarded another speculation. "There is a butcher in Coombe Gilbert, a Mabel Ambrose. But again, a butcher would have access to the appropriate tools for dismembering a body."

"Unless said butcher did not want to draw attention to her capabilities," responded Bodkin. "Anything else?"

Dave fielded this one. "The forensic team has concluded from the nature of the cuts that the body was kept cold prior to its being dismembered. Not frozen, as in a deep freezer, but cold enough to enable clean cutting. A butcher would have access to a large fridge."

"I'll have a little chat with Mabel Ambrose," Bodkin decided. "Dave, you check out all the paperwork at the bank. In addition to the fund transfer, see if you can find anything questionable in any dealings between Anderson and Michael Barton. Jenny, I want you to go through every piece of paper that forensics brought out of Sparrow Cottage. Then I want you to go to Sparrow Cottage to see if anything vital may have been overlooked. We'll meet again this time tomorrow."

In less than five minutes, Jenny was at her desk stacking papers in what she deemed topically appropriate piles, Dave was on the way to the bank and Cora Bodkin was in her shiny new black and red Smart car, on her way to interview Mabel Ambrose.

FIVE: WEDNESDAY

Torbay Express, Wednesday, July 22, 2011
MURDERED MAN IDENTIFIED

Late Tuesday evening, police confirmed the identity of the man whose remains were found in Churston Grove as James G. Anderson, resident of Coombe Gilbert. Mr. Anderson purchased property in Coombe Gilbert seven months ago, but divided his time between England and his other residence in Tampa, Florida. Little else is known about Mr. Anderson at this time as, according to village residents, he maintained a low profile in the local community. An intriguing coincidence is the fact that his remains were discovered by his next door neighbours, Karen Lawrence and Mary Kemp, who apparently happened to be walking through Churston Grove around the same time that the police have determined his body had been placed there. Another interesting connection between finder and victim is that Lawrence and Kemp,

Canadian citizens who worked for several years in the US, moved from the US to Coombe Gilbert just two months prior to James Anderson's arrival. They are considered to be helping with the murder enquiry and are therefore unable to answer any questions from the press. At this time, they have not been charged or identified formally as suspects in the investigation.

"My word!" uttered Mary with a sharp intake of breath, folding the newspaper in half and slamming it on the table, inadvertently knocking the teaspoon out of her cup and into the lap of Karen, sitting across from her.

"Bloody hell," muttered Karen, who had quickly become enamoured of that common English expletive, "what's bothering you?"

A calmer but still simmering Mary replied, "You might like to read this. On second thought, you definitely will not like reading it but read it anyway."

Mary watched Karen's brows begin to knit together in fury as her jaw dropped progressively lower and lower. "How did the newspaper get this information? How can they garble it so dreadfully? How can they make these insinuations? My God! This is going to be just like that Joanna Yeates murder investigation up in Bristol last Christmas, crucifixion of the innocent by the press!"

"Calm down. Let's start with your first question. Who released this information to the press? It can only be Bodkin. I cannot think she really believes we had anything to do with this horrid murder. I think she is setting us up as a distraction to get people talking. If the perpetrator thinks we are suspects, that person might speak more freely, might give himself away somehow. Funny, I automatically assume it's a man. I guess it could be a woman."

At that moment, the doorbell rang. When Karen opened the door, nobody was there. However, a parcel lay at her feet, neatly wrapped in plain white paper. "What's this? Oh no, Mary, it's your gift to Betty. Here's a note:

Dear Mary and Karen,

Thank you so much for your gift but I cannot accept it. I cannot believe either of you had anything to do with the terrible death of Mr. Anderson but the thought of him being found in the Grove right under these masks is too horrible. I don't want them in my house. I hope you understand.

Still your friend, I hope, Betty

"Well," said Mary, sucking in her breath and then blowing it out, "that's an artistic rejection I could have done without."

"I don't believe it's an artistic rejection. I think it's a gut reaction. Let's just put the package aside for now and wait until this is all over. My guess is that she will be happy to accept the gift when the time is right for her."

"Well, perhaps that might be the case. I hope it is." Mary picked up her mug of coffee, designed in art deco style and given to her by one of her nieces in Canada, regarded it ruefully and took a thoughtful sip. "Back to this article. I'd really like to know what DI Bodkin is playing at. It's obvious that she is carefully and deliberately releasing only the information she wants printed. There is nothing about the key or the poor sparrow or even the wallet. They always hold some details back, hoping that the guilty person might give something away in an interview by knowing that detail. I assume the wallet provided the identification but they had that wallet yesterday. Besides, I think identification has to be verified by a relative, if they can locate one, or perhaps by his dental work, if he has had any done here, or by someone respected in the community who knew him."

"That would not be either of us, obviously," remarked Karen, her shoulders tense and hunched in combined anger and frustration. "Respected in the community, I mean, especially after this news story."

"Well, perhaps we need to do something to garner respect rather than simply expecting it."

Karen straightened up and looked around her, as though the walls of the kitchen might provide a clue about how to earn respect. "Mary, I have an idea. At the party after the wedding, when I was chatting with Mabel, Tommy and Sue and with some of the other villagers, including our friends from the Ramblers, we all commented on how there were not enough opportunities for the new people and the long time residents to get to know each other. We've lived here almost ten months and still know very few people in the village, partly because of our lane being on the outskirts of the village but also partly because we are so busy doing our own activities and not mixing with the others in the village except on a business basis. I think we should arrange a few small tea parties to welcome to our home some of the people we've begun to know. That way, we can learn more about them and they about us. Before people can respect us, they need to get to know us better."

"Tea parties! We're being defamed in the newspapers, our neighbour is returning our wedding gift, and you think anyone will come here for a tea party? We'll be lucky if we're not lynched!" exploded the usually calm Mary, still angered by the news story and abashed by Betty's rejection of her carvings.

"No, listen. I've been thinking. Somebody in the village must be responsible for this murder and mutilation or at the very least might be connected to it in some way. The death must have occurred right around the day of the wedding, or perhaps the day after, and I keep visually going over the party in my mind. Looking back, I can recall a number of strange incidents."

"Oh yes, and don't forget Mabel's odd behaviour on the way to the church," added Mary.

"Good grief, she's a butcher. She could easily have..."

"Let's not get carried away. I'm not pointing a finger at anyone. We don't know enough."

"You're right. We don't. We need a way to learn more about those who might possibly in some way be involved. Let's make a sort of storyboard or chart the way they do on New Tricks and some of those other detective shows."

"We can do it in your study, similar to the way you are outlining your novel. We'll do it on the flip chart underneath your novel outline so that if by chance anyone comes into your study, they'll see your outline, not our murder chart."

"OK, that sounds like a plausible approach to organising anything we find out."

"Good. That's sorted. Now then," Mary asked, "tell me more about what you have in mind for these tea parties."

"My idea is that if we invite people into our home, in a relaxing environment, feed them and chat with them, we can get to know them better. And then, perhaps, as we learn more, we might be able to put that information together in such a way that we can determine whether someone in the village was involved in this death or would even have a reason to be involved in this death. It can't have happened without some kind of motivation. And that motivation would need to be very strong for such a horrible disposition of the body. And even if we cannot solve the crime, which we probably will not be able to do, at the very least we might dispel some of the suspicions that have been laid at our doorstep by that ridiculous newspaper story."

"Yes. I agree. Even without this murder and that dreadful story in the newspaper, it's a good idea, just in terms of getting to know more about our neighbours and having them learn more about us. Let's start with Mabel. I'm very curious about Mabel. We can invite her for tea and see what we can learn about her and from her. Should we invite her daughter-in-law Sue as well?"

"That might work. Mabel might be less on guard with someone else. Good idea. Who would be next?"

"I'm not sure. I'd like to chat with some of the men as well. You know, I'm beginning to get a slightly different idea. Instead of a series of small tea parties, let's have a couple of outdoor buffets. There's plenty of space for people to mingle in the garden.

"Good idea," agreed Karen. "We work so hard trying to get into the British culture. Let's show them a good old Canadian barbecue!"

"What do you mean 'a good old Canadian barbeque'? How does it differ from any other kind of barbeque?" asked Mary, who wasn't actually very fond of barbeques.

"Oh, you know, steak, baked potato, Caesar salad, and then strawberry shortcake. Mmmmm. Delicious. We might do it by generation. We could invite Tommy and Sue, Dan and his girlfriend, what's her name? Linda? and Betty and Rob to one of the barbecues, and the older folks -- what a lark to call them older; they're still a generation younger than we are -- to the other. That would be Mabel, Michael, Sam and his wife Adele, Andy and his wife Marge, and Willie. That would be a good group, actually, four men and five women, counting us."

"Slow down. I can't keep up with you. I'm warming to the idea but I think I'd prefer just to have one barbecue with everyone. Would that be too many for any meaningful kind of conversation?"

"You know, now that I think more about it, you're right. One group would work just fine. We have quite a large garden. We could accommodate the whole group. And they would naturally break into smaller groups to chat. Let's do it!"

"Well, that was a fast journey from a series of tea parties to one large barbeque but I do think it is a better idea. We should be able to learn a lot."

And another thing," added Karen, recalling Mabel's rebuff when she apologised for not having contributed to the wedding buffet, "instead of doing a steak, potato, and salad barbeque, which really is just as much American as it is Canadian, let's make it a cross cultural event. Let's provide all the meat but ask folk to bring their favourite salad or dessert. That way, everyone will feel engaged in making the barbeque a success and it will break the ice as we learn the stories behind people's preferred recipes."

"All right. I'll design the invitations. You can plan how we will seat and feed, what, about twenty people if everyone comes? When should we have it?"

"Soon, I think. The sooner the better. Let's see. This is Wednesday. If you can design and print the invitations this afternoon, I can hand deliver them before tea. How about after the church service on Sunday? That gives people time to go home and change and pick up whatever dish they have prepared."

"I think perhaps if we are having the barbeque after the church service and are inviting the people we met at the wedding, we should probably also invite the vicar."

"Oh dear. The vicar? But we aren't churchgoers. Wouldn't that be hypocritical? Besides, he's a little bit weird, don't you think?"

"'Charmingly eccentric' I think would describe him a little more kindly," replied Mary, "and I'm not sure it would be hypocritical. It would be neighbourly. And I think that most of the people we are inviting are regular churchgoers. At least they all seemed very familiar with Reverend Nicholas Potts. And he seems a genial sort of fellow."

"Right. I'll add him to the list and mention that he can bring a guest. I'm pretty excited. This will be our first party since we moved here. And now we need to plan a strategy for information gathering that will not be too obvious."

"My guess is that everyone will be very interested in this murder and will be talking about it. Simply listening and observing might be the best strategy."

***

At 1:00 pm, as requested, DC Johnson and DC Kendal presented themselves in DI Cora Bodkin's office with some findings that they anticipated might take the case to an entirely different level. Bodkin could sense their excitement. "What have you learned? Jenny, you first."

She took a deep breath and plunged. "James G. Anderson went by the name of Gilbert Anderson, Gilbert being his middle name, until just over a year ago, when he began making preparations to purchase property in Coombe Gilbert. Five years ago, Gilbert Anderson was involved in a horrific accident between Dartmouth and Brixham. He had saved the newspaper clipping, which I discovered in one of his drawers when I visited Sparrow Cottage this morning. Let me read it to you."

"No need," said Bodkin. "Just tell us in your own words."

"It was a two-car crash resulting in three deaths. James – or rather at that time Gilbert – Anderson was driving from Brixham toward Dartmouth on one of the local lanes, doing fifty-five miles per hour. He was not legally speeding because the speed limit is up to 60 miles per hour on that part of the road but it was dark, the road is very narrow, he was not familiar with the passing bays and he struck an oncoming vehicle with four people in it. Three died, all residents of Coombe Gilbert: Thomas Ambrose, Amanda Barton, and Margaret Barton. Thomas was married to Mabel Ambrose, who took over her husband's work as the village butcher, Amanda to William Barton, at that time the tenant farmer at Gilbert Farm, and Margaret to Michael Barton, manager of the Coombe Gilbert bank. Mabel Ambrose was also in the car but survived the crash. She was briefly hospitalised with concussion and some minor injuries undisclosed in the news story. Apparently she was the only person in the car wearing a seat belt. Thomas Ambrose was driving. While his speed, at forty-five miles an hour, was within the legal limit on that lane, he was found to be well over the legal limit for alcohol, as were all three passengers, so the cause of the crash was imputed to him. Gilbert – James Anderson, amazingly with only minor injuries, was not charged."

"Did you find out the purpose for his being here five years ago?" asked Bodkin.

"It appears that he came to check out his heritage in Brixham and the surrounding area. It looks from the paperwork as though he was trying to find a connection to the Gilbert family that lived in Greenway and were the original owners of Gilbert Farm. His mother was a Gilbert, which might explain how he came by the name."

"How long did he stay after the accident? Did he have any dealings with either Mabel Ambrose or the surviving spouses and families of the deceased?"

"From what I could ascertain, he did not. Apparently he was scheduled for some medical treatment in Florida. I have a request out for more information on that. He was scheduled to fly from Heathrow to his home in Florida two days after the accident, which meant he had to take the train to London the next day. Not having been charged, he was allowed to leave on his ticketed flight."

DI Cora Bodkin was not only the head of this team, but she had also, in the half hour prior to this meeting, been assigned to mentor Jenny. Generally, the mentor of a recently promoted detective would not also be her immediate superior. However, the Chief Constable of the Devon and Cornwall Constabulary was trying to support female officers, particularly female detectives because of their rarity, and he had emphasised that females should be mentored by females where possible. Budget reductions had eaten away at the numbers of both male and female personnel at every rank and so, contrary to custom, recently hired DI Bodkin was designated to mentor recently promoted DC Jenny Johnson.

Bodkin had never before, throughout her lengthy professional life, been assigned the role of mentor, largely, she supposed, because she did not radiate the kind of warm camaraderie with her fellow officers and detectives that would provide nurturing support for new recruits. She doubted she would enjoy being a mentor but she was determined to do the best she could. She decided that her major responsibility was to ensure that Jenny would progress through the ranks successfully, not only by means of her compliant personality and willingness to work hard but, even more important, through solid and smart detective work, through inductive and deductive reasoning, sound judgement, and the effective application of that judgement. Consequently, while Bodkin's usual response would have been to state as briefly as possible the significance of this evidence with its implications for the team, she instead asked Jenny to do that.

Taken slightly off guard by this shift in their relationship, Jenny nonetheless proved up to the task. "Guv, it could provide a motive. Tommy Ambrose did not seem to have a strong motive before. Now that we know he lost his father as a consequence of Anderson's driving, he does. Additionally, this revenge motive could conceivably apply to Mabel Ambrose, Michael Barton, or William Barton, all of whom lost their spouses in that accident. Also, Michael has a son, Dan, who works as a car mechanic in the village. He might now be a possible suspect. So this widens our range of potential suspects considerably." Jenny gulped a breath of air, unaccustomed to airing her deductions and opinions so extensively. "There are two major problems, though, with considering revenge as a motive. First, Mabel, as the only survivor, would be the only person able to identify Anderson visually but, according to the news story, she was unconscious at the scene and so could not have seen him. There would be little reason for them to assume that the James Anderson who had recently moved to Coombe Gilbert was really Gilbert Anderson. It's a common enough name. Unless one or more of them worked it out somehow."

"Second?"

"The official cause of the accident is attributed to Thomas Ambrose, not James Gilbert Anderson. There is no legal reason for revenge. On the other hand, revenge is generally based on emotion and perception rather than on legal accuracy."

"You are correct in both instances. There would definitely be a revenge motive had any of the spouses or their children realised that James Anderson drove the car that killed their respective spouses and parents and if they presumed, despite the legal ruling, that James Gilbert Anderson was at fault. However, we currently have no evidence that anyone has made either that connection or that presumption. Michael, as the manager of the local bank, might be the most likely person to have discovered his identity, having access to legal documents that would have Anderson's full name on them. We'll start looking into that possibility. Dave, what can you add from your investigations?"

Lured into a sense of ease by Bodkin's unusually temperate treatment of Jenny, Dave responded with less formality than his usual precise and straightforward presentation of facts.

"I didn't half learn a ton about getting mortgages, did I, not that it will help me with mine, I'm afraid." His grin was wiped from his face by a steely look from Bodkin.

He began again. "First of all, Michael Ambrose was cordial and cooperative, giving me full access to all paper files related to his dealings with Anderson, as well as a small table to work at. He even was willing to answer my questions when I wanted to clarify something from the documents." Bodkin's glower softened only marginally. He jumped in more directly. "Most of my queries concerned the mortgage of Sparrow Cottage. Anderson was a US citizen and resident when he initiated the purchase of Sparrow Cottage. As a homeowner in the US, with an excellent credit rating, apparently he thought he could easily obtain a mortgage at his American bank for the purchase of Sparrow Cottage. However, the banking regulations in the US do not favour providing mortgages for properties in other countries, particularly within the constraints imposed as a consequence of the housing and banking crisis. And you cannot take out a mortgage in the UK unless you have a bank account in the UK. But you cannot open a bank account in the UK unless you are resident here. One way around this dilemma is to find a mortgage broker to locate a mortgage lender who is not bound by such stringent restrictions. The mortgage broker will charge a percentage of the mortgage, usually around 1.5% according to Barton.

"Can you draw this out any longer?" queried a foot-tapping Bodkin.

"Sorry, Guv. There was a lot for me to absorb and I need to explain the background because it really is relevant." Dave consulted his notes. "According to my conversation with Barton, on the third of October 2010, Anderson first contacted Barton by telephone from Florida. He introduced himself and explained his interest in Sparrow Cottage, saying that his offer to purchase Sparrow Cottage had been accepted by the vendor but he could not secure a mortgage in the US. He therefore wished to mortgage through the bank in Coombe Gilbert. Barton explained the residency requirement and promised to see what he could arrange. On the tenth of October, Barton telephoned Anderson offering a mortgage at 6% plus mortgage insurance at an additional 1% with a brokerage fee of 1.5%. Anderson agreed to these terms and Barton faxed the paperwork that same day. Anderson completed the bank account form, indicating Sparrow Cottage, Coombe Gilbert as his home address to meet the residency requirement, following Barton's instructions, even though the purchase had not been finalised and no residency had been established. He then faxed the paperwork to Barton the next day. That same day Anderson mailed separate cheques for the deposit, insurance and brokerage fee, the deposit made out to the bank and the insurance and brokerage fee directly to Michael Barton.

Yes, yes, I know, all this is is procedurally unethical and bordering on the illegal," he interrupted himself in acknowledgement of Bodkin's quizzical response to these additional fees, "but it's one of the major causes of the huge fracas the last time Barton saw James." Dave continued reading his notes, "On November 1, Anderson flew to England and took up residency in Sparrow Cottage." He looked at Bodkin. "This much is supported by Barton's notes, correspondence from Anderson, and bank documentation."

"So now tell me the cause of this argument on the last day Anderson was seen alive?"

"It was exactly what you noticed in my overview of the event." Dave once again consulted his notes. "According to the clerk, Anderson stormed into the bank at around 1:00 pm, yelling about charges, fees, and insurance. He bumped shoulders with the assistant manager who tried to assist him, pushed him away and burst through the closed door to Barton's office. When Barton tried to explain the appropriateness of the charges, Anderson stormed out."

"And Barton's take on it?"

"According to Barton, after Anderson moved here, he did some checking around with other banks and mortgage institutions. Based on the information he was given, he was led to understand that he was not actually required to pay the brokerage fee, a hefty £4500 pounds, because Barton was employed by the same financial institution that provided the mortgage. Anderson concluded that both the mortgage insurance and the brokerage fee were unethical additions to his purchase of Sparrow Cottage. He acknowledged that Barton had done him a favour by taking a risk and processing his bank account application as a resident, which is definitely against bank policy." Dave paused, as though searching for the right words. "Although, according to Barton, there are some available loopholes." He heard Bodkin start to interrupt, then silence herself. "Apparently, Anderson did not consider either the favour or the risk worth a £4500 brokerage fee. Furthermore, because he had paid a sizeable deposit, he also did not consider that mortgage insurance had been necessary either. Barton tried to explain that Anderson would not have secured the mortgage from any bank without established residency and therefore, without Barton's help, would have had to pay the brokerage fee to some person anyway if he wanted to find a mortgage but Anderson wasn't buying that argument. Nor did he believe Barton's assertion that mortgage insurance was required when the purchaser lived in a different country. He flung open the door, strode through it, and slammed it behind him. That was the last Barton saw of him."

"Right," responded Bodkin. "You both have used the past twenty-four hours effectively. Regrettably, I have nothing to report from Mabel. She was taken ill the day after a wedding she attended at the weekend and was spending the day pouring her insides out, but not in response to questions. I told her I would give it a day and return tomorrow. It means that she will be prepared for my visit, unfortunately, but your reports have given me information about the accident that I can use. Dave, in addition to the land purchase details, I want you to follow up on Anderson's heritage in relation to the

Gilbert family. See if you can find whatever it is that he discovered. There should be some paperwork in his home or details on his computer. I'm thinking there might be something he learned that prompted him to move here. Jenny, you have a chat with William Barton tomorrow morning around 10:00. Don't telephone in advance. Just show up and knock on his door. I want you to take particular note of his reactions as well as his responses to your questions. Use the information you have about the accident as you see fit.

I will drop in on Mabel Ambrose around 9:30 and walk with her to the bank to visit Michael around 10:00, assuming she's well enough to leave her home. Otherwise, I'll ask Michael to come to her house, but that will lose the element of surprise with him. I don't think any of them knows we are aware that Gilbert Anderson and James G. Anderson are the same person. I'm not even certain that they know he's the same person. Let's try to ascertain whether any of them discovered the connection. And I'll check out whether any information from Florida — family, work, medical files, legal — has come in to provide further background. It's odd we've had no word from any family members or friends wanting to repatriate the remains. We'll meet back here at 1:00 tomorrow."

***

For two days in a row, the butcher shop in Coombe Gilbert had been closed. Villagers accustomed to purchasing their daily meat and poultry as and when they needed it were shocked. Even when Mabel's husband had died five years earlier, the shop was closed only for the day after the accident while Mabel determined what she was going to do. Having quickly decided that she would take over – she had certainly helped her husband at all stages of running the business, including purchasing and butchering the meat – she reopened the shop the following day. Other than Sundays and bank holidays, it had never been closed for a full day since. She even scheduled her husband's funeral for Wednesday afternoon, when the shop was always closed for half a day.

Good fortune, good health and good character comprised the unspoken 21st century golden triangle in Coombe Gilbert and, in many of the villagers' minds, Mabel embodied all three. She owned her own business which had so far survived the discounted fowl and animal flesh of the supermarkets, she had a hardworking son, happily married, who had already given her a grandson with another grandchild on the way, she was never sick, she went regularly to church and she didn't flirt with other women's men. While not the most outgoing of women in the village, she was solidly respected. She had worked for a couple of hours on Monday morning but had closed early and had remained closed all day Tuesday and now again on Wednesday. The sight of her shop closed for one day was shock enough but the villagers had soon learned from her son, Tommy, that she had developed flu or food poisoning or something very similar the day after the wedding. They all understood that flu or food poisoning would hold her down for one day, but two in a row? Not their robust Mabel! While in many villages neighbours would simply knock on a person's door if someone were ill, in Coombe Gilbert people generally waited until invited before going to a neighbour's home. Consequently, her friends, neighbours and customers watched and waited and wondered.

Inside her flat above the shop, Mabel was in a frenzy. She was not sick, or at least not physically ailing from some insidious infection, despite what she had led Tommy to believe. She was psychically sick; she was sick inside her soul; she was sick, sick, sick of the entire mess with James Gilbert Anderson.

Yes, she did know his real identity. She had discovered it almost three weeks before the wedding, when he had come to place his order at the butcher shop and discovered he was short of cash. Apologising that he did not yet have a credit card because all credit card issuers required a year's residency as a condition for approval, he had paid with a cheque. Their conversation about the name on the cheque had alerted her suspicions. Later that afternoon, these suspicions had been confirmed during the meeting she had subsequently arranged with him at the Trout and Salmon, the meeting that Karen had observed and had commented upon to Mary.

Five years earlier, that wretched night of the accident, Mabel had been sitting in the front seat of the car beside her husband, had seen the bright lights of the other car approach in the darkness, but only in the split second of flash before the crash had she glimpsed the shocked and horrified face of the driver. The resultant concussion had knocked her out, preventing her from seeing him again before he left for his home in the United States. That split second had not been sufficient for her to identify him. It was the G in his name that she had been curious about. 'James G. Anderson' was on the cheque he wrote that day he was short of cash for his meat order. "What does the G stand for?" she had asked, not yet suspecting his real identity but merely wanting to engage this reserved new customer in conversation.

"Gilbert," he had replied, fully aware that he was purchasing his meat from the wife of one the three people killed in the car accident five years earlier and fully aware that his answer would enable her, sooner or later, to work out who he was. He had dreaded discovery while knowing it would inevitably come. In a strange way, he was almost relieved.

"Gilbert. Means bright promise," Mabel had responded with a smile, not immediately making the connection. Mabel loved names, had always been curious about names, would have loved to have named her son almost anything except Tommy. She had favoured Archibald – Archibald Ambrose -- because it meant 'precious'. She would have called him AA for short. She liked the sound of Cecil but since it meant 'blind' she would not have chosen it. Cedric was another favourite and she would have been hopeful that her son would live out its meaning of 'literary' which, strangely enough, Tommy actually did with his love of English Literature. But male lineage will win every time with a first and, as it turned out, only son, and Thomas Ambrose – Tommy--it had to be. Thomas – meant twin – but her Tommy had been born all by himself and he was not in any way except physically a copy of his father. His father, killed in a car crash caused by – well, possibly not caused by but definitely contributed to by -- and then the penny had dropped -- a person called Gilbert Anderson. The back of her neck had felt as though a rod of ice were being thrust through it. Her smile had faded and then returned as she said, "This is usually a slow time of day. It's so hot. I feel like a pint. Would you like to join me across the street at the Trout and Salmon?"

They had chosen a small table in a cool, dark corner of the almost empty 16th century former coaching house, Mabel with her cider shandy and James with a half of bitter. Sitting across from him, Mabel had thought what a pleasant man he seemed, courteous without being overly friendly. She had been reluctant to break the serenity of the atmosphere by broaching the subject of the accident and so they had chatted about why he had chosen to live in Coombe Gilbert. He had initially been somewhat reticent beyond rhapsodising about the natural beauty of the area, a topic Mabel could certainly understand and appreciate.

It was at this point that Willie had entered the pub and had noticed the two of them in conversation. Initially he had wondered whether he should join them in order to be polite, but instead had chosen to follow his daily routine: a pint of his favourite pale ale and the Daily Telegraph, to be enjoyed at his customary table, which happened to be in a private little snug, better lit for reading than the dark corner where Mabel and James Anderson were sitting, and behind a partial wall separating him from them. He had sought his own privacy with no intention of encroaching upon theirs. His primary focus had been on his reading and, while he could very slightly overhear the gist of their conversation, he had not been interested in listening.

Mabel had responded to James's praise of the countryside by telling him how her family had lived and worked in and around Coombe Gilbert for several generations and would consider it unthinkable to live anywhere else. When she had married, her husband had wanted to move closer to London but she had been insistent and here they had stayed. Now their son was married and also living in the village. When she mentioned that she had grown up on the farm right across from Sparrow Cottage where James lived, his eyes had lit up and his entire body had shifted with interest. Elbows on the table, he had leaned over to explain that he had been checking out his ancestry over a period of several years. When he mentioned that he had made a trip to the area five years earlier, Mabel's ears echoed the words over and over, so that she barely heard the remainder of his explanation. Anderson had continued to describe how he had unearthed evidence of what appeared to be a direct link to the Gilbert family who had lived in Greenway and had, several centuries ago, owned Gilbert Farm and surrounding lands, in fact much of what is now Coombe Gilbert. Mabel's ears had continued to ring, preventing her from fully hearing anything but the repetition in her brain of his words: "I came here five years ago." Anderson had sensed her distress but could not stop the flow of words, as though he had committed himself, finally, to as much disclosure as he dared. He went on to tell her how, when Sparrow Cottage in Gilbert Lane right across from the old farm had come onto the property market, he had snapped it up. It had seemed a propitious base from which to continue his search for his origins.

If he had noticed Mabel pale when he mentioned his previous trip to the area, he didn't acknowledge it. And neither he nor Mabel had heard the snap of the newspaper on the other side of the partial wall. They had remained submerged in what had become a one-sided conversation, Mabel's head spinning the substantiated realisation that this man sitting a half-metre across from her had killed her husband and her two best friends. No, that was not true. It had never been proven, never even supposed officially or unofficially, that he had caused the accident. The police had very quickly attributed the cause to her Tommy, tipsy as usual, rather more than just tipsy this particular time, driving his wife and his best mate's wife and his best mate's brother's wife back home from their girls-night-out birthday party for Mabel at the Resnova, a restaurant on a boat in the middle of Dartmouth Harbour and their favourite place for celebrations. Because they had wanted to enjoy their wine with dinner without having to worry about driving home, Michael had driven them there and her husband Tommy had agreed to drive them all home. He had also promised not to drink before picking them up but nobody in the group had really expected him to keep that promise.

She had looked at the man across from her, had gazed at his face, worry wrinkles on his forehead contradicting the laugh lines around his mouth, his eyes a slightly faded blue-green, his hair nicely combed, a greying light brown. Their eyes had met only briefly. It had been a long time since she'd scrutinised a man's face so closely. She had actually quivered for the briefest of moments with a familiar tug in her gut, a warmth, embers beginning to glow with the aid of her cider shandy. She had allowed herself to enjoy the feeling for some moments longer and then she doused the fire before it even sparked. But the memory of the feeling lingered pleasurably. She was only mildly surprised at the realisation that she could not hate this man. She had finished her drink, saying she had to get back to the shop, and had left without mentioning the life-changing impact his visit five years earlier had made on her life. So lost in thought was she that she did not even notice Willie around the corner, still apparently engrossed in his paper.

She had remained silent about her discovery of Anderson's identity, not to save Anderson from potentially furious confrontations with Michael or

William or even Tommy or Dan, but more to keep it to herself as a connection, a strangely lovely and private connection between her and her dead Tommy. She could not have explained that feeling to anyone, not even to herself. She and Tommy had grown companionably comfortable in their marriage but the romance, the sizzle, possibly even the love had long gone or had evolved into something else. The last few years of her married life had been largely unremarkable, full of quotidian squabbles, some rare outbursts of anger, usually about his drinking too much, and, except for a few outrageously passionate encounters behind the closed blinds of the butcher shop, mostly mediocre sex. She had not even minded his occasional flirtations with Margaret, Michael's wife, because it had not ever occurred to her that Margaret would find her Tommy attractive or interesting. Certainly she had never, to Mabel's knowledge, reciprocated his attentions.

Mabel could barely understand it but for some reason that brief encounter with Anderson had rekindled memories of her physical connection with Tommy, producing a completely unexpected feeling of satisfaction. Was this what people meant by closure? She didn't know. She had never felt comfortable with the concept of closure. Things happen in life and you get over it and on with it. That's what she had done. But this meeting with Anderson had seemed to bring about a satisfying conclusion to that episode in her life. It was done; it was over. Telling others would somehow have dissipated that satisfaction.

But today, two days after having committed the most horrendous act of butchery she could imagine, that feeling of satisfaction was long gone. Usually calm and sensible Mabel slammed down the phone after demanding that Michael come as quickly as possible. "Get your skates on double quick and get over here," had been her actual phrase.

She paced the room, shoving her hair back from her forehead, banging cushions on the sofa, scraping her calf against a chair, then kicking the offending chair, and finally collapsing into it, her head bowed to her lap, her back heaving in silent sobs. The conversation she'd had with her son Tommy the day before would not go away. He had suffered through the interview with DI Bodkin unaware of what had happened to James Anderson after he had left Sparrow Cottage. After Bodkin had left, Sue had brought him the Torbay Express and a cup of coffee. As soon as he had read the story about the discovery in Churston Grove of the mutilated remains of a man, his insides had soured and his stomach had felt like a cold stone in his gut. He had known immediately that his mother must have been responsible for the barbaric destruction of James Anderson's body. He also had known that she had done it solely to protect him. And, knowing these facts, he had taken the guilt and burden of her deed onto his own shoulders. He had run directly to her flat and had banged on the door. His face, wild and red, had told her everything before he could utter a word. Mabel had tried to hold him, to hug him, but his rigid body had rejected her embrace. Nothing Mabel could say would comfort him. He had walked out of the flat so bowed down with the heaviness of his guilt that she did not know what to do.

Michael tapped lightly on the door and then let himself in. With one look at Mabel, he put the kettle on for tea.

"Pull yourself together, little sister. We can get through this only if we remain calm and talk things through. You look a sight. Why don't you wash your face and comb your hair while I make the tea."

Mabel calmed her heaving sufficiently to sit up, then stand up, and then wordlessly follow Michael's directions. When she returned, she was ready to talk rationally. "That Bodkin detective is coming back tomorrow. What do you think she knows? What am I to tell her?"

The tiny quivering muscle on the right side of his mouth challenged Michael's apparent composure. "I think we can probably assume that our plan to detract attention from ourselves by trying to contrive a ritual murder site has failed. I'm not sure why. I still think it was a feasible way to have the body discovered without any connection to us or to our original plan. And horrible though that way may have been, and actually was," he looked at Mabel and lightly touched her face, as though to acknowledge the dreadful role she had been required to play, "Anderson was already dead when we carried out those atrocities." Mabel looked as though she might begin heaving again and even Michael suffered a swollen gorge in his throat at the thought of it. He swallowed. "On the other hand, Bodkin may simply be fishing. With no leads for a ritual murderer, she has to begin somewhere and the most logical place is where Anderson lived. I don't think she really knows anything. Look how she temporarily fingered the Canadian ladies simply because they found the remains and they live next door to where he lived. That was so far from the mark. No, I think if we make sure that we all inform each other of everything that any of us says to Bodkin, so that we will all be telling the same story, we can see this through."

Mabel sank onto the sofa, her freshly washed face once again wan and pale. "It may already be too late. If she doesn't know already, there is something she will probably learn soon. I should have told you sooner."

Michael moved back a step, but then, realising that Mabel needed all the support he could muster, moved closer and sat down beside her. "Tell me now."

"James Anderson, James G. Anderson, is really Gilbert Anderson, the man who was involved in Tommy's, Amanda's and your Margaret's deaths."

The words hung in the air. Michael wanted to punch them away, make them unspoken, shove them back into Mabel's mouth, anything but have to deal with what he had just heard. He had made peace with Margaret's sudden death eventually but he had suffered dreadfully from Willie's decline over Amanda's death. How had he not suspected anything in all his dealings with Anderson? He was beginning to wish he had charged him an even higher brokerage fee when a much more significant cause for remorse suddenly struck him. Here was a direct connection between Anderson and all of them, a connection that was certain to be discovered during the police investigation, a connection that would make them all legitimate suspects. It was macabre. The tragic accident of five years earlier had in no way influenced the appalling misfortune in Sparrow Cottage just a few days ago and yet might be the one sticky spider web that entrapped them all. They were certainly innocent of any revenge murder but they were definitely not innocent of anything else connected with the death of James or Gilbert whatever-his-name-was Anderson. What a colossal mess! But his first duty right at the moment was to Mabel. He forced himself to focus on her immediate problem.

"OK. Worst case scenario. Let's suppose Bodkin has discovered the connection among all those involved in that accident. God, it makes me sick to have all of that brought up again. But let's assume she knows. You say she's coming to see you tomorrow? Did she give you a time?"

"Around 9:30. That's why I called you over. I need help. I don't know what to say. I can't even anticipate what she'll ask. Do I tell her straightaway or wait until I find out if she already knows?"

The doorbell rang. It couldn't be a neighbour. They all knew better. Tommy would phone first, although who could predict what he might do after their meeting yesterday. Could Bodkin have changed her mind and decided she needed to speak with her today after all? Mabel's composure, just barely under control, began to fray. She did not want to answer the door.

Michael did, to find the vicar on the threshold. Startled, he nonetheless warmly greeted him. Michael, not an avid churchgoer like Mabel and Willie, nonetheless respected the vicar, Reverend Nicholas Potts, with his earnest eyebrows closing in on his forehead then arching heavenward to punctuate the end of every sentence, always when he was speaking and frequently when he was listening. His was a mobile face to match his mobile mind, which would often shift unpredictably from topic to topic. While not a welcome interruption at the moment, he was less cause for concern that almost anybody else might have been. "Good afternoon, Reverend Nick," said Michael, using one of the villagers' customary appellations for their popular vicar. His other nickname, 'Nic the Vic', didn't seem quite appropriate in the circumstances. "What can we do for you this afternoon?"

"Ah, Michael. Good day to you. How thoughtful of you to drop your busy schedule at the bank for awhile and come over to cheer up your ailing sister. I didn't think I'd catch you here today. Maybe I'll even catch you in church one of these days! No, it's not what you can be doing for me today. I've come to see Mabel. I heard that she was under the weather, and I've come to see how she is, if there is anything I can do for her."

At his cheery voice, Mabel rose from the chair to greet him. "Hello, Vicar. How good of you to come. Can I get you some tea?" she asked, politeness only minimally winning out over her strong inclination to ask him just please to go away.

"Ah, a warm cuppa would be lovely, but sadly I cannot. I have several more visits to make. I've heard you were ill and so I have brought you Nursie Bear to look after you," he replied, taking out of a well-used M&S bag an equally well-used soft and cuddly teddy bear kitted out impeccably and quite smartly as a nurse.

"Nursie Bear?" Mabel looked at Michael who was having a difficult time keeping his mouth from giving away his inner amusement about the whole concept of Nursie Bear.

"Whenever any of my parishioners is ill, I bring Nursie Bear, who provides a bit of comfort, at least a warm cuddle when you need it. You can even microwave her if you need a really warm cuddle. Everyone tells me that Nursie Bear works wonders. You've not been ill since I've been in the parish, at least not to my knowledge, so you've not benefitted from her healing powers. But you'll soon see. I'll just leave her with you until you are feeling better," he said, noting the pallor in her cheeks and the unkempt state of her usually meticulous flat."Unless there is something else I can do for you?"

"No, that's fine. Thank you, Reverend Nick. I have indeed not been feeling myself the last two days. I shall return Nursie Bear to you the moment I feel better. This is very kind and thoughtful of you."

As the door closed behind the vicar, Michael and Mabel looked doubtfully at Nursie Bear and then had to hug themselves to stifle their laughter, careful not to make a sound. They would never have wanted to hurt the feelings of Reverend Nick, who, while somewhat eccentric, nonetheless cared deeply about those in his parish. At the very least, Nursie Bear played her role in reducing their stress. It was as though something in the air had cleared away the tension. Mabel even thought she might put a little extra in her collection envelope this Sunday. And then it all came smashing down on her again. How could she possibly think of going to church, sitting in her regular pew with her regular friends and neighbours, singing hymns, and listening to the word of God after what she had done to James Anderson? She slumped back into her chair.

Michael took over. "OK, you were asking about whether you should admit to knowing Anderson's real identity right at the start, before you are even asked. Bodkin's going to find out anyway. That sort of detail is easy to find if you're looking for information about someone. I agree with your inclination to provide that information as soon as appropriate in the interview, so that you appear to be as open and as helpful as possible. Tell her how you found out, and that you chose not to share that information with anybody because.... By the way, why didn't you tell me or Willie?"

"I didn't want a fuss," replied Mabel. *Well, that at least is true, even if only part of the truth.* "I was afraid that telling you would bring back all the misery and unhappiness of that accident, and that you might do something to James – Gilbert – something that you would regret." *Right. Instead my son thwacks him on his temple with his wrench, knocking him down the stairs, causing him to break his neck.*

"That makes sense," said Michael, "because for certain I would have banged on his door and punched him out." He paused, giving Mabel a quick glance to see whether she realised the unlikelihood of his doing anything of the kind. She remained slumped and non-reactive. "And yet, on thinking it over, I would not have told Willie either, not because I would have feared he might become violent but because I think it would have been too much for him. While the pain of losing Amanda has never left him, this kind of information would certainly make it worse, not better. Yes, I think you have a reasonable answer for that one. What else are you worried that she might ask you?"

"My guess is that she will want a complete accounting of my time from whenever they have estimated the time of death until the time the body was found. There are three times I was directly involved. First, right after Tommy called me on his mobile almost hysterical with fear after James -- I'm going to just continue to call him James – fell down the stairs, and you and Sam and I went to see what could be done." She paused for a moment and then indicated with her finger, "second, that same night, putting his body into the fridge when you and Sam brought it to me after the wedding party, and third," she stopped to swallow the rising gorge, shook her head, looked down, tried to raise her head to look Michael directly in the eyes but couldn't. And then she could, and did. Her voice like steel, she continued, "And third, the following night, preparing him for the ritual murder scene."

"OK, let's work through them one by one. I'm confident we can work out plausible and verifiable activities for you for each of these times."

SIX: THURSDAY

"Mummy, mummy, MUMMY," shrieked Little Tommy. "Tuck. Want tuck. Want fie tuck."

Sue, in the midst of preparing lunch, was already in a fluster. Tommy had not yet left for work today, although she knew he had at least three jobs slated throughout the village and those small jobs would bring in the cash needed to run the household. But she was worried about more than the money. He had been acting strangely ever since the day of the wedding and even more strangely after the visit from DI Bodkin. He would leave the house for hours at a time, taking his tool kit, but missing some of his scheduled jobs. He had never before missed a scheduled job that she could remember. To make it worse, he would not talk about what he had been doing while he was gone. But it was the news story about the man found in Churston Grove that had really pushed him over the edge. Sue had known that Tommy would have to leave right away to complete the job he had been working on when Bodkin had insisted on his coming home to speak with her. Even so, to provide some comfort before he went back to work, Sue had brought him a cup of coffee, a freshly baked chocolate muffin, and the Torbay Express, which she had picked up earlier that morning at the newsagent but had not yet had an opportunity to read. As she passed it to him, she had noticed the horrific Mutilated Male headline covering the front page but did not in any way connect it with her husband. After reading the story, he had placed the newspaper onto the table so very slowly, ironed it flat with the palms of his hands and put his head down on top of the paper.

When he lifted his head several moments later, his eyes were dead. That's the only way she could describe it. There was no life at all in them. He had looked at her but without seeing her. He had stood up as though manipulated by a string, as though if whoever held the string let it go, he would collapse. He had walked out of the house and walked away. Grabbing Little Tommy, Sue had followed him, somewhat relieved when she saw him go into his mother's flat above the butcher shop. When he returned, his eyes had changed yet again. They were no longer dead but they seemed to look inside his head instead of outside at his surroundings. He looked at her, he saw her, but there was no smile of happy recognition or openness to being comforted. He simply said that his mother was not well and he was tired. If anyone asked after his mother, say she had the flu. Then he had gone to bed for twenty-four hours, saying nothing about the job he had been working on before Bodkin had required his presence at home.

That had been two days ago. For most of that time, all he had done was sleep, sometimes deeply, more often fitfully, waking up hot and sweaty from his thrashing. When she had suggested calling the doctor, he had wrenched himself into a rage. Her Tommy, thoughtful, considerate, patient, rational, had spiralled into a rage so black and forceful that she feared he might have a heart attack. Sue was dumbstruck. She had no idea what to do, nobody to ask what to do, especially with Mabel also sick. She certainly had not wanted to involve the neighbours by asking any of them for assistance because she suspected that Tommy must somehow, although she could not see how, be involved with that unfortunate mutilated man in Churston Grove. Why else would DI Bodkin have come to their home? Why else would Tommy have been so upset after reading about it in the paper? So she had played with Little Tommy and cooked and cleaned until the house sparkled and the fridge was full of Tommy's favourite foods. He would go out with his tool kit from time to time, return, and go directly to the bedroom. The last time she had checked on him, he had been lying in bed, clutching Little Tommy's red fire truck, the very truck that Little Tommy was now clamouring for.

***

Sam Mason came into the grocery shop at midday, grabbed Adele around the waist, and announced, "I've got tickets on the Eurostar. Let's spend a few days in Paris."

"What? You've never wanted to go to Paris."

"But you have, my dear, and Majestic Holidays is offering a terrific deal on a long weekend, under two hundred quid each."

"Four hundred pounds! We don't have four hundred pounds to spare. And what about the grocery shop? And your work? You promised the Jacksons to attend to their brickwork this week. And you have other jobs waiting."

"They can wait a few more days. And you can get Betty to look after the shop. She's had three days of honeymoon. Time enough to unwrap her presents and get settled into the cottage. We had it pretty well all ready for her and Rob."

"We also have that barbeque the Canadian ladies have invited us to. Such a lovely invitation. Beautiful calligraphy, with a gorgeous kestrel, all hand drawn. And I've already accepted for us."

"Well, you can easily unaccept. They'll understand when you tell them your handsome husband is whisking you off to Paris."

"Never mind the handsome stuff. Handsome is as handsome does. What I want to know is why Paris and why now?"

Sam thought how to answer that. No man wants to tell his wife that he is frightened. But word was getting around about the investigations of the red-headed detective lady. So far she had just focused in on Michael,

Mabel and Tommy and on the Canadian ladies, even though they'd had nothing to do with anything. Michael had rung Sam soon after his meeting with DI Bodkin and they had discussed what to do and say. As things stood, there was no direct connection that Bodkin could make between him and James Anderson. He hadn't even done any work for him that could have been charged the additional ten per cent, having focused more on building brick garden fences and driveway gates for the newcomers in the large homes on the hill. But if the plan to fund the deposit for Lark Cottage were discovered, all the connections would be exposed. Everybody in both families would be affected, their lives ruined. Michael thought that the fewer people Bodkin could focus her sights on, the more he could manage what was said and not said. Besides, Sam had a tendency to lose control of his tongue in stressful situations. Michael had recommended that Sam and Adele take a well-earned break to the continent for a few days before Bodkin could start sniffing around in their corner.

Sam had been relieved at the suggestion. What they had done in the Grove had been churning inside him, unspeakable to anyone, even his wife. Adele had known of the ten per cent plan and had even participated, when possible, in the grocery shop. But he had not told her the details of that night of the fishing trip, particularly his role in it.

He'd made a pig's ass of himself that night and that was the truth. In the light of day, he could not believe that he could take that dead sparrow, wasn't young, must've died of old age, lying right beside the chalice and stuff it into poor Anderson's mouth. It had seemed funny at the time, sparrow in the mouth of the guy who had lived in Sparrow Cottage.

It didn't seem funny anymore. It seemed sick. It seemed nasty. It seemed as though something had taken away a slice, a huge slice, of his humanity and that slice would never grow back. He was frightened of being arrested, yes, but he was at least as frightened of the person he had become that night.

"Adele, I'm scared. I haven't told you everything about what went wrong with our plan the night of the wedding but you must have put two and two together and realised that I'm involved in something terrible, something illegal, something that could ruin us for the rest of our lives."

Adele certainly had put two and two together and had been working very hard to determine how she was going to fit the sum of that equation into her life. She had suspected that the so-called fishing trip had been something quite different and the newspaper story the following day had confirmed her suspicions. But suspicions were just potential energy in her mind. Unspoken, they were powerless unless she gave them power. She knew James Anderson solely from his visits to the shop and, just like the others, had overcharged him by ten percent whenever it was possible. It wasn't easy in a grocery store where most of the prices were set and where Betty was often nearby but she could add on a bit when weighing the fruit and veg. James Anderson hadn't noticed or, if he had, he hadn't commented. Certainly he did not deserve what had happened to him from her point of view. But he was not her family. Sam was her family. Sam and Adele were a unit; they had been together since the fifth form, since they were fifteen years of age. If she did not give voice to her suspicions, they would eventually vanish and not come between them. They would fester only if she allowed them to. So she had focused on her work, and had, for the most part, succeeded in making no compartment in her mind to house her fears.

"Say no more, my love. I'll ring Betty to see if she can look after the shop. Then, if she can, I'll call the ladies and let them know, with apologies of course, that our plans have changed for the weekend. Let's pack our bags. I'd love to go to Paris."

***

In preparation for her interview with William Barton, Jenny pored through the papers brought from James Anderson's cottage as well as printouts Dave had made from files on his computer. She was looking for any communication that might have occurred between him and Anderson in relation to the accident. As she had expected, the papers yielded no new information. The computer printouts, on the other hand, provided an entirely new dimension.

Anderson had been discovering his ancestry and developing his family tree for over five years and had unearthed a number of documents related to property in the area that had been owned by the Gilbert family. He was not interested in property that had been sold off, such as Churston Court, but rather property that had at one time been entailed through the male line. Gilbert Farm appeared to be one such property. He also had seemed very interested in the current patriarch of the Gilbert family, impressively titled The Right Honourable Doctor The Lord Gilbert, who lived at Compton Castle in nearby Paignton. While Anderson's connection to the Gilbert family seemed on the face of it to be tenuously matriarchal, he had uncovered some scandals that hinted at incestuous relationships and concealed births directly traceable to the male line, to entailments, and to inheritances. It was extraordinarily complex and quite beyond Jenny's understanding of heritage and the laws related to heritage. Even so, as she read through each document carefully, it seemed to her that Anderson had been attempting to build a case of entitlement to Gilbert Farm.

She decided to consult with Dave, who had been working on issues concerning the delay of the transfer of funds for a property transaction. She hoped there might be some connection between the property transfer and Anderson's interest in Gilbert Farm.

He answered his mobile immediately. "I'm at the bank. I haven't unearthed anything yet that will shed any additional light on the case. How are you faring?"

"I'm wondering whether we might talk through some of your findings and my findings. It might be possible to piece them together in some meaningful way. Do you have time for a coffee? "

"I do indeed. Meet you at the Trout and Salmon in five?"

"Can you bring the files you are working with?"

"Certainly. I'll show you mine if..."

"See you then." Jenny cut off the call, not wanting to encourage any silliness between the two of them.

Café latte in hand, she selected a table in a corner, the same table Mable had chosen for her chat with James Anderson. Dave arrived a minute later, ordered a large filter coffee and dropped his files on the table. "As requested."

Jenny summarised for Dave what she had learned so far from her preparation for the next day's interview with William Barton. The Bartons had held the tenancy of Gilbert Farm for twelve generations. Until the three-year drought coupled with six cases of bovine tuberculosis in 2005 and four more in 2006, the farm had prospered under the stewardship of William Barton. The farm was even marginally profitable going into the third year of the drought, the year of the accident. 2006. This much she had been able to glean from public documents.

So had James Anderson, apparently, according to Dave. Anderson had all the facts and figures on Gilbert Farm, including the loss of the tenancy, as part of his huge electronic folder on the property. William Barton's name appeared in relation to this loss as did the generations of William's forebears in relation to the long-held tenancy.

"Have you found any connection, either legal or financial, between Anderson's interest in the farm and William Barton's history with the farm?" asked Jenny, thinking that this information might provide a key to establishing some kind of connection between Barton and Anderson.

"There's really nothing to indicate any sort of connection with each other. The farm itself is the only thing in common between the two of them. And, of course, the accident but we don't know yet whether Michael Barton was aware of that connection. However, it is pretty clear that Anderson was trying to establish some kind of legal claim to Gilbert Farm through his ancestry."

"What about the land transfer transaction?"

"Well, it seems as though the current owners of Gilbert Farm are selling some acreage and Anderson was hoping to bid for it. However, with all the international regulations about transferring funds, Anderson seemed to be having difficulty getting the funds over here. But that's a bit complicated because it almost seems as though Michael was not facilitating the requested transfer in any way. In fact, it could be interpreted that he was putting up roadblocks to the transaction."

"Have you questioned him about that?"

"He's pretty smooth on that one. Says that since he crossed the line somewhat on allowing Anderson to open an account while not yet resident in the UK, he wanted to be certain to cross all the t's and dot all the i's on this transaction and do it according to all the regulations."

"What's your take on that?"

"Hey, you're sounding like Bodkin now."

"Sorry. I'm just wondering whether he could have been setting up obstacles that could be overcome with a little bit of extra cash."

"Oh, you are growing cynical. On the other hand, I must admit the same thought did cross my mind but I can't locate any evidence to support it."

Jenny closed the James G. Anderson file and opened her William Barton file.

"Here's something that might be important. William was born in 1963, the first child of Mary Ashcroft Barton and John Gilbert Barton. Could William, and his siblings Michael and Mabel, also have blood connections with the Gilbert family? Or was it because the Gilbert family had lived in the area for so many centuries and had owned so much land, with so many workers and tenants, that hundreds of people have Gilbert in their name?" To Jenny, the name had seemed seared in red on the paper even though its actual presence was a fading and commonplace black.

"What are you suggesting?"

"I'm wondering whether the entire Barton family discovered not only Anderson's identity but also his interest in Gilbert Farm. I'm wondering whether they also began to research their heritage and discovered some link. From what I understand, there are social networks for people with the same name searching for a common heritage. The Bartons and James Anderson might have connected on one of these sites. But it's really a far-fetched theory. And even if they did discover a link, you would think it would result in a collaboration rather than a murder. Unless, of course, the Bartons worked out that James Anderson was the same person as the Gilbert Anderson who was involved in the death of their spouses."

"You're right. It's a far-fetched theory but it is a theory. It's feasible. We'd need to learn whether any of the Bartons were engaged in researching their heritage. I didn't find anything on Michael's computer suggesting that he did. Of course, that was his work computer, since our mandate right now with Michael involves only his financial work with James Anderson. He might also have a personal computer at home but we'd need a warrant for that and we have no basis upon which to request one. And besides, it's no crime to look up one's heritage."

"Yes, it's a very tenuous stringing together of a mixture of facts and ideas. I agree. Far-fetched and much too speculative." Jenny and Dave finished their drinks and headed back to work.

SEVEN: FRIDAY

For the fourth day in a row, the butcher shop in Coombe Gilbert did not open promptly at 9:00. This time, however, Mabel had placed a sign on the door announcing that she would be open for business at noon and apologising for the inconvenience. Fortified by her previous afternoon's planning with Michael, Mabel felt mostly confident. She had been able to lie quite effectively as a child, seeking and then concealing experiences her parents did not want her to have but she had rarely experienced anything to lie about as an adult. A bit of emotional faking on the domestic side, as all married women too exhausted with raising children, preparing meals and working to be able to relax at the end of the day are able to appreciate and understand. And this past ten months of overcharging foreigners and newcomers by ten per cent in order to contribute to the deposit for Lark Cottage could be considered a distortion of the truth. She really did not count that as lying, however, but rather as equalizing the distribution of assets for a very good cause. And, of course, that was finished now. Mission accomplished. But with one tragic outcome to resolve as best she and the others involved could. She hoped her youthful experiences with deception would enable her to get through the interview with DC Bodkin without too much trouble.

She had tidied herself and her flat to their usual immaculate state. Neither she nor her flat were striking in any way, other than their similarity to each other: good quality, sturdy furniture built to last, without exceptional colour combinations or any particular flair but spotlessly clean and tidy. The same could be said of her shop.

Punctually at 9:30, DI Cora Bodkin rang the bell.

***

"That was Adele," said Karen, putting down the telephone. "They can't come to the barbeque after all. They're off to Paris for the weekend. Adele seems quite excited about it. Apparently Sam chose the holiday as a surprise for her."

"Wow! Nice surprise. It should be lovely and warm, crowded, but not as bad as it will be in August. Too bad they won't be here, though. They both seem so bouncy and affable. How many do we have now for the barbeque?"

Karen counted on her fingers. "Betty and Rob, Michael, Dan and Linda, Mabel if she's feeling better, Sue and Little Tommy, and possibly Tommy, who is also under the weather, Andy and Marge, Teresa and Marvyn, and Eve and Rowan. That makes 15 plus us, only 13 if Mabel and Tommy can't make it. Oh, and Willie is coming. And so is the vicar. He's bringing a guest, his older sister who recently moved to the area. So between 16 and 18, however the health bug sees fit."

"That sounds like a good number. We won't be crowded, and there will be lots of opportunity to chat with people."

Again the telephone rang, not a common occurrence in the Lawrence-Kemp household. Raising her eyebrows in a wondering query, hoping it would not be another cancellation, Karen lifted the receiver.

"Good afternoon. This is Reverend Potts. I hope I'm not disturbing you."

"No, that's fine, Reverend."

"I'm calling about your barbeque for Sunday after the service."

"Yes?"

"This may seem a strange request I'm about to make but let me give you some background. Our church has been involved for several years in providing support for abused children, particularly those who are abused while in the foster care system. One of the fundraising mechanisms we have used is to provide fortune telling sessions at carnivals, festivals, beach parties, and outdoor events in the community, such as your barbeque. We don't actually charge anything but rather suggest a voluntary donation of five pounds for anyone who wants their fortune told. Would you be interested?"

Taken aback, Karen's mind fluttered for a moment to find an appropriate response. "Oh, dear. I think your charitable cause is very important. In fact, I am hoping to do some volunteer work myself in the area of abused and neglected children after I become more familiar with the culture and the problems in our local area. But Mary and I have always shied away from inviting people to our home and asking them for money, even on a voluntary basis."

"What's that?" asked Mary.

"One moment, please, Reverend Potts. I just want to share your request with Mary."

Mary thought a moment. "It could be a lot of fun. Betty and Rob just asked me this morning if they could set up a croquet game during the party and I said yes. How about if you and I each contribute fifty pounds to the cause? Then anyone who wants to can participate in the fortune telling without feeling the need to make a donation."

Karen relayed the message to the vicar, who was delighted. "Of course, I won't be directly involved in the fortune telling. It wouldn't be deemed appropriate in the same parish where I preach. However, my sister, whom you are graciously welcoming to the event, has been predicting fortunes for the cause whenever she has the time. And one or two of the local ladies have a real knack for it as well. Would either of you be interested in doing some fortune telling yourselves?

"Oh, thank you, but no, I couldn't. I wouldn't be able to do it well enough," replied Karen, even as part of her was jumping up and down and silently shouting, "Oh yes, I'd love to."

Reverend Nick heard Karen's unspoken response just as clearly as he heard her spoken one. "It's very easy. It's not really fortune telling as the trained professionals or the spiritually gifted would do it. Rather it simply draws upon your interest in people to start a conversation which leads to logical predictions. There are some basic questions you can ask and behaviours to observe and then it becomes a chat during which you just let your imagination take you where it will. I organise this kind of event fairly often, not only locally but also for other organisations contributing to the same charity. In fact, my sister and I were even in Covent Garden last spring on behalf of my sister's church when she was working and living in London. We made almost five hundred pounds that day for the charity. I could give you a quick lesson prior to the barbeque and we can even establish a rota for the fortune telling so that you can pick the people you will feel most comfortable with."

"I know that Mary would prefer to ensure that the food and beverages were all set out properly and that people were comfortable. But you've convinced me. I would love to try. I used to have my Tarot read, and my palm, and my tea leaves, and many of the readings were extraordinarily accurate. I think I will really enjoy this."

"That's wonderful. If you would like to pop into the vicarage, you can pick out the costume that most appeals to you. I have several costumes, a couple of wigs, jewellery, robes and all the trimmings. I'll also show you how to use the electronic box of sounds and sights that add to the atmosphere. Which reminds me, do you have an external plug point for the electronics?"

"Yes we do. Right by the door to the garden."

"And is there room nearby the door for a small tent?"

Karen had been visualising a table placed in the garden. At the mention of a small tent, an idea popped into her head. "What about putting the tent at some distance from the house, so that we would not be disturbed by people coming and going through the back door? We have a couple of long extension leads. If you have another one, we could create quite a long connection almost into the public green, and have the tent removed from the hustle and bustle of the party. Would that work for you?"

"That sounds like an excellent idea."

"I have a question for you, Vicar."

"Yes?"

"Well," Karen paused, wondering how to phrase her question in a way not to offend the vicar. "I always thought that organised religion was against mystical practices such as tarot, palmistry, teacup reading, and other aspects of fortune telling."

"Hmmm. Yes, that's a good question. The Church of England has broadened its doctrine considerably in recent years and, while it does not officially condone such practices, it does see their utility for raising funds for societal needs. Before I became a vicar, I used to participate considerably in spiritual and mystical practices. I could say that these actually brought me closer to the spiritual presence of the Lord in my life. I see a kind of reciprocity or at least resonance among spiritualism, mysticism, and religion. Nonetheless, in the presence of my own parishioners, I generally ask my sister if she will do the mystical honours while I attend to the spiritual well-being of my flock."

Karen and the vicar made arrangements for her to drop by the vicarage and then ended the call. Karen turned to Mary with the look of a cat licking milk from its whiskers. "I have a plan that might help us learn if any of our neighbours are involved with James Anderson's murder or mutilation." As Karen explained how she would use fortune telling as a means of asking questions, Mary countered with a dry observation that the question-answer process usually went the other way around and that a fortune teller would be answering rather than asking the questions.

"Ah, but it's like teaching and learning. Teachers learn a lot about their pupils from the questions the youngsters ask. Then they build on what they have learned about what their pupils already know or want to know and raise their own questions in a discussion that engages both the teacher and the pupils in learning more. That's the method I intend to employ."

"Well, good luck to you. How are you coming with your chart of suspects and possibilities?"

"Not particularly well in terms of hard fact or verifiable evidence. But really very interesting in conjecture. Do you have time now to run through it with me? Or do you need to practise the piano or work in your studio?"

"I should do both but I don't actually feel like doing either at the moment. I'm curious to see what you've done so far. Let's go into your study and you can show me your chart."

"It's not much of a chart. More like listing ideas as they come and then going back and adding notes as I think of potential connections. I fear mostly that I'm making a lot of connections that probably don't exist, primarily because my knowledge is limited by whom I've met and what I've heard and experienced. It's like brainstorming before writing. Before you write down anything, everything is a possibility. But you put down one word or name or idea and suddenly you have a focal point. You put down another word or name or idea and then your mind wants to make a connection between those two focal points. So that every time I write a name or an event or an idea down, I'm opening up connections among a restricted group. If I've left out someone or something important, my connections will not add up to anything meaningful." Karen brushed her fingers through her hair, almost as though massaging her head would help her think. "But I can only work with what I know or can make a guess at. So, for what it's worth, here's what I have." Karen read her notes aloud, not because Mary couldn't read them for herself but because she thought it might help her hear or see something she missed, some connection she had not yet made.

Mabel: tense; butcher — could dismember a person. Nervous when talking about Tommy's presence in Sparrow and Lark. Met with James Anderson at pub. Husband killed in crash possibly involving J.A.

Michael and Sam: developed 10% plan

"Hold on," said Mary. "What are you talking about? What 10% plan?"

Karen managed to look simultaneously tentative and pleased with herself. "It's these connections I was telling you about. When you put everything down, they leap out at you. On the other hand, they could, as I mentioned, be quite wrong because I don't really know anything for certain. But here's my hypothesis. In order to raise the money for Lark Cottage, Michael and Sam developed a plan. They said as much at the wedding. Thinking of their conversations with Mabel and Tommy and others in the family during the wedding, it seems that several others in both families were involved in this plan. Then we discovered in our conversation with Eve and Rowan and Teresa and Marvyn that there was a 10 per cent differential in charges to locals and newcomers, a differential that began roughly at the same time as Betty and Rob's engagement. So, putting it all together, I think that Michael and Sam took the lead in organising and overseeing this plan."

"Clever you. See what you can figure out when you put your mind to it!"

Basking in Mary's infrequent praise, Karen beamed. "Oh, but there's more about Michael and Sam."

Fishing trip morning body found (Seen returning the boat at Galmpton --overheard conversation in grocery store) No fish. Possible to get to Churston Grove by water, but a challenge (found out by looking at map and asking the ramblers, some of whom are also sailors). Michael good boatsperson (asked Eve). Michael's wife killed in accident, possibly involving JA.

Karen grabbed her felt marker and started writing. "Aha – I'm going to add Sam's sudden decision to go to Paris for the weekend."

"Why? Do you think it's suspicious? How can that be?"

"Sam was involved in the plan with Michael, went fishing with Michael the night the body was placed in Churston Grove and had not planned to go to Paris until today according to Adele. It might not mean anything, but I'm just putting down everything that comes to mind."

<u>Tommy</u>: *charges us and other newcomers more than locals; kept finding things to repair; something new would go wrong each time he finished a job; Father killed in accident possibly involving JA (same with Dan, who lost his mother in same accident).*

Again Karen grabbed her marker. "Ah, another thing to add. I just realised the last time we went out that the key worked so much more easily in the door. Could Tommy have repaired it without telling us? If so, why? But I'm not sure when it was done, because I didn't really pay attention to it until just now, when I re-read my notes about the other repairs."

"What's that got to do with anything?" asked Mary, looking dubiously at Karen's list of tentative suppositions and speculations.

"I'm not sure. But we've always thought of Tommy as a man of integrity. If Tommy overcharged new residents as part of the plan and if he created little problems that required fixing in order to have more opportunities to overcharge, then perhaps once the deposit was made for Lark Cottage, he felt he ought to repair any problems he had created."

"That's an interesting theory," mused Mary, "but it seems a huge speculative leap."

"Well, I agree, but that's the purpose of this chart, to act as a catalyst for possible solutions to the problem of who murdered James Anderson. But you're right. Even if he did try to make up after the wedding for deliberately causing damage that needed to be repaired prior to the wedding, it still does not involve him in the murder."

"No, but you still might be onto something. He was at Sparrow Cottage the day of the wedding."

"And that could have been the day of the murder. Remember how upset Mabel was when we mentioned that we had seen Tommy at Sparrow Cottage that afternoon."

"But it's still all conjecture based on coincidence. It's not evidence."

Karen looked crestfallen. "It's just a way to help us think through what we have discovered to see if we can come up with some plausible scenarios to explain a horrible occurrence in this beautiful village populated by ordinary, hardworking people."

"Don't be so hyper-sensitive. It wasn't a criticism. I was just making an observation. Carry on."

<u>James Anderson</u>: newcomer. Dealt with Michael at the bank. Met with Mabel at pub. Possibly involved in accident that killed Mabel's husband, Michael's wife and Willie's wife.

<u>Willie Barton</u>: lost his wife in accident possibly involving JA

<u>Betty</u>: lost mother same accident

<u>Unexplained</u>: the wallet, the sparrow and the missing key: is there meaning to the sparrow? To the key?

<u>Assumptions and tentative conclusions to date:</u>

<u>Possibility 1</u>

Michael and Sam devised 10% plan overcharging newcomers. This money collected over several months to provide the deposit for Lark Cottage. We've paid Tommy about £2000 pounds for repairs and painting, so that would give £200 toward the deposit. We've paid Dan about £800, so that would be

£80. If there were 25 newcomers paying roughly the same, that would still provide only about £7000. If 50, then about £14,000. Michael might have been adding significant charges at the bank. Thatched roofs (Andy) and bricklaying (Sam) would bring in a lot. James Anderson discovered the plan and confronted Tommy the *day of the wedding.(Mabel's tension about his presence at Sparrow). Something went wrong somewhere, resulting in J A's death. Elders of family helped out in a gruesomely macabre way (explained by all the conspiracy the night of the wedding).*

"The problem with this first possibility is that I cannot imagine any of them doing something so horrible. So, on to the second possibility."

<u>Possibility 2</u>
James Anderson accidentally killed Amanda Barton, Margaret Barton, and Tommy Ambrose five years ago in a car crash. One or more of the spouses or children of those killed discovered JA's identity and killed him.

"That's where I'm stuck now. Again, I can't visualise any of our neighbours in the village doing this, but revenge born of anger and huge loss can do strange things to people. What do you think?" asked Karen, interlacing her fingers and hoping for a positive response.

"I think you have a very creative imagination and that you are confusing an evidence chart with a work of fiction. That said, you've certainly opened up some sinister speculations here. I am somewhat amused, though, at your conclusions. You obviously think that people will behave more bizarrely over revenge for loss of a loved one than over money."

"Well, yes."

"Well, not necessarily, my good friend," chuckled Mary. What's your next step?"

"I think I need to develop a list of questions to determine which possibility is the more likely or whether we are completely on the wrong track. We might be able to conduct some research on the accident to explore the second possibility a bit more. I've been wondering ever since I discovered that news story about the crash. Why was Anderson here five years ago? A tourist? Or did he have some business here? I still think it's more than coincidence that he called himself Gilbert prior to the accident and then started using James after the accident and five years later moved to a cottage on Gilbert Lane opposite Gilbert Farm. At the very least, one could presume an intention to deceive. But whom and to what end? I should be able to find something out about that. And we might be able to learn some answers to our questions about the first possibility at the barbeque.

"Have you thought what could happen if we do work out who killed James Anderson?"

"What do you mean?"

"If we solve the problem, or even if we discover evidence that may help to solve the problem, we have to notify the police, and that means we would have to inform DI Cora Bodkin."

"Snitch on our friends and neighbours to Bodkin? "

"Karen, less than a week ago you were moaning about not knowing many of our fellow residents of Coombe Gilbert. Now they're our friends and neighbours?"

"They've always been our neighbours even if we don't know them very well. And going to Betty's wedding has made a difference. People were all so friendly and they've all accepted our invitations to the barbeque. I am starting to feel as though I belong here. No, that's not quite right. I have always felt I belonged here, right from my first step into this cottage. But now I'm starting to feel accepted and liked here."

"But we'll still have to call the police if we find anything that would implicate any of them in the murder."

"Oh no. Oh damn. I didn't think. I was so caught up in the idea of discovering the murderer that I didn't think of the potential consequences. In fact, I was even more selfish than that. I was thinking of actually basing my novel on this murder mystery."

"You can't do that. These are real people living their lives. If they are caught up in this gruesome event, it might simply be coincidence. The event happened near where they live. I don't think there is any hard evidence connecting any of them to the death of James Anderson. You can't just cannibalise aspects of their lives, make wild speculations and then use them for your own purposes."

"How is my using and reshaping events in the lives of others and drawing upon human characteristics in people I meet to create events and characters in my own work of fiction any different from your making miniature artistic copies of the masks created by the students from Brixham College?"

"Oh, Karen. I'm surprised you even have to ask that. The difference resides in the public nature of those masks in Churston Grove. They were created expressly for the public domain, for the community, without copyright as far as I can tell. And I am not passing off my masks as original designs but rather as miniatures of existing works of art. It's different with people. People have a right to live their lives without fear of finding themselves in someone's book published as a work of fiction."

Karen, chagrined at her own thoughtlessness, scratched her head, thinking over Mary's words. "Well, I was planning to change a lot of it in the creation of my own story."

Mary flipped through the chart. "Based on that chart, you'll have to change quite a lot." She looked out the window across Gilbert Lane to Gilbert Farm. "This discussion is intriguing but rather removed from solid evidence of any criminal acts. It might be good if it remains that way. If you actually do find real evidence of the involvement of any of our neighbours in this death, you will have a dilemma on your hands." She turned to face Karen."Because if you do, you will definitely have to turn that evidence over to the police. You have no choice."

Karen looked stunned and then defiant. "I do have a choice. I don't know at the moment what choice I would make but I do think that I have a choice. Perhaps not legally. I suppose legally if I learned something and withheld that information from the police, I would be considered an accessory after the fact or to be perverting the course of justice or some such thing. Morally and ethically, I'm less sure about that." Karen joined Mary at the window and they both turned to look across the lane at the green fields and stone outbuildings of Gilbert Farm, simultaneously shrouded in shadows and bursting with brilliance in the afternoon sun, depending upon where they focused their attention. Karen was pale, shaken by her growing understanding that by playing author-detective with speculations based on hearsay and suppositions, she might actually have stumbled upon something that had the potential to ruin the lives of several people in the community.

Mary put her arm around Karen's waist in an uncustomary gesture of support and spoke gently. "What is legal is not always just. We both know that. The law is set up to define almost all human behaviour as either legal or illegal. You and I both agree that human behaviour is much more complicated than a simple separation of right from wrong. Just consider that recent case of the sympathetic euthanasia of a suffering spouse that resulted in the surviving husband being sent to prison. Was the custodial sentence just? Probably not.

But it was required by current law. We need to abide by current British law. We cannot be rogue players in the legal system of the country we have chosen for our retirement. We have to live within the rules, within the law." Mary sighed in sympathy with Karen's contrary viewpoint. "If we do uncover any hard evidence of illegal activity, we have to report it."

Karen stared outward, pondering Mary's words. She fully realised that following the law would be the easier choice and probably the wiser choice but questioned whether it would it be the most humane choice. "Wouldn't circumstances determine whether keeping silent or informing the police would be the more just choice?" she asked, still looking out the window and not at Mary.

"You can't make that decision. You're not judge and jury. You can't be a situational ethicist where crime is concerned. We live in a society organised by laws and traditions."

"I disagree. I mean, yes, of course we live in a society organised by laws and traditions, but I still think the individual, in this case me, I still think I have a choice, not a legal choice, but a choice based on humanity rather than on legality."

"You'd have to be prepared to go to prison for your right to make that kind of choice."

"Well, I'd be following in the footsteps of some great thinkers who championed civil disobedience," Karen spat out in frustration, then calmed herself. "But you're right. I'm not prepared to go to prison to save someone from the legal penalties for wrongdoing."

"Anyway, it's all far too hypothetical at this point. And besides, it's much more likely that Bodkin and her team will figure it out long before we can. Even so, you need to give a thought to what you will do if you manage to discover evidence which supports either of your possibilities. Or opens up a third."

***

"Hello. How may I help you?" Willie opened his door to discover an attractive young woman on his doorstep, displaying her credentials.

"Good morning, Mr. Barton. I'm DC Johnson. I'm sorry to disturb you, but I have some questions I would like to ask you concerning the death of James Anderson."

"Oh yes, a terrible thing that was. Right here in Coombe Gilbert. I could hardly believe it. I walk past his cottage quite frequently on my daily constitutional. Yes, please come right in, Detective Johnson. Would you like some tea?"

"Tea would be lovely, thank you," replied Jenny, thinking she could take advantage of Willie's going to the kitchen to look around his sitting room. It was a very tiny sitting room, very tidy and very sparse. But freshly cut hedgerow flowers in a medley of vibrant pink and pale lavender were in a vase on the window sill and several photos of two females, likely his wife and daughter, were placed so that, no matter where Willie was sitting, he would have an image of his loved ones nearby or in his sightline.

"Please take a seat." Willie graciously led Jenny to the most comfortable-looking piece of furniture in the room, a well-worn Queen Anne-style chair upholstered in faded rose-coloured damask set within a well polished mahogany frame. Only after she was comfortably settled did he leave for the kitchen, another tiny space almost entirely visible through its arched entrance from the sitting room. In less than five minutes, he carried in a tray with an elegant fine china teapot, two matching china teacups, sugar, cream jug, and a buttered toasted tea cake, cut into quarters, with two quarters on each of two china bread plates. He placed the tray on the small dining table, there being no room for a table in the kitchen, and poured the tea.

"My daughter Betty made tea cakes for me," he said, "fresh baked this morning. I hope you enjoy it. That's her, with my late wife, in all of these photos."

"They're lovely," replied Jenny, with inclusive reference to both the tea cakes and the photos.

"Thank you. My favourite is this one when Betty had just received her O level grades. She had done very well and Amanda baked her that cake to celebrate. They were laughing and having so much fun. Betty was married last weekend and very shortly I will have her wedding photo to take pride of place. It's being framed. It will be just Betty. My wife was killed in a car accident five years ago, just a few weeks after this photo was taken. But Betty wore her mother's wedding dress and looked so much like her that the photo will be like having them both together again."

Following up on Willie's fortuitous introduction of the very topic she had been assigned to explore, Jenny offered her sympathies. "It must have been terrible for both you and Betty to lose the person dearest to both of you so suddenly."

"We don't ever talk about the accident. You're right. It was sudden, like falling down a dark pit with no warning. For a while I thought I would never hit bottom so that I could begin to climb up and out but Betty proved the stronger of the two of us. Without her, I'd still be falling. But I'd prefer not to talk about that time."

Not sure how to proceed in response to Willie's stated unwillingness to talk about the accident itself, but thinking it might be helpful to remain in the same time period, she asked about Betty. "Did Betty continue in school to do her A levels or did she look for work after completing her O levels?"

Willie's pride in his daughter shone through his eyes. "Oh, Betty was clever in school. She had planned to do her A levels. She enjoyed learning. She had hopes of becoming a veterinary surgeon. But circumstances worked against her goals." He paused, not wanting to step further down the path to the past but determining, finally, that it was inevitable. He sighed deeply. "I was ill for quite awhile after Amanda's death and let the farm go. I'd been having some trouble with it but we'd been managing to keep body and soul together and stay in the black. Just. So when I became ill, Betty tried to manage the farm and look after me but she was only sixteen, almost seventeen, but still so young. It was far too challenging for her to handle. I see that now, of course, but I did not see anything much for several months after losing Amanda. I'm sorry, this is much more than you wanted to know. I'm just an old man babbling."

"Not so old at all, Mr. Barton, but the loss of someone we love can make us feel ages older than we really are." Jenny tried to smile. She was on unfamiliar territory here, talking about emotions instead of getting to the facts. But her instincts told her that she had to establish an emotional bond before she could get to the nub of what she needed to know. "I understand that your family had been tenants of Gilbert Farm for several generations and so you have lived here all your life. Did Amanda come from around here as well?"

"Yes, Amanda was Devon born and bred, in Paignton, although there was some Canadian blood in her through her paternal grandfather." Willie stopped and looked at Jenny calmly and directly. "Detective Johnson, it's very charming conversing with you but none of this has anything to do with James Anderson. What is it precisely that you wish to know?"

With that query, Jenny was on firmer ground. Willie's directness warranted equal candour from her. "Mr. Barton, I would like to know if you are aware that

James Anderson was driving the other car in the accident that killed your wife five years ago." She remembered Bodkin's command. Observe. What people do and how they react can reveal much more than what people say.

Willie sat still. The fingers on his right hand moved first, drumming a slow pattern on the arm of the chair. When he spoke, after almost a minute of silence, it seemed as though he weighed each word very carefully. "I did not know for certain but I had wondered. The name Anderson in itself did not at first capture my attention because I had known the name of the driver to be Gilbert Anderson, not James. But when I heard that James Anderson was from Florida and knowing that Gilbert Anderson had returned to Florida almost immediately after the accident, I did wonder . But of course one cannot come right out and ask such a question. I knew he was conducting his financial affairs through Michael's bank and I am confident that Michael would have informed me had he made the connection. I don't actually know what I would have done had I known that he really was the driver. Amanda is gone. That's the reality of my life." Willie suddenly stopped speaking, as though it had cost him all his strength. He reached for his teacup. His hand, which had not shaken throughout the making and pouring of tea, was now trembling. He replaced his teacup without drinking. "Detective Johnson, while I live with the constant awareness of Amanda's absence, I try not to relive the horror of the accident that took her away from me. I'm very sorry but I cannot help you any more with your investigation. My brother Michael, who handled James Anderson's financial affairs, has probably spoken with him more often than any other person in the village. If anyone can provide any information at all about him, it will be Michael."

"*Well and truly dismissed am I,*" thought Jenny, unsure whether Willie had cannily taken over the direction of the interview or whether he had truly been overcome by having to recall the accident and learning for certain that James Anderson was the person involved. Everything taken all together suggested he was genuinely upset but some deeper intuition was nudging her to think she might have been manipulated. "Mr. Barton, thank you so much for your time. I do have just one more question for you."

Willie's countenance seemed to dissolve, as though his muscles could no longer support the face he had managed to put on for this unanticipated conversation. "Yes, Detective Johnson, what would you like to know?"

"Apparently James Anderson had been looking into his heritage, specifically connections to the Gilbert family. I noticed in my preparation for this chat with you that your father's middle name was Gilbert. Since your family had lived and worked on Gilbert Farm for generations, did you ever try to learn whether you had any hereditary links with the Gilbert family?"

Willie's eyes answered before he did. He also noted that Detective Johnson had caught the answer in his eyes. He paused only a few seconds before starting his response. "Well, yes, in fact, I have been doing some research. Betty gave me a DVD to get me started on genealogy research last Christmas, saying that it would be something for me to do during these winters that seem to be getting longer and colder every year. She had to keep nudging me to get started on it. I already knew a lot about my family because we have excellent records for the past several generations in the books and accounts kept as part of holding the tenancy to Gilbert Farm. I didn't know much about Amanda's family but for some reason I didn't really want to research that. I knew her. I loved her. I lost her. That was enough for me. I'm sorry. I still don't understand what any of this has to do with James Anderson's death."

There was nothing more she would learn from William Barton during this interview, Jenny decided. "Thank you Mr. Barton. I may need to ask you more questions. If you think of anything that might help our investigation, please ring the number on my card." With that she passed him her card, which he took and placed on the table. Willie then accompanied her to the door, shook her hand, and gently closed the door behind her.

***

The day had started well for Sue and she was allowing herself to feel a bit better about Tommy. He still was not back to his normal cheerful and outgoing self but at least he had almost leapt out of bed this morning bright and early. He had played with Little Tommy for a few minutes and then, after a quick breakfast, had taken his tool kit and left to begin to work through the jobs that had been slated for his attention this week. Midway through the morning, he had rung to ask her to bring him a sandwich rather than take a whole hour off to come home to eat lunch. He also asked her to fetch Sam's mid-sized wrench since he had apparently lost or misplaced his and he needed it to repair a loo in one of the houses where he would be working in the afternoon. Little Tommy had been happy for the opportunity to visit his daddy at work and for the ride in his stroller. Sam, who had been just about to leave for the train station to begin his journey to Paris when Sue rang him, said he would drop off the wrench at the address where Tommy was working, as it was on his way. Sue had just given Tommy his sandwich when Sam and Adele pulled up. Sam brought the wrench to Tommy, slapped him on the back in friendly greeting, chucked Little Tommy under the chin, and jumped back into his car.

"Got to catch the 13:13 into Paddington," he called. "See you in a few days."

While Sue waved good-bye to Sam and Adele, Tommy slowly sank onto the front steps of the house, sandwich in one hand and wrench in the other. He looked first at the sandwich and then at Sam's wrench. The image of the other wrench, his wrench, his last action with that wrench and everything that had happened since filled his head until the weight dragged it down, down, into his chest, down to his knees. In less than ten seconds Sue watched her husband's newly-found energy drain away. Frightened, she used the only weapon she had. "Little Tommy, give your daddy a kiss. Tell him you love him. Quickly now."

"Luv you Daddy."

A flicker of light came back into Tommy's eyes, illuminating such inner pain that Sue could hardly bear to look. "Love you too, Son." He hugged his little fellow, looking over the top of his head, mouthing to Sue, "Get him out of here, please, right away."

Somewhere within her, Sue found the strength to say "No! You're coming with us. Daddy's going to come home with us for a little while, right Little Tommy?" She felt miserable using their little boy as ammunition but she also felt she was fighting a battle for her husband, one that she and Little Tommy might lose. One that they all might lose.

Tommy stood up, suddenly enraged, not at Sue or Little Tommy, but at his never-ending battle with himself. He lifted his hand with the wrench as though to strike the sky, took one step forward, stumbled on the step, dropped the wrench, and sank into himself. "Yes, take me home."

It takes awhile to collapse a child's stroller and install it as a reconfigured car seat into a vehicle and then to help a grown man who has lost control of his muscles to stand up sufficiently to be more or less pushed into that same vehicle and then straightened out and strapped into his seatbelt. Sweating from the effort, Sue also found the presence of mind to ring the bell of the house where Tommy had been working and inform the householder, an older woman whom she did not know very well, that Tommy was ill and would finish the job as soon as possible another day. Then she picked up the tools he had been using, including the wrench Sam had brought over, wiped them more or less clean with the cloth Tommy kept for that purpose in the van, placed them into his took kit, and hoisted it into the boot. Only then did she take a swig from the flask of hot tea she had brought for Tommy.

Back home, with Little Tommy fed and napping, she sat down across from Tommy at the kitchen table with a jug of water and his favourite biscuits and directed him to tell her everything, to hold nothing back. "Save the chocolate coating for the biscuits," she had said, with no trace of humour in her voice. "I want the whole story, no matter what."

***

DC Johnson and DC Kendal lined up in front of DI Bodkin feeling like cannon fodder. For all their hard work the past twenty-four hours, poring over papers and computer screens, Kendal checking with forensics about the murder weapon, the dead sparrow, and the lost key, and Johnson talking with William Barton, neither of them had anything solid to report. They were certain they'd be in for a lashing. What they could not have anticipated was that DI Bodkin was in the same position.

"Damn," was the first word she uttered, after she had heard their reports and prior to making hers. "Mabel Ambrose and Michael Barton were both so well prepared that they almost had their lines memorised. Not a moment's pause between question and answer. Both of them, questioned individually and together, had complementary stories, each supporting the other and together covering the entire time from when the murder might have occurred until the body was found. The only possible hole in Michael's story was his time spent fishing." But Bodkin had tracked that down after chatting with him and his story was backed up by his son, Dan Barton, and indirectly by Sam Mason, who had just left with his wife to Paris but who had talked about their pre-dawn fishing trip in the Trout and Salmon and in the grocery a couple of days earlier. Bodkin had then spoken with Robbie James, the publican at the Trout and Salmon and Betty Ambrose, filling in for Adele at the grocery, both of whom had overheard talk of Michael and Sam's participation in the pre-dawn fishing trip. She had also learned that Sam's brother Andy had been with them. All spoke about having planned the fishing trip for the night after the wedding as a kind of lads' night out for the older generation, the uncle of the bride and the father and uncle of the groom, all three having been mates since childhood. On the surface it had all seemed logical and harmless. But Bodkin's antennae were humming.

"I'd like to have forensics check out Mabel Ambrose's butcher block but we really do not have sufficient solid evidence to make such a request. I'd like to check out Tommy Ambrose's tool kit, and Sam Mason's too for that matter, just to see if anything would match the indentations in Anderson's skull. But we don't have sufficient evidence to request that either. And based on what you've told me just now, Jenny and Dave, I'd also like to requisition William Barton's computer and Michael Barton's home computer. Again, there is insufficient evidence for such a request. We'd be accused of being on our own fishing trip."

"So where do we go from here, Guv?" asked a tired and dismayed Jenny.

Dave spoke up. "McKenzie has now confirmed that all three indentations on the skull were made by the same instrument. When I spoke with Keith just before coming to this meeting, I asked whether he could speculate on the type of instrument. That, as you might guess, was a non starter. I had asked the wrong question. Because Tommy Ambrose was the last known person to see Anderson alive, and, according to his own report, he was repairing the U-bend on the upstairs loo, I asked instead whether a wrench could have made the indentations. The answer was yes, a wrench could have. Based on that response, I think we might be able to make a case for a warrant to examine Tommy Ambrose's tool kit."

"I agree," replied Bodkin. "Good work. That kind of specific connection is precisely what we needed."

"There could be a problem, however, getting the warrant approved."

"Why's that?" asked Bodkin.

"None of the blows can be established as a direct cause of death. According to Keith, it is possible that the first blow knocked Anderson off balance, causing him to fall down the stairs, but it was not sufficient to kill him. The last two blows, however, seem to have been delivered after he was already dead. In fact, it is possible that neither the blows nor the fall itself actually killed him and that he died of something else during the fall. Keith is carrying out further tests to discern just what it might have been."

DI Bodkin had a choice. She could rip Dave apart for his inability to see how to make his case or she could patiently explain. In the competitive environment of the Met she would have chosen the former without hesitation. But her role as Jenny's mentor was having a surprising effect on her and so she spelled it out. "Dave, we still can make a strong case. If the first blow caused Anderson to fall to his death, then it is primary evidence of either murder or manslaughter. If the second two blows occurred after death, the wrench could be considered evidence of the crime of desecrating a dead body, again, serious enough to seek a warrant. So there should not be a problem." But there was a problem, she thought, with Dave. He was sharp and yet he had missed an easy and obvious aspect of making a case for a warrant. This was an unusual lapse in his performance. She would have to scrutinise his understanding of the rules and regulations for requesting a warrant very carefully. Or, she reconsidered, regarding him more carefully, might he be ill?

Dave was abject. "I should have known that. I should have been able to work it out. I'm sorry. I'll get right on the paperwork." He pulled on his tie as though to straighten it and brushed his fingers through his hair, feeling his damp scalp, furious at himself for his solitary overindulgence of scotch the night before and its impact on his thinking.

"Good. If you have it ready for me within the hour, I can sign it in time to have it approved before the end of the day. One other thing you both might find interesting is this report that was faxed from Anderson's doctor in Florida. Evidently, he was a very sick man."

***

"So I was almost done repairing the loo and was just tightening the nut with my wrench when I heard the front door open." Tommy's brow was already soaked from the effort of revealing the plan and his shameful part in it and then having to relive that eventful afternoon. He was just getting to the part where it all went wrong. Sue was trying to listen to Tommy's story without betraying any of her reactions or judgements. She was keeping her tone neutral and calm, her hands relaxed, not wanting to say or do anything that might spook Tommy into lying or saying nothing so as not to upset her further. Internally, she was anything but calm. Anger at many of Tommy's decisions, sorrow over his distress and fear of what all this would mean for their family warred inside her, competing for her attention, distracting her from her need to stay impartial and unruffled. Little Tommy had woken from his short nap a few minuts earlier but Sue had been prepared. He was now occupied in the adjacent sitting room with his favourite snack of sliced apple, banana, and orange and his favourite DVD about a friendless little car that finally proved its worth and made many friends.

"I didn't know what to do. He came upstairs before he realised I was there and when he saw me he just lost his temper. He yelled at me, accused me of deliberately breaking things so they would need to be repaired, which I had to admit was true. I had hoped that owning up to it would calm him down but it enraged him even more. He yelled, 'You and your bloody uncle Michael, the pair of you, you're a couple of damned thieves. I'll be reporting both of you to the authorities, you just wait. Now get the hell out of my house!' I reached for my tool kit, which was awkward because it was behind where he was standing. I accidentally knocked it against the back of his leg as I tried to pick it up and that was it. He grabbed me by my shirt and shook me and shook me until I thought my head would fall off. I asked him to stop but he wouldn't. He kept pushing against me as I kept trying to get to the stairs and get out, my toolkit in one hand and my wrench still in the other. When we reached the top of the stairs, he shook me so hard, I lost my balance and started to fall. I reached up with my hand, he swooped against me somehow, and I swung my wrench right into his temple while trying to balance myself with my toolkit. It was a hard swing. I was falling and I was scared and I don't know how it happened. It was all so fast. But I did swing at him and I did hit him. And then he stopped shaking me and just went slowly backwards and sideways down the stairs. I followed him to the bottom. He was splayed out on the floor at the foot of the stairs and he wasn't breathing."

"You're sure he was dead?"

Tommy nodded affirmatively.

"And then what did you do?"

"I thought first of calling an ambulance but since he was already dead I thought that would not be of any help. Then I thought I had better call the police. I reached for my mobile, it was in my toolkit, and just as I grabbed it, it rang. It was Uncle Michael, calling to let me know that Mr. Anderson had stormed out of his office about fifteen or twenty minutes earlier and might be back home before I expected him. He said he would have called sooner but his staff were so upset with the row that Mr. Anderson had made that he had needed to calm them down. In all the tension that had been generated, it then slipped his mind that I was in Sparrow Cottage. I just listened and said nothing. I couldn't actually speak. Finally, Uncle Michael must have realised I hadn't said anything, not even hello. He stopped speaking and asked me if anything was wrong. I told him I had just killed Mr. Anderson and asked him to come over to Sparrow Cottage as quickly as he could. He told me to stay put, close the curtains and open the back door so that he could come along that little path edging the green and not be seen. He also insisted I was not to call the police." Tommy paused to look at Sue for her reaction.

Sue kept her eyes wide open and focused on Tommy's face, working hard to show only her support for continuing to listen to his story, trying to prevent any hint of reproof from registering itself in her face. Inwardly she was seething, not so much at Tommy but at Michael, for being so adamant that the police should not be called. "And then?" she asked.

"I drew the curtains closed. I couldn't look at the body. It was too horrible, twisted, and still. So very still. I unlocked the back door so that Uncle Michael could come in. He was followed almost immediately by my mother and Sam, whom he had obviously contacted. I can still hear every word of their conversation. It's etched on my brain.

Mum said right away, 'We should call the police.'

Uncle Michael said most definitely 'No. Let's think this through.'

I asked, hoping against hope that I'd be wrong, 'He's really dead, isn't he?'

Sam walked around the body and asked, 'Could we make it look like an accident? Like he just fell down the stairs?'

Again, Uncle Michael spoke with his usual authority. 'Never. Not the way he looks.'

Mum looked at her watch. 'We've got to get to the wedding. We'll be missed.'

Sam asked the question everyone was thinking. 'What'll we do?'

I was so wrought up from having caused this terrible mess that I began to blubber, 'I'm so sorry. This wasn't meant to happen. I didn't...'

But Uncle Michael wouldn't let me finish. Instead, he said those words I will never forget. 'Leave it to me. I'll figure something out and let you know after the ceremony.'"

Here Tommy paused, looked directly into Sue's eyes and took both her hands in his. "Sue, I was so scared that I just reacted with relief that he was taking the responsibility off my shoulders. I should have known better. I did know better. I did know the right thing to do was to call the police. But I was terrified that not just me but everyone involved in the plan for the Lark Cottage deposit would be arrested because it would all come out. Then we'd have to give the money back, Betty and Rob wouldn't have the home we'd put the deposit on for their wedding and many of us would go to prison. It was too much. I had caused the problem but if I turned myself in I would cause problems for my mum, my uncle, my cousins, my friends. I didn't know what to do." Sue wanted to scream away his words, as though obliterating the sound could obliterate the event. Instead, she remained calm, held his gaze, and said nothing.

"Mum looked at me with such sadness that I will never forget it as long as I live. She left first, then Sam, both by the back door the way they had come so that nobody could see them. Uncle Michael nodded for me to leave by the front door, since my van was parked in front of Lark Cottage and he left by the back door. I took one last look at James Anderson, at the trouble I'd caused, grabbed my tool kit, and left. That was the last I ever saw of James Anderson." The story told, Tommy let go of Sue's hands and collapsed.

Sue could think of nothing to say that would comfort her husband, face down on the table, heaving his silent sobs. She stood up, came around to his side of the table and hugged him. "I am here for you and always will be." At that moment Little Tommy's movie ended and the doorbell rang. Tommy was completely unresponsive. Sue took charge. "You get Little Tommy. His hands and face will need washing after his snack and your face needs a little freshening up as well. Make a game of it, where you wash his and he washes yours. He knows the game. We do it all the time. It will cheer you up, I promise. He's pretty good at it. I'll get the door."

Little Tommy was always ready for a game, any kind of game. Tommy grabbed his son's hands, swung him onto his shoulders, and carried him up the stairs for their face washing, just as Sue was greeting DI Cora Bodkin at the front door.

"Good afternoon, Mrs. Ambrose. I'd like to speak to Tommy Ambrose, please." With a smile, she added, "the tall Tommy, not the little Tommy."

Emotionally exhausted from her husband's story of the death fall of James Anderson, Sue gathered her wits together as best she could. "Please come in, Detective Bodkin. Tommy and Little Tommy are both upstairs but should be down in a minute or two." Sue guided Bodkin into the sitting room, settled her into the most comfortable chair and picked up the remains of Tommy's snack. "May I get you some tea?"

"Actually, you can get me something but not tea. I have a warrant here to search Tommy's tool kit. Could you please show me where it is?"

Sue hoped against all hope that the quaking she felt inside was not broadcasting itself to Detective Bodkin. Keeping her voice as light as possible, she replied, "It will be either in the boot of the van or in the garage. Just a moment please and I'll ask Tommy where it is."

"Where what is?" smiled Tommy, freshly washed and looking much brighter, giving Little Tommy, also fresh and sparkling, over to his mother. "Good afternoon, Detective Bodkin. How may we help you?"

"Good afternoon, Mr. Ambrose," responded an intentionally frosty Bodkin. Seeing right through what she considered to be Tommy's false charm and bravado, her bloodhound instincts honed in on the red rims lingering around his eyes. "I have a warrant here to check your tool kit. We could actually impound it but I know how crucial it is for your work. All I would like from it is your wrench."

Sue took Little Tommy into the kitchen, her mind a whirl. She could still see the image of her Tommy hitting James Anderson in the temple with his wrench. But the wrench in the tool kit was not Tommy's wrench; it was Sam's. Her face was too full of mixed emotions to expose it to Detective Bodkin's scrutiny and so she poured a glass of milk for Tommy and put the kettle on for tea.

"Certainly," replied Tommy. "It's in the van. Shall I bring in the entire kit for you to see or do you just want the wrench?"

"I'll come with you," replied Bodkin.

She was impressed with the spotlessness of the van, knowing from experience that the vehicles of handymen, because of the nature of their work, are often full of wood chips, paint chips, cleaning cloths, roughly folded dust sheets, odd bits of wood and plaster and general job-related clutter. But Tommy's van was just as meticulous as his house and his mother's house. Cleanliness seemed to run in this family. The tool kit was no exception. Every tool was wiped clean of the day's work, ready for the tasks of the next day.

There were three wrenches in the kit, but only one the approximate size of the indentations on James Anderson's skull. Even so, she decided to take all three for forensic examination.

"How long before I can have them returned?" asked Tommy. "Most of my jobs require a wrench at some point or other, although I can substitute some of my painting jobs for a few days."

Bodkin was beginning to realise that the change she had observed in Tommy when he came down the stairs, compared to her initial interview with him, was not a false bravado. He seemed to have acquired a calmer centre, as though he were confident, no, perhaps not so much confident as more comfortable with the circumstances of being investigated. She wondered what had brought about that shift, particularly as she had anticipated exactly the opposite.

"It can take awhile," Bodkin replied, testing this new level of comfort Tommy was exhibiting.

"May I ask what role my wrenches might be having in your investigation?" Tommy asked.

"You may ask but I cannot answer that," replied Bodkin. "Good afternoon, Mr. Ambrose. Unless you have anything you would like to add to what you have already told me about the last time you saw James Anderson."

"I haven't thought of anything to add," replied Tommy, "but if I do, I will certainly ring you. Good afternoon."

EIGHT: SATURDAY

DI Cora Bodkin's eyes popped open at 5:20 a.m., not with any startling new revelations that had come to her during the night of restless sleep but with the need to sort through all the evidence she had collected to date and to work out her next step in the Anderson investigation. Flinging her bedclothes aside for their regular Saturday morning adventure in the washer and dryer, she then flung herself into the shower for her own morning ablutions. Only after brushing her hair one hundred strokes, brushing her teeth for four minutes with the best Oral B electric toothbrush on the market, donning a loosely flowing cotton skirt topped off with a bright blue jumper selected from the colourful stack of jumpers she wore in her private life and preparing a pot of chai tea was she ready to carry out the mental work that had startled her awake almost an hour earlier. Pouring the correctly steeped tea into a china mug, she allowed herself the luxury of one slow and deep inhalation of the spicy aroma, took the first long and lovely hot sip of the day and then marched into her study, ready to work.

Cora Bodkin did not speak any more than she needed to at work but at home, living alone, she talked to herself constantly. Taking advantage of this habit, she had developed the routine of using a digital recorder to capture her thinking throughout the course of an investigation. She pressed the power button and began sorting through the major threads of the investigation.

"OK, potential suspects. First we have the two Canadian ladies who found the remains of James Anderson and who live next door to him. They moved here recently from the States just two months prior to Anderson's moving here and they have miniature copies in their home of the masks in the trees at Churston Grove, where they allegedly 'found' Anderson's remains. Several connections, all circumstantial and tenuous. No intuitive vibes. At this point in the investigation I feel confident eliminating them as suspects.

Second, the last known person to see James Anderson alive, Tommy Ambrose. Very frightened, exudes guilt. But is it guilt for murder? Guilt for some association with the murder? Guilt for knowledge of the person or persons who committed the murder and desecrated the body? A simple eyeball of all three wrenches confiscated from his toolkit against the temple revealed no match. A recent assumption of self-assurance. Did not give off any indications of guilt or remorse at most recent meeting. A weakening potential candidate for the murder but still one to keep on the list.

Third, Mabel Barton, the butcher. Quite capable emotionally as well as professionally of dismembering the body. She admitted knowing that James Anderson was driving the other car in the crash that killed her husband. Guilty about something, but what? I don't see her as a murderer. Possibly an accessory after the fact, especially if her son Tommy is implicated in the murder. That seems most likely. Alibis for the crucial time period all verified by her brother, Michael Barton. Strong candidate for accessory after the fact.

Michael Barton, the banker. Financial arrangements dodgy but not illegal, though mortgage brokering is unethical when his bank handles the financial dealings of the client. Capable, then, of unscrupulous behaviour. Very smooth and self-assured. On the face of it, he seems capable of murder, though motivation is missing, unless he also knows that Anderson was involved in the death of his wife. If Mabel knows, it makes sense that Michael knows. Possible role in helping Mabel as an accessory. Possible candidate for murder; strong candidate for accessory after the fact if Mabel is involved in the murder.

William Barton, a man of scruples and honour according to everyone interviewed during the course of the investigation. Beware those, I tend to think. Jenny Johnson's report indicates that William Barton considered the possibility that Anderson might be the driver of the other car in the accident that killed his wife but never actually confirmed that he knew for certain. Wife and daughter of supreme importance in his life. Seems to have collapsed after wife's death. Possibly the strongest in motivation but seems very weak and frail. Definitely could not carry out the dismemberment and placement of body parts. Murder? He's the wild card in this investigation, I think. Possible candidate.

Dan Barton and all the Masons, Sam, Andy, Rob, and Betty, are all well-covered by alibis verified by several individuals.

So, that's my list if we think the murder involves people in the community. There is insufficient evidence to bring any of them in for formal questioning. Engaging Detectives Kendal and Johnson in further investigation would not be the most efficient use of resources. That new mother and infant homicide that came in on Thursday, Charlene and Baby Annie Gillespie, with a suspect already identified but with several open ends, that recent series of sexual abuse cases involving juveniles in the area both urgently require attention and we're stretched so thin. Unless something breaks over the weekend, Kendal and Johnson should probably be reassigned on Monday morning to the burgeoning backlog of cases.

Alternative line of inquiry: first impression of ritual murder. No ties to any other known ritual forms of murder so initially ruled out. Motivation? So many unknowns and possibly unknowable unknowns in this area. I need to review once again any crimes in or near Churston Woods and Churston Grove and to research motivations for and traditions of ritual murder. I'll pursue this line of reasoning on my own for the weekend, and then make my decision whether to follow it up further on Monday morning.

One final factor relating to whether to request more time pursue this case: To date, we have been unable to locate any living relatives of James Anderson. Nobody has claimed the remains. His solicitor has no record of a will although he did say Anderson had spoken with him recently about drawing up a will. Police in Florida have been unable to locate any neighbours who had more than a nodding acquaintance with James Anderson. He seems to have lived an extraordinarily solitary existence. If he is on a victim protection plan there is no available record. Without pressure from family or American law enforcement for repatriation, it is unlikely that our resources will be stretched much further for this investigation." She reached to turn off her recorder, then paused.

"And yet, until last week, he was a thriving, living human being. Well, actually, not so thriving. He'd been undergoing chemotherapy and radiation treatment for a brain tumour. Had laser surgery shortly before he moved to Coombe Gilbert. Apparently unsuccessful. Death could come at any time and he came here knowing that. Even so, he had been on this earth almost fifty years, had been at one time in his life part of a family, had worked, had resided in a neighbourhood. How could nobody care?

How could he be so alone? Attention must be paid. Somehow."

She stopped recording. She then telephoned headquarters to request all files related to any strange or ritual murders in the Devon or Cornwall area to be brought to her office within the next three hours.

She brewed another pot of chai tea, refilled her china mug, emblazoned with an emerald green fire-breathing dragon, and gazed out the window of her study onto her small garden, mostly laid to lawn, but with one small apple tree, heavy with its abundance of Devonshire reds, blushing into the very early stages of maturity. She thought, as she often did when observing her apples in the sunlight, of the biblical version of original sin in the Garden of Eden.

How easily human beings had regressed from angelic creatures of paradise to disgraced and shamed sinners. How easily evil entered life and became a part of someone's essential being.

She had long been curious about that process. She could remember her first lie, a deliberate choice on her part. She had been three years old, visiting her aunt and uncle while her parents were on holiday. Together with her three cousins, older by only a few years, she had gone into her uncle's study, a room forbidden to the children. Something was disturbed or broken, not her fault, and the children were all lined up, Cora at the end of the line. Her oldest cousin, David, about nine at the time, said he had been there but none of the others had and he was responsible for whatever it was that had happened. But the uncle had gone all the way down the line anyway, asking each of the three other children. They had all corroborated David's story. She had known even at the age of three that it was wrong to lie but if she told the truth she would make a liar of David whereas if she lied she would make a liar only of herself. David would be punished regardless of what she said but she would be punished only if she told the truth. She had been old enough to work out all of that but not old enough to realise that deciding to tell the lie was in itself a form of punishment. She could not yet recognize that her uncle probably had known that they had all been in his study and so would forever more know her as a person capable of lying. Even worse, from then on she would know herself to be capable of lying to save herself from punishment. That was her first bite of the apple, she thought to herself, gazing at the richly laden tree. So many apples ready to ripen. So many opportunities to invite evil into one's life, to decide to take the wrong path.

The gates to memory lane already open, she proceeded further along. She recalled the first time she had taken something that was not hers, one of four shiny shillings her younger brother Nick had proudly saved; the first time she had gone somewhere she had been forbidden to go, a film classified as adult when she was only fifteen. *Anatomy of a Murder* with Lee Remick. She smiled briefly to herself as she remembered how she had rationalised those decisions, step by step acclimating herself to disobedience, possibly the slightest form of evil, much as a child's body acclimates itself to germs, arguably a form of biological evil.

Since her teenage years she had been fascinated by how the mind accepts the intrusion of evil, allowing it to co-exist with all that is good in someone. During her career she had met very few people "born bad," as her parents would have called it, with evil an essential part of their nature from a very early age.

Most of the criminals she had dealt with at the Met either had endured the perpetual grinding of a merciless socio-economic crucible from which they had emerged at an unbelievably early age already hardened and cynical and capable of enormous cruelty or, in adulthood, had become so excessively acculturated to the material world that they readily committed criminal acts for money, power, or both.

The people she was dealing with in Coombe Gilbert did not fit into either category. They were, it seemed to her, decent folk living decent lives. For some reason, they had invited something evil into their lives and they were dealing with it. In the case of Mabel and Tommy, she felt certain she had observed them undergoing the process of acclimating their psyches to evil during this investigation. She wished, not for the first time in her career, that she were doing a research study on this case rather than conducting a police investigation.

After refreshing her tea yet again, she switched on her computer, beginning what she thought would probably be an interesting but ultimately fruitless research into ritual murders in Devon.

***

"Oh this is simply gorgeous!" Karen was back home from her jaunt to the vicarage, modelling for Mary the costume that Reverend Potts had selected for her forthcoming stint as a fortune teller. The golden robe of satin taffeta shimmered with sequinned stars and bugle beaded moons that cascaded down to purple velvet slippers with toes that curled up to tiny points. Her red silk turban, with innumerable folds, cleverly disguised tiny remote switches which, by pressing her forehead in seeming concentration, she could activate to wirelessly produce a limited but intriguing range of light changes and sighing or moaning sounds from the electrical transformer box. The vicar had been a genial and informative tutor, modelling his technique by telling her fortune, showing her how to use questions to gain information which could be recast later during the fortune telling episode into a form of prophecy. Simple examples such as asking Karen whether she had any children, and, learning that she had one son, could then be used to "predict" later on in the session that she would be spending some time with her son in the near future. "Let me practice on you, Mary," asked Karen.

"You already know everything there is to know about me or at least everything that I want you to know. It would be too easy for you to tell my fortune. But the costume looks sufficiently exotic. It makes you look quite different. With makeup and some change of voice and accent, perhaps the guests won't even know it's you."

"That's even better!" replied Karen. "Now what I need to do is go through my chart and develop very specific things I want to know from each of the people I have listed. Reverend Potts said that I could let him know which of the guests I would feel most comfortable with to tell their fortune and he would develop a rota so that their turn would come up while I was on duty as the fortune teller and his sister would have the others. So I now will have one-on-one information gathering opportunities with Tommy, Mabel, Michael, Andy, and William. He suggested six in case one or more of those on my list did not want their fortune told and so I added Sue. I initially thought of Betty but she would have been far too busy with her wedding to be involved with anything concerning James Anderson."

She whirled around one more time and then began to take off the elaborate robes, placing them carefully in the well-worn shopping bag the vicar had provided. "Oh and speaking of Betty, that reminds me. I have a question about your miniature masks. The vicar will be bringing a small tent which he usually decorates with lights, pictures, and carpets. No candles for two reasons. One is, of course, the fire hazard. The other is to enable the electrical cord leading to the tent to be visible without giving away its use to power the little transformer box that controls the lights and sounds. It will instead be assumed to power the lights at the door and within the tent. There is a little table inside the tent with a red velvet covering that goes all the way to the floor, concealing the transformer box. He showed me photos of how he decorates the inside and outside of the tent with evocative secular scenes of romantic love, familial love, happiness, distress, anger, war, exotic landscapes, and so on. I was wondering whether we could add your miniatures of Churston Grove around the inside of the tent. It might spark a response from someone if he or she had anything to do with placing the remains of the body there."

"Certainly, but might it be better to mount them outside the tent, all around it, similar to their being all around the Grove?"

"But then I wouldn't be able to see the response."

"That's true, but wouldn't it be interesting if someone came for their fortune telling, noticed the masks, and decided to forego the reading?"

"Hmmm, that's an interesting possibility. But the same thing could happen if the person entered the tent and decided not to stay. Each way has its advantages. How many masks have you finished?"

"I have nine miniatures, the complete set. But I have also been working at making some full-size copies of the masks and have four done. What if you put the miniatures inside and the four full-size ones outside the tent?"

"That sounds fantastic."

"Good," replied Mary non-committally, willing to help but not anticipating that anything useful would be revealed during this fortune telling enterprise.

***

Michael and Mabel were enjoying an after dinner brandy at Michael's home, both more relaxed than they had been all week. Mabel was quite chuffed over how the interview with Detective Bodkin had transpired. "It was brilliant," she told Michael, for about the tenth time. "Every question she asked, I could answer, just as we had planned. I caught her looking at me funny after my second answer and supposed it was because I had been too quick with my replies and was too certain of where I had been and what I had been doing at the particular time. So when she asked me about the third time period, I waited a while, looked a bit puzzled, and hemmed and hawed a bit until finally pretending to recall the answer you and I had agreed on. And when she walked me over to your office and you accounted for those same three periods of time almost exactly the same but with different words, there was nothing she could do."

"You did well, little sister," said Michael. "And that Detective Kendal, a nice young man, does not seem to have settled on any problems in all the paperwork I put at his disposal."

"Do you think it's over? That they'll start looking elsewhere now?"

"I honestly don't know," replied Michael. "It seems too easy." He noticed the change in Mabel's face. "Oh, I know it wasn't easy for you. You had probably the toughest part of the job. You were a brick."

"I don't feel like a brick. I still feel dirty whenever I work at the block. I'm pleased that I got through the interview all right but I don't think I will ever get rid of the blight inside of me. The only thing that keeps me sane in all of this is looking at my Tommy and thinking that what I did, what we did, will protect him from going to prison. He's a good man. He didn't mean for all this to happen. He's already told me he would gladly have confessed if there had been a way to do so without implicating all of us in the plan for Lark Cottage. You said I had the toughest part. I think every one of us has found this week probably the most difficult week of our lives. It's hard to look in the mirror and not see what the events of the week have done to our insides, to our souls. I've changed, Michael. I don't feel proud of who I am anymore. I don't even feel comfortable with who I am."

Michael took a slow sip of his brandy and reached over to place his hand over Mabel's hands, which were tightly clenched on her lap. He wondered about himself, why he did not feel as torn apart as she did. He still had not told her, had not told anybody, about his return to Sparrow Cottage before the wedding. Nobody had asked him to explain why he had been late, probably assuming that Willie had been slow getting ready. Of the four of them who had been at Sparrow Cottage that day, only he knew that Tommy could never be convicted of murder or manslaughter because only he knew that James Anderson had still been alive when they had all left the first time. Barely alive, but nonetheless alive. He was definitely not alive when Michael left the second time.

***

"Zoom! Zoom! Zoom! Fire! Fire!" screeched Little Tommy, racing his red fire truck to an imagined catastrophe on the other side of the sitting room. Tommy and Sue were together on the sofa, holding hands, watching their son and feeling tentatively contented. Sue's support the previous day, after he had confessed everything to her, had affected him far more powerfully than he would ever have thought possible. It was not that he had doubted her. He knew he could count on her. But that she could so completely love him and support him despite his reckless response to James Anderson's physical threats, despite his injudicious and criminal behaviour and despite the physical and emotional weakness he had manifested this past week was almost beyond his comprehension. It was certainly beyond anything he felt he merited. In that moment, at his most vulnerable, head down on the table, Sue's arm around his shoulder and her quiet voice assuring him of her love, he had grown up. At least that's how it had felt. He had ceased feeling helpless almost immediately. When he had taken Little Tommy up to wash his face and Little Tommy had looked him in the eye and said, "Luv you daddy," and then laughed as he smudged the warm, wet washcloth all over his daddy's brow, his cheeks, down his nose, around his chin, and then his neck, they had both broken into laughter. And that laughter had cleansed away the last of the vulnerability. He had come downstairs not only as master and protector of his home and family but also as master and protector of himself, of the essence of who he was. He was a husband, a father, a son, a handyman, a man basically good and decent. Whatever happened as a consequence of what he had done, he could take it in his stride. He would do what needed to be done and say what needed to be said. Sue saw and fully apprehended the difference. What neither could know was whether it would last. But for now, life felt comfortable. Cautiously comfortable.

***

Willie turned the key in the latch. The wooden door was large and heavy, out of proportion to the interior of his annexe. Despite the lengthy summer evening, it seemed to him that he was walking from twilight into darkness, particularly when he was still resonating with the bright happy joy that filled his daughter's new home. He'd spent a delightful evening at Lark Cottage with Betty and Rob, enjoying her cooking once again. She'd prepared his favourite meal, salmon steak in a white wine sauce, Brussels sprouts, slender green beans, and parslied new potatoes, accompanied by a respectable pinot grigio, It had been an extravagance for them but their pride in their new home and their love for each other sparkled so much that they could all have eaten weetabix and been happy. Willie had contributed a smooth and silky port to enhance the post-prandial conversation. Warmed by good food, pleasant drinks, enjoyable conversation, and the obvious mutual adoration between Betty and Rob, he had walked home in a contented and mellow mood. All that changed as soon as he stepped inside.

His home seemed so empty, so bereft of all that had made it bearable to him after losing Amanda and the farm. He poured himself a glass of port from the bottle on his sideboard but this second glass did not recapture of the warmth of his first glass in Lark Cottage. He picked out one of his favourite albums of photos and skimmed through them but they could provide no solace for him this evening.

It had been an extraordinary week for him. He had dreaded losing Betty but was comforted by the thought that she was in good and capable hands. Rob would love her well and truly. He had no doubts on that score. And that lovely little cottage. That plan hatched by Michael and Sam, still the two wily rascals they had been as children, had resulted in so much happiness for his little girl. However had they and the others managed all that without his knowing anything about it until the very end? Very strange and definitely not ethical but it never paid to look too deeply into other people's thoughts and deeds. He hoped that Betty and Rob would never learn of the details of the plan and the resultant tragedy. That business with James Anderson had been shocking, appalling and completely irreconcilable with how he wanted to think of himself as a human being. Both Michael and he had concluded their dealings with James Anderson in a manner that did not bear thinking about. He had observed and listened all week long and had taken note of the changes in Michael, Mabel, Sam, Andy, and Tommy. He didn't know specifically what role each of them had played in this family drama and didn't want to know. He already knew much more than he could ever comfortably life with. Virtually invisible in his customary place in the quiet, almost hidden little snug in the Trout and Salmon, he saw and heard everyone come and go, dropping snatches of conversations which he had threaded together into a quilted narrative, a quilt with lots of holes in it. So many holes he hadn't even realised what was going on with Lark Cottage until the day of the wedding. But in the days following, he had learned something, not much, of the villagers' speculations about what had transpired in Sparrow Cottage. He wished he didn't know the truth.

He was weary. He was not yet sixty, but he felt totally drained.

NINE: SUNDAY

The sunbeams smacked Karen awake. At least that's how she felt as the hot bright shafts of light penetrated her eyelids in those first moments while she was still half asleep. "What a magnificent day for our party," she said to herself, shaking the slumber out of her head and bounding out of bed. Looking out the window, she could see the lane below, still quiet in the early dawn. Her nose informed her most pleasurably that Mary was already in the kitchen preparing breakfast. She quickly jumped into the shower and then threw on a pair of jeans and a bright blue t-shirt. "Ready for the day!"

"So, have you determined your strategy for your fortune telling this afternoon?" asked Mary as Karen warmed the teapot, preparatory to brewing her tea. She selected the special brew she had purchased at Fortnum and Mason the last time she had been in London. Chai tea, her favourite.

"No, I was hoping you could help me."

"Hope away. I've got my work cut out for me today setting up the back garden for the barbeque. I think we have all the food we need and all the accessories taken care of. What if you spend an hour or so in your study after breakfast, working out your approach for each of the people you'll be meeting with? Then we can talk it through over morning coffee."

"Sounds like a great plan. Thanks for the time. I really should be helping you with the preparations. On the other hand, I did sort of indicate to the vicar that I might attend the service this morning."

"You what? That's not like you."

"That's true, but he was so nice getting me all kitted out for the fortune telling and giving me a tutorial on how it's done. I thought it was the least I could do, especially since he will be coming here for the party."

"Yes, I can see your point. As for the garden, I have it all planned out in my mind. I'll probably be much more efficient working alone. If I need help hanging any of the decorations, we can do it together after you return from church."

"Good thing we both woke up so early. I still can get some work done on the questions before I leave."

Following their customary breakfast of poached eggs and fresh fruit salad, Karen took her pot of tea into her study and began to analyze her chart. She quickly realised it was hopeless. The hypothetical and the unknown completely eclipsed anything that could be considered fact. As a set of ideas for her novel, the notes were fine; as a means of determining any kind of answer to the problem of who killed James Anderson and why, there was absolutely nothing concrete. There was no way that the chart could provide any openings for reasonable, sensible questions that might yield productive information.

She found herself tensing in frustration and quickly realised that would not help in any way. She had written down everything she knew about the crime, which, admittedly, wasn't much. She had applied all the rational thinking she could and had come up with nothing. Possibly she needed an escape from what was rational in order to achieve some conceptual leaps to a new way of looking at the information she had. She began to mutter to herself, "I think I'll try what I used to advise my students to do when they were completely stuck. It sometimes worked for some of them. Perhaps it will work for me. At the very least, it will shift my focus just a little and help me look from a different angle." She tore off the three pages of her chart that she had already written and placed them on the floor. She then took a red biro from her desk, lay on the floor beside the papers, closed her eyes and used a technique she had learned from drama classes to completely relax her body and mind. Starting at her head, she tensed it as tightly as she could and then made it feel as heavy as possible, as though it were sinking into the floor, until she couldn't feel its weight any more. She did the same with her arms, her back, her pelvis, her legs and finally her heels until she felt weightless, almost floating on the floor. When she was completely relaxed, she lay still for three or four minutes, allowing her mind to wander freely. Usually under these circumstances, images would drift into her mind or at the very least colourful shapes that her mind would begin to interpret. This time there was nothing. Just black. She waited patiently for the black to turn into shadows that might bring something to mind but the black remained solid and impenetrable. Disappointed, but not yet finished with this particular technique, she very slowly sat up, keeping her eyes closed, located the spread out pages with her hands and moved them around so that she did not know the order they were in. With the biro still in her hand, she then drew a narrow elliptical shape the width of the page on each one. She opened her eyes to discover that she had circled "get to Churston Grove by water," "key: is there meaning to the sparrow?" and "Elders of the family helped."

She took a fresh sheet of paper and wrote these three phrases on it. At that moment, Mary came into her study. "There's a dead sparrow in our back garden. I'm quite prepared to simply throw it in the garbage but I know you might feel differently about its disposition. What would you like me to do?"

"A dead sparrow? I can't believe it! I just wrote 'is there meaning to the sparrow?' on this piece of paper. Look!" Mary peered at the page but was less impressed than Karen was with the coincidence. Karen continued, "Show me where the sparrow is."

Together they went to the back garden, to the area where Betty and Rob had said they would like to set up the cricket hoops. The sparrow lay there, looking asleep. It did not seem to have been attacked. It was not a baby. There was no tree nearby from which it might have fallen. It seemed to have fallen from the sky.

"Strange," mused Karen. We see sparrows all the time in this back garden. I think of them as vital and alive. But I suppose they must die as everything does. I wonder why we don't see more dead birds when it comes right down to it. But this is the first we've come across here, right?"

"It's the first one I've encountered in our garden, that's certain," replied Mary. "So what do you want me to do with it."

"I'm not sure yet," said Karen, "I'm thinking."

"Well, think away! I have other work to do. I'll leave the disposal of the sparrow to you."

Karen brought out a paper towel from the kitchen, picked up the sparrow with it, and took it into her study. She looked at it intently, more thoroughly than she had ever observed a live sparrow. She explored its delicate markings, the intricacies of the feathers, the complexities of its structure. She marvelled at its completeness. She thought, not for the first time, of the extent to which she too frequently took the marvels of the world for granted. How many hundreds, more likely thousands, of sparrows had she seen in her life? Pondering that question visually, she recalled the first time she had ever seen a sparrow, almost sixty-four years ago. She had been three and half years old and had come across a nest that had been blown down in a storm. In this nest were four squalling beaks, wide open, surrounded by little balls of fluff. Her mother had put on gloves "to prevent the mother sparrow smelling my human touch on the baby sparrows or on the nest" she had explained to Karen, and then she had carefully placed the nest back in the tree, fearing the mother sparrow might never return to feed her hungry babies. Karen hadn't thought of that incident for a long time. It bothered her that she couldn't remember whether the sparrow mother had returned or not.

In some ways, James Anderson was similar to this sparrow. In the most trivial and purely coincidental sense he had inhabited the shell of a sparrow with respect to his home in Sparrow Cottage. Like this sparrow, he had died alone, unmourned, it seemed, and unmissed by others. No apparent family members or friends had shown up to collect his body, to contribute to the investigation, to close his house or to see to his possessions. Or rather nobody had been reported in the local paper or had been seen coming to the house. He had lived almost unnoticed just as dozens of sparrows flitted about in the garden every day, anonymous in their brown and grey sameness, not appreciated nearly as much as the vibrant kingfisher, the gravity-defying kestrel, or the warbling lark. One day James Anderson lived unseen next door and the next day he didn't live anywhere at all.

Pondering the death of the sparrow lying on her desk, Karen was reminded of the line from *Hamlet* where Horatio is trying to persuade Hamlet not to fight with Laertes, referring to inauspicious circumstances. Hamlet replies:

> *...we defy augury. There is special providence in the fall of a sparrow. If it be now, 'tis not to come; if it be not to come, it will be now; if it be not now, yet it will come—the readiness is all. Since no man, of aught he leaves, knows what is't to leave betimes, let be. V.ii,217-224*

"We defy augury," Karen mumbled to herself. "To determine the fall of my sparrow, whether it be this little one on my desk, or James Anderson next door, augury or fortune telling will not help. All will unfold itself in due time. This little sparrow fell according to its special providence. Could the same be said of James Anderson? She didn't think so. She rarely attended church as an adult but she had attended Sunday School as a child and church as a teenager. She knew the connection between Hamlet's speech and the Gospel of St. Matthew:

> And fear not them which kill the body, but are not able to kill the soul: but rather fear him which is able to destroy both soul and body in hell. Are not two sparrows sold for a farthing? and one

of them shall not fall on the ground without your Father's permission (Chapter 10, KJV).

Was the fall of this little sparrow a warning to her not to explore the death of James Anderson any further, the warning coming from some special providence that she did not fully understand? She did not believe that could be the case. Discovering the dead sparrow in the garden the day of the barbeque was pure coincidence. But can coincidence ever be pure? Isn't the perception of coincidence already a contamination of the mind perceiving similarities in two or more disparate events? Is one person's coincidence another person's circumstance? Karen threw up her hands in despair. "I'm going around in circles," she muttered to herself.

"Fear not them which kill the body, but are not able to kill the soul," Karen repeated to herself. "James Anderson's body was certainly killed. But his soul?" Karen's understanding of the concept of soul was more secular than religious. She embraced a Whitmanesque view of a collective unconscious, an ephemeral mass of energy, combined with a half-developed notion that some souls remained in ghostly concentrations of energy, separate from the collective mass, to complete something left unaccomplished during a lifetime. She had always thought that the two sparrows being sold for a farthing represented the minuscule monetary value accorded to the commonplace. Could it possibly be that the two sparrows are the body and the soul? If a special providence looks after the body, it would certainly seem that it also looks after the soul? Or would it?

"Ready for coffee?" Mary poked her head through the door of the study. "Yuck! You've brought that dead creature inside the house? Whatever for?"

"Yes on the coffee. Yes, guilty of bringing the dead sparrow into the house. But on the 'whatever for' I am much less definite. I feel I am circling around an idea, but I can't swoop down into the centre. I think perhaps that going to the church service, leaving all this behind, might help."

Mary stared at the three focal points Karen had blindly selected and had written on a sheet of paper:

- *get to Churston Grove by water*
- *key: is there meaning to the sparrow?*
- *Elders of the family helped*

Karen explained the process by which those three phrases had been selected. During her explanation she began to realise that, taken together, they provided the foundation of a narrative for one of the possibilities she had proposed two days earlier. If the elders of the family had helped, then the actual killing must have been done by one of the younger members. Michael, with help from others in the family, somehow got the remains of James Anderson to Churston Grove during the so-called fishing trip. Mabel must then have been the one to dismember the body. The key has never been found, unless the police have found it and are keeping it secret. And possibly there is no meaning to the sparrow. The mind desperately wants to ascribe meaning to what we see and hear. But perhaps there is no special providence. Perhaps things just happen. A sparrow has died and someone just puts it into James Anderson's mouth because the sparrow is there and James Anderson lived in Sparrow Cottage and it seemed like the thing to do at the time. It could all be as simple as that.

But of course that narrative is not simple. Knowing that the story she had created from those three snippets was entirely conjectural and almost totally unrealistic, Karen for a moment pretended to herself it was true. If true, what then? If she knew it to be true, and could prove it to be true, at least a half dozen people she knew would have to be arrested, their lives ruined. James Anderson's life had been ruined, no doubt about that. His body had been ruined. Had his soul? She couldn't answer that. But she did know that if she somehow managed to learn that her neighbours had participated in the mutilation of James Anderson's body and if she informed the police, they would indeed all be ruined, body and soul. What a dreadful responsibility. She suddenly felt dizzy. "Thank heavens it's all speculation," she uttered aloud to Mary.

"Coffee. Now. Let's get you out of this room. You look as though you've seen a ghost. We'll attend to that sparrow later."

With relief, hot mug of coffee in one hand and a buttery toasted tea cake in the other, Karen sat in one of their outdoor chairs. It was a quiet morning, the only sound the twittering of the birds in the hedge. She surveyed Mary's decorative handiwork for the barbeque, almost completed, and then went in and dressed for church.

***

Cora Bodkin was reviewing the files that had been placed on the desk in her office the previous day. She had intended going into her office on the Saturday afternoon but had become so engrossed in her computer search of ritual murder that it was time for afternoon tea before she switched off her laptop. And while some might consider Cora Bodkin to be a workaholic, she never worked past tea time on a Saturday afternoon. Her routine was either to prepare herself a proper cream tea and then sit in a comfortable chair with a good book or to go out to the theatre or a concert or a film. London had been a mecca for her Saturday late afternoon relaxations with its endless array of choices. She had wondered, when she decided to transfer to a less politically fraught posting in the Southwest, whether she would have many options for her weekly cultural adventures. But since moving not even a month ago to her new home in the Torbay area, she had already learned about the excellent Picturehouse Cinema in Exeter and the rustically sophisticated Barn Theatre at Dartington Hall, as well as the many local and regional theatres, including the highly respected Theatre Royal in Plymouth, even though she had not yet had an opportunity to visit any of them.

This Saturday, her choice had been to settle into her favourite chair, a large, overstuffed and cosily comforting sanctuary, to read a book. She was almost halfway through A. S. Byatt's *The Children's Book*, which had been shortlisted for the 2009 Man Booker Prize. While a part of her resisted selecting her reading on the basis of the critical praise of others, she had come to respect the Booker selections for the wide range of intellectual worlds created by the short-listed authors and now made a point of enjoying the finalists every year. Or rather, she purchased the books of the finalists every year. In terms of actually reading them, she was two years behind. Once she opened the pages of any book, however, she found that the characters, events and atmosphere of the book swirled through her imagination between opportunities to read. Sometimes she welcomed these mental intrusions while at other times, when they threatened to colour her thinking through a case, she tried to resist them. Following the intriguing adventures and misadventures of the brilliant potter, Benedict Fludd, in *The Children's Book,* she had begun the mental construction of a giant urn based on the mesmerising details of the Anderson case. She decorated the urn to resemble Churston Grove, with its masks, carved trunks and the central chalice. Her imagined design displayed the horrific head of James Anderson not only in the chalice but also in different guises on each of the masks. The visages of Mabel, Michael, Tommy, and even herself formed and reformed in endless combinations and recombinations on the four trunks that curled around the base of the urn. The creation emerged and evolved despite her occasional resistance, twisting and intertwining in labyrinthine distortions. Unable to escape its constant presence in her mind, shifting and shaping and reshaping, she had finally fallen into a fitful sleep.

Having woken early, unrefreshed by sleep, she had eaten a hurried breakfast of toast and coffee and had driven directly to her office, determined to focus on a different line of inquiry, if only to eliminate it as a possibility. Her internet search had yielded almost no ritual murders involving human sacrifice in Devon or Cornwall in the 20th or 21st centuries, although she had learned more about ritual animal slaughter and sacrifice than she had ever wanted to know.

The online history of druidic sacrifice, particularly the bloodstained alters of Anglesey in Wales, as well as in Cornwall, Devon and Dorset, had been thorough, interesting and informative but not particularly helpful in relation to this case. The stack of files she had requested and which lay pristinely on her desk awaiting her attention was very small, only three in number. The first two cases involved ritual animal slaughter and sacrifice which had required police investigation because of the accidental dismemberment of a participant in one and an accusation of animal theft for the sacrifice in the other. Neither was relevant to her current investigation. The third captured her attention. The victim, a Cornish parish councillor named Peter Solheim, fifty-six years of age, had been found almost exactly five years earlier, on the eighteenth of June, off the Lizard Peninsula, drowned, with several unexplained bodily injuries. Subsequent investigation had established the unfeasibility of his body floating from Mylor Harbour, where his empty dinghy was found, to the site where his body had been discovered. Neither wind nor tide could be held responsible for the directional flow that would have been required.

While it was a bit of a stretch, Bodkin could see some similarities: age of the two victims, both male, time of year reasonably close to the summer solstice and inexplicable post mortem injuries to the body. Solheim had been a practising druid. Anderson, according to his file, had apparently wanted to become a mason but had not been accepted. Could there be a connection? Both the masons and the druids are cloaked in ritual and mystery. Moreover, the official date of the death of James Anderson, established by Keith McKenzie, was June 18, 2011, precisely five years later. And Anderson had been visiting here at the time. Could he have somehow been involved? Could his death and mutilation have been some form of ritual retribution? The more she thought about it, the stronger the similarities became but her experience over twenty years of detective work had accustomed her to this phenomenon and she knew to be wary of being lured into premature conclusions based on coincidence. At the same time, she respected the words of her first superior officer, who would almost daily assert, "There is no such thing as coincidence."

She put down the file and considered. The department's resources were scarce. The new homicide that had come in on Thursday, a pregnant mother and infant child knifed to death, apparently by a friend of her partner, seemed on the face of it to be straightforward but Bodkin knew from experience that the most obvious was not always the easiest or even the correct approach. There was a backlog of domestic abuse and child abuse cases requiring follow-up from Detectives Johnson and Kendal, as well as three missing teenage girls, one of whom had been missing for over two weeks. Even though other DIs had been assigned either to oversee these cases or to work with her on them, everyone's caseload was overly full. Her superior officer would be expecting either a result or a rationale for continuing the investigation of the death of James Anderson, a recent immigrant without extended residence status, whose home country and family were not clamouring for follow-up or even repatriation. The living and the dead, all requiring justice, with insufficient police personnel to provide that justice. In an ideal world, there would be sufficient personnel to – no, forget that thought. In an ideal world, police personnel would scarcely be required at all. Fortunately, the decisions of whether to reduce, stop, or increase resources for particular cases were not hers to make. Nonetheless, she would be expected to have a strong argument for continuing an investigation that had yielded, as of yet, no substantial evidence.

Cora's gut instinct, which she had learned over the years both to trust and to mistrust at different times during the arc of an investigation, shouted to her that the murderer was one of the suspects she had interviewed in Coombe Gilbert. Possibly, and quite probably, more than one. But whenever she pointed her finger at Mabel, she could find reasons why it couldn't have been her. Mabel could have dismembered the body but did not seem capable of anything other than that and her alibi for the time of the killing and the transporting of the body was well supported. Of course, the support came from Michael, who might also have been involved. Mabel, Michael, William, and Tommy all had motivation, except that James Anderson had never been faulted for the accident which had resulted in the deaths of their spouses and, in Tommy's case, his father. No, she really could not convince her super that she had good reason to bring in any one of them. And a good defence lawyer could locate the Peter Solheim case in Cornwall as easily as she had and point out the strong similarities, thereby raising sufficient doubt to quash any possibility of a conviction. But she wasn't ready to throw in the towel quite yet.

She did have one card left to play before she had to meet with her super on Monday morning but was unsure whether or not to play it. She was getting ready to leave to visit her brother when she heard the fax machine printing out a communication. When she saw it was from Florida, she waited.

***

Reverend Potts was not expecting a huge crowd for the morning service this Sunday. It was gloriously sunny and warm, the kind of day to celebrate the generous bounty of the Lord outside, paddling in the sea or rambling on the moors or sailing on the Dart. That's what he would have been doing, except for his obligation to offer a church service regularly on Sunday mornings, no matter what the weather, in addition to his other duties. Funny thing about church attendance, he thought. The days with the most inclement weather brought in the most people. His topic for this day, "Justice, Mercy, and Humility: God's Prescription for Happiness," was unlikely to attract the hordes but it was a subject he liked to explore with his parishioners from time to time. The discovery of James Anderson's body and the subsequent attention of the police had caused considerable concern and stress in the village. Nobody had come to speak to him about it but after twenty-five years of ministering to the spiritual needs of others, he readily recognised feelings of guilt and discomfort in people. Mabel had certainly exhibited these feelings early in the week, as had Tommy. Oops, no longer Tommy. Two days ago, he had let it be known to everyone he met that he was just Tom now and his son was to be called Tommy rather than Little Tommy. Full stop. He hadn't made a fuss of it. Rather he had quietly informed anyone who addressed him as Tommy that he preferred Tom. Dignified and manly had been the vicar's impression at the time, as though Tom had been imbued with a more mature sense of himself.

"And here he comes now," he thought, as he saw Tom, Tommy, and Sue walking up the drive. "Good morning," he greeted. "You are all looking fit and well, ready to enjoy this lovely day."

"Yes," replied Tom. "Tommy is looking forward to the barbeque after the service. We've been talking to him about the fortune telling. He's never had his fortune told and he's very excited. I think we might even get Sue into the fortune telling tent." Sue grimaced just slightly, as though in accord with Tom's assessment of her reluctance, and then smiled to say she was looking forward to it.

"And how is your mother today? I noticed that she returned Nursie Bear while I was out and so I am assuming she has recovered?"

"Oh, she's fit as a fiddle now. It was just a temporary illness, something bad passing through her system," replied Tom. In the past, he would have inwardly congratulated himself on his little double entendre but his newly acquired inner peace had rendered him much less self conscious. "She's coming this morning. She should be here shortly."

And sure enough, Mabel came walking up the path, together with Michael. "Morning, Reverend Nick. Lovely day."

"Miracle of miracles," thought the vicar as soon as he saw Michael escorting his sister to church. Betraying no surprise, he warmly greeted them both.

And, for the first time since she had moved to Coombe Gilbert, came Karen Lawrence walking up the lane. While Mary and Karen supported church-sponsored concerts, markets, and charities, they did not generally attend services. Reverend Potts welcomed Karen with obvious delight. "Did the tent arrive? I asked one of the neighbouring children to carry it over to your cottage this morning."

"Oh, yes, thank you. Mary has already put it up. She's having a wonderful time organising the garden and setting everything out for the barbeque. She sends you her greetings and looks forward to meeting your sister."

Wanting to ask more about his fortune-telling sister but realizing that others were behind her waiting to be greeted by the vicar, Karen moved into the church, taking a place at the far end of one of the unoccupied pews near the rear of the church. She was not sure whether some people had regular places where they preferred to sit and so thought it safest to sit in an empty pew. A few minutes later, Willie slipped into the same pew, but much closer to the aisle. He nodded his head and smiled in silent greeting, polite and gracious as always, and then focused on the prayer book.

And still more came, the loyal and faithful, the wayward returning, the stalwart persisting, the frail limping, the hale and hearty striding, happy in their good fortune. In all, forty-two villagers warmed the pews of the church, ready to worship together, to sing together, and to contemplate, for this morning's service, issues of justice, mercy, and humility.

Reverend Potts rarely delivered sermons. Instead, he used the twenty to thirty minutes of the service usually devoted to a sermon in most church services to engage his congregation in structured discussion. He had two major ways of organising these discussion times. Sometimes he would start off with a theme and a short Bible verse, have people mix up so that no two family members were in the same group, and allow roughly ten minutes for them to chat amongst themselves. Then they would return to where they had been sitting, and, as individuals, share any new insights they had gained or state any significant questions that their group had raised but could not answer satisfactorily. He would try to bring these collective insights and questions to some sort of conclusion, sometimes using one or more of the unresolved questions to begin another "collective sermon" at another service a month or so later, having allowed the ideas to permeate his parishioners' minds in the interim. His second method was to develop two or three questions around a theme or topic and ask the congregation to think of an answer or response, share their response with the person beside them, and then talk about how their answers compared. In this method, people were not required to change places and so very often it would be husband and wife or other family members or close friends who would be sharing their responses with each other. One of his main objectives in the latter method, in addition to exploring the actual topic, was to help people realise that disagreements can lead to deeper understanding rather than continued discord. Sometimes it worked. At the very least, everyone was engaged. Nobody could sleep through the sermon in Reverend Potts's church.

Today he had decided on the latter method. He had developed three questions for them to explore:

1. What is the relationship between mercy and justice?
2. What role does humility play in this relationship?
3. Thinking of the past week, in what ways have mercy, justice, and humility contributed to your own happiness or to the happiness of someone you know?

He was aware that all three questions were difficult not only because of their open and abstract nature but because they were combining these concepts in ways not generally experienced in day-to-day life. Few people would combine justice and happiness in the same thought or humility and happiness. Even the consequences of mercy are more coloured by fear of punishment or relief at reprieve than by happiness. But thinking of justice, mercy, and humility working together to contribute to happiness could potentially help many of his parishioners deal with some of the problems and challenges of their daily lives. He hoped the openness of the questions would invite some helpful exploration of the concepts and would stimulate conversation in the areas most germane to each of his parishioners.

"Anybody here not wanting to be happy?" began the vicar, after preliminary announcements, readings and hymns, looking around the congregation. Up came the heads, eyes met his and one or two smiles graced the faces of his parishioners. "Good. We're all aiming for some form of happiness, which is why the topic I've chosen for today's discussion is 'Justice, Mercy, and Humility: God's Prescription for Happiness.' As we read in Michah, 'He hath shewed thee, O man, what is good; and what doth the Lord require of thee, but to do justly, and to love mercy, and to walk humbly with thy God?' (KJV). Today we are going to explore what that means in our everyday lives, how we deal with each other and how we steward ourselves through life. Let's start with the first question, the relationship between mercy and justice. You all know the procedure. Just talk with the person beside you. If there is someone in a pew without a partner, then pair up with someone in another pew. Otherwise, join the group of two nearest to you. Take a couple of minutes on your own to gather your thoughts together and then take another five minutes to share your ideas with your partner."

Nobody wanted to be first to break the silence and so many simply looked at each other, shrugged, and looked down, as though their prayer book or hymnal would provide an answer. A couple of parishioners actually leafed through one or the other book to see whether they could find some concept upon which to hang their deliberation.

"Give me mercy every time," said one person, rupturing the solemnity and providing the needed catalyst for others to speak.

Mabel, a Sunday regular and therefore familiar with these discussions, turned to Michael, a much less frequent attendee of Sunday service, who had accompanied her on this occasion primarily to show his support for her over this past difficult week. "I've always thought that real justice must include mercy. It doesn't always happen that way. I think sometimes justice, as we experience it in real life, too often excludes mercy."

"I've never really thought about it," replied Michael, less comfortable than Mabel talking publicly about this topic in the midst of others, most of whom were among his regular clients at the bank. "But before you spoke, I was thinking almost the opposite. Justice is more objective and therefore more apt to be the better choice. Justice is generally based on some kind of agreed upon expectations. Mercy is more individual, reliant on sympathy more than on regulations or laws. Mercy implies weakness, softness. Mercy occurs between two people. Justice occurs between people and the law."

Mabel pondered her brother's response, realising that it was partly true but still did not capture the essence of the relationship for her. She wondered how to get to that essence. "I have a question for you," said

Mabel. "Thinking of the events of this past week, would you prefer to be treated justly or mercifully?"

Michael did not have to reflect long before giving his answer, looking rather sheepish as he did so. Concurrently, Sue and Tom, as well as the other members of the congregation, were exploring the issue from their perspectives.

"There can be no true justice without mercy," said Sue, not looking directly at Tom, not wanting to jeopardise any of the delicate bond they had forged over the past two days. "Justice without compassion is for rule followers. It does not allow for decisions based on humanity or circumstances."

"Well, it could, couldn't it?" asked Tom. "Like all words, there's justice as some people think of it, as you just described it, following strict rules and expectations, and then there's justice as we all would like to think of it, justice that includes mercy."

"But that's a logical tautology," said Sue, who had hoped to read philosophy at university and now relished any opportunity to draw upon the philosophical foundations she had learned doing her A-levels. Recalling one of the maxims drilled into her by her teacher, she pointed out that "Reverend Nick has already separated the two in the question. Consequently, you can't recombine the two in your answer. You have to relate the two, which is different."

"Hmmm," thought Tom. There was a flaw in Sue's reasoning but her strength in logic far surpassed his. He'd have to make it concrete for himself before he could identify the flaw. "OK, are mercy and justice analogous to apples and oranges or to hammer and nails?"

"What?" asked Sue, so taken aback she was able to look directly at Tom. In so doing, she realised that the hard won new level of harmony and understanding between them would not be harmed by their disagreement on this issue.

"I mean are we thinking of blending them together in a relationship or are we thinking of one as a tool to use with the other, so that the relationship is a supportive one?"

"Interesting question" replied Sue, becoming increasingly engaged in the discussion. "Blending them together makes me think of soup or juice." She giggled softly, just to let off the frisson of tension she had initially felt. "In soup or juice, the individual qualities of each ingredient are combined to make something which obscures the essential taste or texture of one or more of the ingredients. Just as when you make apple-orange juice, you can never fully recapture the taste of the apple or the taste of the orange. So a blend of justice and mercy might not necessarily be either truly just or truly merciful. It seems somehow a weak relationship insofar as diminishing the integrity or essence of each item. The hammer and nails analogy is more interesting. Which is the hammer and which is the nail? It seems that if justice is the hammer and mercy is the nail, all is lost. If mercy is the hammer and justice is the nail, you might have something useful." She shook her head as she ended the thought, not sure that she had actually said what she meant. Apple-orange juice could be both delicious and healthy. Would it matter that the separate ingredients going into it became indistinguishable?

Tom also paused and thought about what she had said. "You know, I've been thinking of that line in *Hamlet* where he says something like, 'treat a man according to his own just desserts and none of us would escape hanging.' That captures the essence of the relationship for me. Every one of us has either intentionally or unintentionally committed so many wrongs against our fellow creatures that justice alone would have most of us in prison. Mercy needs to be the hammer hitting the nail of justice or we'd always be constantly punished."

The vicar, as was his custom, had spent most of this artificially-induced discussion time about relationships between abstract concepts observing the very real relationships between his flesh and blood parishioners. He had discerned in Sue's and Tom's conversation the very kind of phenomenon he enjoyed most. During the first exchange, Sue and Tom had been looking into their respective minds, unearthing ideas, their focus inwards to delve into their thoughts. Gradually, however, as they listened to each other, they began first to look at each other's faces while they were talking, and then directly into each other's eyes, respecting each other's ideas and actually enjoying the challenge to combine disparate starting points into a better understanding.

What he could not observe, however, were the catalytic circumstances that had laid the foundations for what was currently going through their minds. Had he been able to, he would have seen both of them drawing upon the countless similar conversations they had enjoyed in school, especially in the sixth form, where their courses had been structured very similarly to these sermon discussions and where disputation and debate were common occurrences in the curriculum. They had both intended going to university after their A-levels, Sue to read philosophy and Tom to read English, and they had both enjoyed debating abstract ideas, blending or contrasting their different disciplinary perspectives. The announcement that the universities, which had always been free to those who had earned a place, were going to charge tuition fees the year they would be eligible had blighted but not completely shattered their dreams. They had thought they could work through their gap year and save sufficient money, at least for their first year, and possibly work during term time and the summer recess to earn the tuition fees for the ensuing years.

The plan might have come to fruition except for that terrible night when Tom's father was killed in the crash. His emotional distress and Sue's comforting arms had generated a disastrous combination for teenage hormones. Their plans for university had been forced to morph into plans for making a home together to raise the new life conceived in the midst of such terrible loss of life. Until this week, their domestic conversation had revolved mostly around Little Tommy, budgets, work schedules and the daily business of being a family. As a change from their household exchanges and a return to their youthful dreams of further education, they both relished the sermon-discussions at church but never before had the discussion brought them right back home, to what they had been wrestling with all week. They read all that in each other's eyes and saw not anguish but an acceptance of whatever was about to happen, knowing that together they had the strength to get through it. Reverend Potts could not possibly apprehend all of that but he certainly took note of the robust connection between the two of them.

He interrupted the conversations with a clapping of his hands and asked the congregation to consider the second question, the role that humility plays in this relationship between mercy and justice.

Karen turned toward Willie, with whom she had discussed the first question, or rather he had listened respectfully while she had rambled on, but he did not turn back to her. Instead, he stood up, moved to the centre of the aisle, and declared in a voice surprisingly sonorous for his thin frame, "'Vengeance is mine,' sayeth the Lord." He paused, as though astonished by what he had said, turned, and left the church.

***

"That was a short service," said Mary, as Karen came through the cottage and into the back garden. "I didn't expect you for another half hour."

"The vicar let us all out early," replied Karen, realizing she sounded like a skiving school girl. "It was all quite dramatic. Willie stood up, looking at least six inches taller than his normal height, raised his right hand high above his head and almost roared out, 'Vengeance is mine, sayeth the Lord.' We'd all been in the midst of a discussion about mercy, justice, and humility and everyone suddenly stopped speaking and froze. Willie walked with what I can best describe as a solemn dignity down the aisle and out of the church. I thought Betty and Rob might follow him, or Michael, or Mabel, just to check up on him to see if he was all right but nobody did. We all just sat there, watching him leave, watching him descend the path, and then, almost all together, we turned to face the vicar.

I could see his mind working to determine what best to do. He looked around, realised our concentration had flown out the door with Willie, and made his decision. I was rather struck with what he said and took some notes, so I think I have it almost word for word, or at least quite close to the meaning." Karen consulted her notebook. "That is, if I can read my scribbles and shorthand. Here goes. He began by repeating what Willie had pronounced: 'Vengeance is mine, sayeth the Lord. What Willie has done for us, in a rather spectacular manner, is to sum up his view of the relationship among mercy, justice, and humility. If justice is seen to be a form of social vengeance for some crime, and if vengeance is the purview of the Lord, then it is not ours to administer but rather His. We are freed from the need and the responsibility to punish for revenge or even for justice. Humility comes in the realisation of God's role and our role and in the supposition, promised in the New Testament, that God's mercy is all powerful and everywhere present. And if mercy is omnipresent, then it is in each and every one of us. It follows, then, that our purpose is to be merciful and to put justice in the hands of the Lord.' He then thanked everyone for our contributions to the discussion and asked us to stand for the closing hymn."

"Wow. There are some pretty strange leaps there. For example, how can he conflate vengeance and justice? What is the role of the legal system in all of this?"

"Betty and Rob and I talked about that on the way home," replied Karen. "We wondered if he could have been referring to the events of this past week. Apparently everyone's been talking about the death of James Anderson. It seems to have slipped out that he was the person in the crash that killed Betty's mother and, of course, Tom's – everyone seems to be calling Tommy 'Tom' now for some reason – father and Dan's mother. The whole village knows it. I'm always amazed at how quickly something like that spreads. Betty said that the vicar was quite concerned about the spiritual health of a community trying to deal with something catastrophic in its midst, first the three deaths in the car accident and now, five years later, the death of the man in the other car involved in the accident. She had overheard him chatting with some of the villagers while she was covering for Adele in the shop. Apparently she learns a lot about what goes on in the village when she's working in the shop." Karen paused for breath. "I'm wondering if Reverend Potts is deliberately moulding theology to address what he perceives as the psychological needs of the village."

"He probably isn't the first vicar to do something like that. It makes me like him more. From what you've described, he seems to make adherence to ideology subservient to the circumstances and needs of the people in his parish. That actually makes me interested in going to one of his services."

***

Betty and Rob were the first to arrive, Betty proudly carrying a Victoria sponge, Rob's favourite cake, made from her mother's recipe. Rob brought the croquet set and, while Mary and Betty chatted in the kitchen, began to set it up in the garden. "Wow!" he called through the back door. "It's amazing what you've done out here. Betty, come and see this."

Mary had a sudden cold chill, recalling Betty's reaction to her wedding gift. She had set out their round Victorian wrought iron tables and chairs near the hedges that made up the three sides of their garden, leaving space between the tables and the back hedge for the croquet set-up. This had the charming effect of turning the entire back garden into an outdoor tea room surrounded by flowering hedges. She had moved the large worktop from her studio onto the rear patio to accommodate the buffet food, decorating the paper tablecloth with large, colourful strokes suggesting local birds in flight, most particularly the kestrel, the lark and the sparrow for the three connected cottages. Adjacent to the patio was the massive and imposing stone and brick barbeque, originally a 19th century outside stone oven that must have served some function in the former schoolhouse. In the centre of the garden was the small tent which the vicar had sent over, gleaming gold on the top and the doorflap, with scarlet sides. Astonishingly, Mary had even found the time to create a poster with dazzling gold and scarlet letters announcing Fortunes by Lilith and Pandora which she had placed in front of the tent. And around the tent, Mary had installed her full-sized renditions of the Churston Grove masks.

Betty gasped, but not with horror. "What an amazing transformation! Who would have thought you could turn an ordinary back garden into a place of mystery and enchantment. Who's Lilith? Who's Pandora? I mean, I know who they are in the Bible and in mythology, but who will be portraying them?"

With relief at her reaction, Mary explained that the vicar was bringing his sister, who had recently moved from London to a nearby town, to the barbeque, and that she, as the person who had initially introduced the vicar to fortune telling, had volunteered to entertain this afternoon's guests. As reading fortunes was apparently a hobby for her, she frequently raised money for charities, using Lilith as her spiritual name. The identity of the other fortune teller, Pandora, was to be a secret.

Within a half hour, the garden was bustling, the sounds and smells of sizzling meat were tickling the nostrils and the buffet table was sagging with the bounty of salads and cakes. Karen and Mary ensured that all of their guests had their first drink in hand and then instructed them to help themselves from then on. Rob had volunteered to cook, as had Dan and Tom, and so the three of them established a rota, relieving their grateful hosts of the task. A ring of the doorbell announced the arrival of the vicar in his funky off-duty clothes, comprising cotton tartan trousers and a bright green t-shirt, and his sister, robed and masked exquisitely as a lushly exotic Lilith. In the meantime, having taken care to welcome and chat with each of her guests, Karen quietly took her exit and prepared to dress as Pandora, the name she had chosen for her first foray into telling fortunes. Since she feared opening up a trunk load of troubles, she had considered Pandora an appropriate avatar for this afternoon's performance. Mary had concurred.

Karen was feeling not just excited but also nervous about this venture. She had a passing familiarity with teacup reading, Tarot cards and palmistry, through having experienced several readings, especially in her late teens and early twenties. She had just enough knowledge, however, to realise that her exposure was hugely inadequate. Reverend Potts had been helpful but he had years of experience as well as an effervescent charm. All Karen had was a general curiosity about other people and a particular curiosity about whether any of her neighbours had committed the barbaric acts against James Anderson. Initially, she had been overjoyed at the opportunity to meet one on one with her neighbours in this mysterious way but as the minutes ticked away and the time for her performance drew nearer she started to realise just how poorly prepared she was. She thought about the mystical aspects of scrying, a form of fortune telling using the observation of natural elements, such as tea leaves, water, crystals, and the like. Perhaps she could gather together some objects and have people arrange them and then talk about their arrangement. Out of that, she might be able to piece together some sort of reading.

And then, almost through a side door of her consciousness, a possibility suggested itself to her. She could use items representing the elements of the story as she had experienced it or later heard about it. Thinking about the placement of the remains in Churston Grove, she determined that she could use the miniature masks made by Mary since they were already in the tent, she could use the dead sparrow, which still lay limply in her study, their own brass door key, a leather wallet, what else? A small boat? She recalled a carving of a fishing boat in Mary's studio. A butcher's cleaver? We don't have that, she thought, but we do have a cheese cleaver, and Mary has knives for carving wood. Painting on her masked face, donning her robes and turban, Karen mulled through her options. She had plenty of time. Lilith would be telling fortunes for at least another forty-five minutes before it would be her turn.

Michael arrived late, cheeks flushed, eyes bright and rapidly darting about, his whole body looking as though ready to explode from trapped internal energy. Mary welcomed him, gave him a Guinness, and showed him to the buffet table. Within less than a minute, a hastily filled plate in one hand and his Guiness in the other, he headed straight for Mabel, a man on a mission. Her attention, however, was completely absorbed by another male, her grandson Tommy, whose parents were enjoying a game of croquet with Dan and Linda and Betty and Rob. With all the cooks at play, Marvyn had volunteered to keep the barbeque going in case anyone wanted another sausage or burger, Karen and Mary having quickly given up on the idea of steak for such a large group.

"What kept you?" Mabel asked, taking Tommy onto her lap so that Michael could have a place to sit.

Michael thumped unceremoniously down into the vacated chair, in his haste spilling some of his salad onto the lawn. "I had the most extraordinary telephone call from America, from a lawyer in Florida, advising me that he was faxing me a very important document. I then had to go to the bank to retrieve the document, a copy of a will that James Anderson had made over here a couple of weeks ago with a firm in Exeter and had arranged to have it mailed to his lawyer in Florida last week. It must have been only a day or two before his death that it was mailed. It arrived at the lawyer's office late on Friday. The lawyer hadn't returned to his office until early Saturday morning, having been in court all day Friday until quite late. When he discovered the will in his mail, he of course notified the Tampa police officer who has been serving as liaison with DI Bodkin and went through the process of verifying the witnesses and ensuring the will was legally correct. That took most of Saturday, by which time it was the middle of the night here. First thing this morning, Florida time, he contacted me."

"What's it to do with us?" asked Mabel, holding a suddenly very squirmy Tommy on her lap.

"Potty," said Tommy. Adamantly.

"I'll be right back," said Mabel. "Sit and enjoy your dinner."

Michael's jaw dropped. He had amazing news but nobody to tell it to. He looked around for Willie.

Eve burst out of the tent. "That was fabulous," she announced to nobody in particular. "Lilith is truly amazing. She's the best fortune teller I've ever gone to. You're next, Rowan. I think you're the last one for Lilith and then they are changing over to Pandora."

"Now that will open a box or two of trouble," quipped her husband as he stood up to go into the tent.

***

Willie had not yet left for the barbeque. His exit from the church, so dramatically unlike anything he had ever done before, had shocked him as much as it had the others in the congregation. It exhibited the extent to which he had altered over the past three weeks. His wife's death, the bovine TB, the drought, the loss of the farm – all these events and conditions had acted upon him and had ground him down over a period of years. In the process, he had lost all sense of control over himself and his circumstances. He had allowed his daughter to look after him because he had not felt sufficiently confident or competent to look after himself. And now, because of the past three weeks, he felt once again poised to take charge of his life. James Anderson had played a role at both ends of this personal drama. Anderson's part in the loss of his wife which led to the loss of his confidence in himself was well understood by everyone he knew. Totally unknown to anyone except himself was Anderson's role in his recent rediscovery of his own personal strength of character. And known only to Michael and himself was the one act which threatened that rediscovery.

Willie had indeed overheard the conversation between James Anderson and Mabel in the Trout and Salmon a few weeks earlier and, like Mabel, he had immediately realised this must be the man responsible for the crash. Tommy Ambrose may have been legally responsible, but, drunk or not, Tommy Ambrose had known these roads intimately, had not been speeding and had a history of being a reliable and responsible driver. James Anderson may have been sober and may have been driving at a legal speed but he had been a first time visitor to the area and did not know the roads. He was to that extent, and to that extent only, responsible.

Willie had pondered a day or two before making his way to Sparrow Cottage.

James Anderson had greeted him without surprise. "Good afternoon, Mr. Barton. I've been expecting you might call."

"Willie. Please call me Willie. Good afternoon, Mr. Anderson."

"And likewise, please call me James. Come in."

They had talked. For several hours they had gone over the crash, the moments leading up to the crash, the need for James Anderson to return on his ticketed flight after the accident for scheduled treatment of an inoperable brain tumour. He had told of the consequent five years of continued therapy and intermittent relapses, his return to the area and his search to locate the surviving relatives of those who had been killed in the crash. He had not wanted to resurrect any pain by letting them know he was the person responsible and so he had used his first name James rather than the name he had always preferred, Gilbert.

"Why on earth did you want to know who we were if you did not want us to know who you were?" Willie had asked.

"That's a reasonable question. I hope you find my answer reasonable as well." James continued in a voice more registered in logic than in emotion. "I'm going to die very soon. I'm a bit of a coward. To tell the truth, I did not want any confrontations, any recriminations, any more guilt heaped upon me than I had already heaped upon myself."

"That's understandable. But why did you want to know about us?"

"When I was here five years ago, researching my ancestry, I had hoped to discover some relationship to the distinguished Gilbert family who at one time owned much of this area. At that time, my motivation was simple curiosity. It seemed that everyone I knew was researching their heritage and I just followed the herd. What I learned was that there is no direct legal relationship even though there is most probably a direct blood relationship. As you might expect, it is drenched in scandal and well hidden in any existing paperwork, other than two private and unsigned letters which I had found among my mother's things after she died. I have no living family. I was an only child, I never married and have no heirs." James Anderson paused, not in any anticipation of a sympathetic response from Willie, which was not, in any case, forthcoming, but rather because he was not a talker by nature and he was uneasy explaining himself and his motivations.

"When I left here so quickly after the accident, I was still in shock. I found it beyond my capability to realise that I had caused the death of three people. I did not want to meet their surviving relatives. I did not want to see their faces, their anguish," he had paused to look directly at Willie, "to see your face, your anguish, as I am seeing it right now. And, of course, I was scheduled to

Begin some rough chemotherapy and radiology treatments, both of which made me very ill for quite some time. When the treatments ceased, having postponed the inevitable for a year or two, I began to think more clearly. I am not a wealthy man but, with some astute property investment, I reasoned that I might, before this tumour achieves its inescapable result, make some sort of restitution for the pain I had caused."

Willie had stirred, as though he might either affirm or contradict the claim of responsibility for the accident assumed by James Anderson but Anderson had raised his hand to forestall interruption and had kept speaking.

"I thought if I purchased property here before I died, I would state in my will that it be sold, the money to be divided among the three spouses and three children of those who had died in that disastrous accident." Willie's mouth opened to respond but again James raised his hand to prevent him from speaking. "I also discovered that a small portion of Gilbert Farm is up for sale and I have been trying to arrange for money transfers to secure that property. For one reason and another, there have been delays in the transaction, both at the US end, because of the limits on funds that can be brought over to the UK at any one time and at the England end, to ensure that there is no money laundering. Funds need to be held virtually in limbo for several days, possibly even two or three weeks, so that I may not be able to conclude the deal before someone else beats me to it or this tumour wins its battle, which could occur any day. It's frustrating but I am working on it. This property, you may be interested to learn, I intended to bequeath to you, Willie, as I had learned that the death of your wife that tragic day contributed to your losing the tenancy of Gilbert Farm. All of this was intended to be a surprise following my death. However, as they say in the movies, my cover's been blown."

At last silence. James had looked at Willie with an open invitation to speak his mind. And Willie decided to do exactly that. He had begun with a quiet trickle, a calm statement in full control acknowledging that both their lives had indeed been turned upside down and inside out from the accident, leaving them both shells of their former selves. Willie had spoken of his life with Amanda, of how every morning he had opened his sleepy eyes, thrilled to watch her lying beside him, of how he would creep quietly out of bed and into the kitchen to brew her cup of tea, and of the beaming smile she would give him every time he brought it to her. And then the calmly described image of their morning ritual ran into other images of their life and love together, one, two, three events flooding into his brain, rushing, intermingling, colliding, until the dam burst and he was drowning in the past, swept into the current of his memories, submerged in joy, happiness, pain, frustration, anger and sorrow, talking and talking and sobbing and finally silent. All the anguish that had festered unspoken for the past five years had flowed out of his soul and into the ether of James Anderson's sitting room and then evaporated. Willie had felt empty. Completely drained. And then, most astonishingly, he had felt relieved. The heavy ball he had felt inside himself for so long was gone.

James was not a sentimental man. He had risen quickly and had walked to his liquor cabinet, bringing back a bottle of 30-year old port. "I know I'm not supposed to drink but I do. Would you care to join me?"

Over their port, they had agreed on that day, just over three weeks ago, to say nothing about the will or about James Anderson's intentions until after his death. Since that first visit to Sparrow Cottage, Willie had become accustomed, during his daily constitutional, to drop in on James from time to time.

Shaking his head sadly at the memory of that first meeting, Willie's musings jumped to his final meeting with James Anderson. He had walked to Sparrow Cottage the day of Betty's wedding to see whether James wanted a lift with his brother Michael or was feeling sufficiently fit to walk. He had thought that his daughter's wedding might provide a good opportunity for Michael to be told about James' true identity. He could have rung James but Willie generally preferred to speak to people face to face and Sparrow was along his usual route. When there was no answer to the doorbell, Willie had knocked. Hearing no response, he had tried the doorknob and found the door unlocked."Unusual," he had thought to himself because James had always kept the door locked, even when he had been expecting that Willie might visit. Crossing over the threshold, Willie had been devastated to find his new friend sprawled at the foot of the stairs.

He had checked his wrist and found no discernible pulse but the body was warm. He then had checked his neck, willing his own pounding heart to quiet itself so that he could feel whatever might be feebly pulsing through James' arteries and veins. Something fluttered. He had felt it in his fingertips. He didn't know what to do and so he had begun to stroke his neck down toward his chest, as though to encourage the blood to flow into the heart and be pumped out again. It didn't work that way, he knew, but it was an automatic reflex. He searched for the phone to ring for an ambulance but did not want to take his hand away from the tiny bit of life force he was certain he could feel. He could not fully comprehend the intensity of what he was feeling. In the three weeks since he had first knocked on the door of this cottage, he had come to know and respect James Anderson as a man similar in many ways to himself At that moment, Michael had walked into the house as though he had expected the door to be unlocked.

Willie's phone rang, startling him from his reverie. It rang several times before Willie realised he could not recapture the intensity of his recollection of the last time he saw James Anderson and so he finally answered. "Yes, I'm fine," he told his worried daughter. "I'm just leaving."

***

"Mary, may I have a word?" Michael drew Mary slightly away from the group of Rambler friends she had been talking with. "Please excuse us for a moment," he said to them in his most charming voice. "I won't be long, but I do need to speak with Mary urgently."

Startled, Mary almost dropped her glass of wine. Instead, she spilled a little of it over her wrist and onto the lawn, but quickly composed herself, wondering what possibly could be the problem. Could something be the matter with Willie? He hadn't shown up yet.

"Mary, I need to request a huge favour. Something that concerns everyone in my family has just come to my attention. I would like to be able to speak with my family in private for a few minutes, perhaps longer. Would it be possible for us to use your sitting room?"

"Of course," said Mary. "Will you need more chairs? I've brought a couple of chairs from that room outside, but we can bring them back in again. You need room for..."

"Mabel, Dan, Tom, Willie's on his way, and Betty. So, that would make six, counting me. I'll help you set up enough chairs while we wait for Willie."

"Would you like me to bring in some drinks or tea?"

"Thanks, but no," replied Michael, not wanting to provide opportunity for any interruptions. "Ah, there's Willie now. I'll collect the rest of the brood. Thanks again for the use of the room."

***

Pandora was ready, encased in golden taffeta and red and purple velvet. She had used a Venetian mask to hide the top half of her face, and, drawing upon her make-up skills from amateur theatricals in her youth, had reshaped her rather thin lips into a lushly scarlet smile. She had located an intricately decorated gilded box in Mary's studio and had filled it with the objects she intended to use. Coming down the stairs very carefully, since the mask obscured most of her peripheral vision, she was surprised to see all the members of the Barton family filing into the sitting room. They were equally astonished to behold Pandora, her slow descent transfigured into sweeping majesty by her costume. Michael, as usual, took the lead.

"I presume you are Pandora?" He bowed slightly, in deference to her robes. "I understand that I am scheduled for a fortune telling session with you in just a few minutes. However, an urgent matter has arisen involving all members of my family and so we will need to delay our meetings with you for at least a half hour, possibly longer."

Karen/Pandora had no idea why the Barton family was taking over the sitting room. Since they were all there, looking healthily curious about what was to transpire, she dismissed her initial fear that some tragedy had befallen them, and, with her singleness of focus, surmised that something must have come up in relation to the death of James Anderson. Using the slowness of her descent to gather her thoughts, she searched for something to say that might suggest she could read what was on their minds. She wished she could be wisely prophetic, like the Delphic Oracle, whose words could be interpreted to fit whatever might happen, whether fortunate or catastrophic. She settled her voice into the lowest range she could manage in order to sound as mysterious as possible, caught Michael's eyes straight on, and replied, "Good afternoon, Michael. Today, as a family, you will learn what you need to know to forge ahead through all the uncertainty of this past week. Your combined humanity will resolve all problems. The generosity of others will become your generosity. Pandora has spoken."

They all paused their progression into the sitting room as though frozen and looked at her uncomprehendingly. All except Michael, who wondered how she could possibly know what he had just learned. She then dramatically caressed her gilded box, keeping it tightly closed, and looked directly at each one of the Bartons. She saw Betty's eyes, still softened by the romance of her new marriage, unclouded by any sense of foreboding. Mabel's eyes were wary but resolute; Tom's eyes were calm; Dan seemed uneasy, not sure of what was going on. Willie's amazingly serene blue eyes met hers with equanimity, almost defying her to discern anything that he did not want her to see; and Michael's pale blue eyes retained their coolness but with a glint of excitement. He signalled everyone into the sitting room, and closed the door.

Pandora, her heart thumping with the audacity of her prophecy, turned to walk through the kitchen into the back garden, almost bumping into Lilith, who had finished her set of guests for the evening and had come in to freshen up. "That was quite some prediction," she stated, in her throaty Lilith voice. "Nick told me you were new at this. I think you might be a natural."

Pandora, again, was caught off guard. What should she say to this person who had been telling fortunes for years, for decades, according to the vicar. Lilith, in her luminescent robes richly embroidered with entwined snakes, apples and angels, intimidated her but not intentionally, she thought. It was more that she was allowing herself to be intimidated, meaning that, if she willed it, she should be able to stop that feeling. She tried to separate her Pandora self from her Karen self, allowing Karen to remain intimidated but forcing Pandora to present herself on equal footing.

"Good evening, Lilith. Reverend Nicholas has told me so much about you. I'd love to chat with you for awhile. But you must be tired after your stint in the tent. Have you had anything to eat yet?"

"Yes, I have been well looked after," replied Lilith, chuckling inwardly, fully aware of Karen's/Pandora's use of hospitality to try to regain her equilibrium. "But I have an idea. I also would like to chat with you. Give me five minutes and I shall join you in the tent. Since all of the people on your list are now in the sitting room, perhaps we can read each other's fortunes."

***

In the sitting room, all eyes were on Michael, who was placing some papers on a small table. Without fuss, he began. "What I am about to tell you has taken me completely by surprise. It will make us all feel wonderful, fearful, and horribly ashamed, all at the same time. It will also reawaken the pain we all experienced five years ago with that horrific accident and again one week ago with James Anderson's death, and it will connect all those feelings together."

Everybody looked around at each other, not knowing what to think. "Michael, get off your high horse and get on with it," quipped Mabel.

"Mabel and Willie, you both already know that James Anderson was really Gilbert Anderson, the man who drove the car that killed my wife and your mother," he nodded at Dan, "your mother," he nodded at Betty, "and your father," he nodded at Tom. Without waiting for Dan, Betty, and Tom to process this information, even though he could tell from their faces that they were stunned, Michael continued. He explained why Gilbert Anderson had returned so expeditiously to Florida after the accident, why he had moved here to Coombe Gilbert, and why he had not let any of them know when he learned of their relationship to those who had been killed in the accident. There were short outbursts from time to time, as each person came to realise that Mabel had known for almost a month and that Michael and Willie had known for a week and that not one of them had said anything about it.

"Makes me almost glad..." Tom began, but Michael stopped him. "No, Tom, you don't believe that for a minute."

"You're right. There is nothing to feel glad about that afternoon in Sparrow Cottage."

"You might be surprised. Let me go on. Last week James Gilbert Anderson died. We all know that. What none of us knew is that he had made a will only a few days prior to his death and had mailed it to his lawyer in Florida. Apparently his treatments for his brain tumour were not working. Prior to his moving here, he had been told he had only weeks or at best a few months to live. That was over eight months ago."

"So why did he go to all the effort of moving here?"

"I'll get to that because it concerns all of us. In a nutshell, he has left Sparrow Cottage to the Barton family, to be sold and the income to be divided equally amongst Mabel, Willie, Betty, Tom, Dan, and me." Once again, he continued without allowing any of his astonished family members to speak. "Additionally, he had initiated an application to purchase the small plot of land on Gilbert Farm that had been put on the market. Acceptance of the application had been held up because of US banking policies. The US bank finally transferred his funds to our bank on Friday, and, since his application to purchase a part of Gilbert Farm had already been approved subject to receiving the funds, he also now owns that land, or rather that land now belongs to his estate. He has left that property in its entirety to Willie."

Michael sat down, wishing now he had accepted Mary's offer to bring in some drinks for everybody. For two seconds there was silence. Betty had played no part in either the death or the cover-up, neither of which had yet been spoken of, and so was completely elated at this turn of events. She could not fully appreciate why everyone was so quiet. Michael, noticing her confusion, nodded at Mabel, who quietly turned to Betty and asked her if she would like to leave the room to tell Rob about the legacy. Betty took the cue and got up to leave, feeling a strange combination of happiness, curiosity and anxiety. And then she remembered Michael's opening words, that this news would cause everyone to feel 'wonderful, fearful, and ashamed.' She felt the wonder. What was there to be ashamed of? To be fearful of? She turned to her father. "Dad, do you want me to leave?"

Willie was unsure what he wanted. When Michael strode into Sparrow Cottage the night James had died and discovered Willie bending over James Anderson's body, Michael had told him the entire gruesome story. Well, not the entire story. At first, all he had told him about was the scene at Sparrow Cottage with Tommy and then with Mabel, Sam and him. Then Michael had seized the wrench, which had fallen from Tommy's hand and had tumbled down the stairs with James, ending up partially obscured under James' left shoulder. As soon as Willie had realised what Michael intended to do with the wrench, he had grabbed at Michael, and they had fought as they used to fight as boys, not hitting or punching, but grabbing, holding, and shaking, as though one could outshake the other by brute force. "Willie, sit down and listen to me. James is dead. You can see that he is dead. You can see where Tommy hit him with this wrench, hit him out of fear, not with any intention to cause his death. I'm going to take this wrench and throw it into the sea. But first I am going to hit James one more time, so that the indentation is slightly different from the one made by Tommy."

"But he's not dead. He's still warm. Feel him. I was feeling for his pulse when you came in."

"He's dead, Willie. I also thought I saw a faint pulse when we left this afternoon, a kind of jerking in the main artery in his neck. I came back now to make certain he was dead. I don't want to think what I might have done had he still been alive. But look at him. Feel him. He's definitely dead."

Willie had cried, cried all over again for the loss of Amanda, and then cried for the loss of James. James, who had reconnected Willie with Amanda simply by his existence here in Coombe Gilbert, but who no longer existed, just as Amanda no longer existed. Michael had held him, had let him cry, had rocked him very slightly, very gently, very slowly, and then had stopped. He had given Willie his handkerchief and then made the most bizarre request, made it in the most oxymoronically gentle and caring voice one could possibly use to make such a request. "Willie, to help Tommy, do you think you could take this wrench and hit James with it, right close to where Tommy hit? Just to confuse the angle and the strength. You can just do a light tap if you like. He is really dead. I'll go first, and then you."

"I can't believe what you are asking me to do. I can't understand what you are intending to do. I don't understand it at all. Why are we not calling the police? If Tommy did not intend to hurt him, if he hit out in self defence, then it's a manslaughter charge at worst. If we do anything else, it takes the crime to an entirely different level, one I don't even want to contemplate. No, of course I will not do this. Nor will I condone your doing it."

At that point, Michael had been forced to tell Willie about the ten percent plan, about how the entire family, other than Betty and Rob, as well as many of their friends were involved. If Tommy were arrested and brought to trial, everything would come out. Betty and Rob would lose the house since the deposit had been funded with money gained through fraud, everyone involved would lose their reputations and many would likely do prison time. He told Willie of Mabel's idea to hide the body in the open, making it look like a ritual murder during, or at least very close to, the summer solstice.

Willie had been dumbstruck. Poor James, about to be sacrificed and desecrated on the altar of family loyalty. Because he had understood immediately how it must be. He had understood his role, an unwelcome but necessary role. He also had understood he had to get through the wedding as though he knew nothing of what had transpired here today or of what was about to transpire in the next two days. He had taken the wrench and he had swung a solid blow, right on top of Michael's.

"Dad, are you okay? Dad. Dad."

"Oh, Betty, yes, yes, dear, I'm fine. But there are some things we need to discuss here that you were not involved in and that you would be better off not becoming involved in. I would very much prefer it if you would leave now. We just have a few more items to discuss and then we'll all be out in the garden. If you could ensure that there was a cup of tea, or, better yet, a glass of sherry waiting outside for each of us, we'd be most grateful. We'll be there directly."

Betty turned to go, and then turned back again. "Dad, please understand what I am about to say. Rob and I are not without eyes and ears. We know that Uncle Michael and Aunt Mabel and Tom and Dan are involved in some way with the death of James Anderson and all that happened afterward. We don't know the details but we think it might also be related to our being able to live in Lark Cottage. If that is so, then we are most definitely involved. I would like to remain. I shall remain." With that, Betty sat down again, turning her face away from her father to look Michael straight in the eye.

***

During the drama in the sitting room, the rest of the party had been winding down. Rob had taken apart and put away the cricket game, Eve and Rowan and Teresa and Marvyn had left to prepare for an early evening ramble on Dartmoor, up to the old quarry behind Haytor, and Sue was ready to take Tommy home for a late afternoon nap. Mary had been in the kitchen much of the time, making tea and coffee for those about to leave in a few minutes. She had been able to overhear murmurings of the conversation in the sitting room, but not sufficient to make out what was being said. Pandora and Lilith had mingled minimally with the other guests on their way to the tent.

Lilith took the fortune teller's seat, leaving Pandora to assume the role of client. "I predict that your induction into fortune telling is about to be delayed," said Lilith. "not just for a few minutes but for some other time entirely."

Pandora chuckled. "I don't actually mind one single bit. I had been looking forward to it, of course, but the closer it came to the time, I was dreading it because I realised how unprepared I was."

"May I ask how you were going to approach it?"

Pandora looked closely at Lilith. It seemed an innocent question, a natural professional curiosity, but something in the tone and inflection of the voice reminded her of someone. Unable to think who it might be, she answered the question with another question.

"Has your brother told you about the terrible death that occurred here this past week?"

"Oh yes. I'm pretty well informed about that. Why?" responded Lilith, who could barely believe that gleaning information from Pandora/Karen would be as easy as the proverbial taking candy from a baby.

"Did your brother tell you that Mary and I discovered the remains of the body?"

"Mmm, yes, I was aware of that."

"Well the detective assigned to the case somehow suspected that Mary and I were involved, which of course we were not, and the newspaper printed a reprehensible story so replete with innuendo and supposition that we feared others might think that we had been involved. We'd been at a village wedding the night of the murder -- or possibly the night before the murder, we're not sure – and noticed a lot of strange behaviour that might be explained by...oh gosh. As I say it now, I realise I've made so many suppositions that have no basis in any kind of evidence. It seems completely crazy now but I had thought that if I could talk alone with some of the people whose behaviour sparked my curiosity, I might learn something. On the other hand, I'm not sure I really want to discover that any of my neighbours was involved in this terrible deed."

"Why is that? Isn't learning the truth about the murder important?"

"Of course. But I am beginning to know these people. I like them. I don't want to be responsible for anybody from this village going to prison, particularly as a consequence of my own selfish curiosity."

Lilith was willing, actually eager, to travel further along this philosophical path, but first wanted some concrete information. "So how were you going to approach getting your neighbours to talk about the murder? Does that box have anything to do with it? Pandora's Box, releasing all forms of evil into the world?"

"It all seems quite silly to me now," said Pandora, forgetting to use her mysterious voice. "Here's what I had put together." She opened the box to reveal the dead sparrow, the key, the wallet, the little carved boat, and a tiny carved cottage with a picture of a lark pasted onto the roof.

Lilith almost pounced but remembered her role and forced herself to become as relaxed and languid as possible. "How very interesting. Tell me about each of these."

Pandora noticed the initial force of energy and sensed Lilith's self-compelled relaxation. All her senses pricked up. *Who is this Lilith?* she asked herself. *Why is she so interested?* "Actually that's the question I was going to ask the people who came to have their fortunes told. Then I was going to use their answers to make some vague kind of prediction."

"How did you come to choose each of these items?"

Pandora knew that no mention had been made in the newspaper of the sparrow, the wallet, or the key. The boat and the lark on the cottage were connections she had made on her own. How much should she explain? Why was this woman asking so many questions? Questions. 'I ask the questions; you answer them.' That was a phrase she would never forget. She looked Lilith straight in the eye. Her eyes. They were bright green, startlingly green, green just like her brother's and green just like DI Cora Bodkin's. It couldn't be.

"I see you have just realised who I am," said Cora, calmly, unapologetically.

Karen was livid. "Out! Get out! You were not invited. You have no right coming into our home as our guest, in disguise, pretending to be someone else. That is completely unprofessional. Please leave." Karen/Pandora stood and swept open the tent flap.

Cora/Lilith remained seated. "Karen, please, I did not come here to snoop or spy or anything of that nature. Please close the tent door and let's talk. Not as detective and citizen but person to person. If it helps, we can retain the Lilith/Pandora personae or we can just be ourselves. But I sincerely would like to talk with you more about your suppositions."

Karen did not want to talk with Cora Bodkin. Every hair on the back of her neck prickled at the thought. But she was intrigued by the fact that Cora seemed to want to talk with her, not as a detective but as a person. Perhaps Pandora could talk with Lilith about some of the aspects of the case. It was worth a try. She sat down and picked up her box, speaking once again in the low and mysterious voice she had adopted as Pandora. "There are secrets in this box, secrets I had thought were known known only to Mary and me but are probably also known to you. The sparrow, key, and wallet you know. The boat is in here because Mary and I think that James Anderson died or was killed in his house, dismembered elsewhere, and transported by boat to Churston Grove. The little cottage with the picture of the lark is in here because we think there was some sort of village plan to acquire Lark Cottage for the newlyweds, that the plan somehow backfired, James Anderson found out, and his death resulted. We don't know any of this. It is all speculation."

"Ah, Pandora, your box certainly does contain all the evils of this investigation. Does hope still reside in your box or has it long ago fled?"

"Oh, there is hope indeed, Lilith. As long as people are living and breathing there is hope."

"And what is Pandora's hope?"

"Pandora hopes that when this investigation has concluded, James Anderson is laid to rest in peace and with respect and dignity and that nobody in the village has to be held legally responsible."

"What if somebody or some persons in the village are guilty?"

"I've been thinking very hard about that question for the past few hours. I'm not sure I fully understand the concept of guilt. If we do something wrong, we are responsible for rectifying whatever we have done wrong and compensating for any damage. Nobody can rectify a death but there are circumstances around every death, be it murder or manslaughter or suicide or natural causes, that require specific determinations and judgements. The law punishes the guilty with social disgrace and imprisonment. I'm not convinced that social disgrace and imprisonment are the best means, in all cases, of having people take responsibility for the consequences of their crimes. That's not to say I'm a 'bleeding liberal' about crime and punishment. I just think that when trying to determine the best way to deal legally with someone who commits a crime, one size fits none."

"Isn't that why we have judges and juries? To make these determinations?"

"The legal system is becoming increasingly politicised and often the determinations of juries and the resultant sentences are restricted by policies that may apply generally but not always specifically. And these determinations and sentences almost always involve social disgrace and punishment. And disgrace and punishment rarely serve anybody's best interests."

"So, Pandora, imagine I am a client coming to you for a fortune telling session. I have had an altercation with a man that has resulted in his death. I have tried to cover it up in order to protect others who were tangentially involved in some questionable business dealings with him and with others. These others have helped me with the cover up by committing atrocious desecrations of the body this man. What is your prediction for my future?"

"My prediction would be different, depending upon whether I knew the person and whether I had reason to respect the character of that person."

"Assume you don't know the person."

"Then I would react as I think most judges and juries would react. My prediction would be something like the following: 'I see a large building, with small windows with very little penetrating light. I see you living in this lightless, soulless building for a long time, long enough that you will be in danger of becoming soulless as well. I see your accessories in the crime in a similar place, in similar danger of losing the essence of who they are. I see your friends and family suffering and waiting for you, worried that by the time you leave this large building and return to them, you will not be the same person they knew and loved."

"If this unknown person were to ask you for advice, what would you say?"

"I would recommend immediate contact with the police."

"Okay, let's do it again. This time you know the person. You know it's a male, hardworking and conscientious, supporting a young family. You know his accessories in the crime are law-abiding members of his family trying to avoid any of them having to go to prison. What do you predict? What do you advise?"

Pandora realised that Lilith/Cora was articulating her assumptions about the death of James Anderson, assumptions that fundamentally mirrored her own. Less than an hour ago, as she was preparing for her Pandora role, she had enjoyed watching Tom and Sue and Tommy playing croquet; she had seen Michael and Mabel chatting, she had revelled in Betty and Rob's honeymoon adoration of each other. These people had been strangers a year ago; now they were neighbours becoming friends. She saw the trap Lilith had set for her. "Lilith, this is too difficult. I cannot be judge and jury over people I know and yet I just acted as judge and jury over a stranger."

"That's why we rely on the legal system," Lilith said quietly, "because it can factor out that kind of emotional involvement."

"But if you factor out emotions, what's left? Person A is different from Person B. Circumstances, motivations, opportunities all differ from case to case. Life is not objective. Crime is not objective. How can justice be served if individual situations are not taken into account?"

Lilith smiled. "Circles are good in fortune telling but terrible in a logical discussion. And we are beginning to transcribe a tautological circle here which will lead us nowhere. You know who I am. Have you wondered at all why I chose Lilith as my alter ego?"

"Actually, no. I haven't had time to digest that you are really DI Cora Bodkin. And I don't know all that much about Lilith. Nor do I know much about DI Cora Bodkin for that matter."

"Interesting, because Lilith and Pandora have a lot in common, the major similarity being that they both are ascribed, through myth, with bringing all manner of evil into the world. I recognised something kindred in you when I first met you in the Grove. And when Nick told me you had chosen Pandora as your alter ego or avatar for fortune telling, my intuitions were affirmed. Why did you choose Pandora?"

"Because the day your brother rang me, Mary and I were discussing what my responsibility would be if I really were to discover evidence implicating any of our neighbours in the death of James Anderson. I think 'opening a can of worms' was the operative metaphor at the time. When your brother asked me if I would like to try a bit of fortune telling, the can of worms evolved into Pandora releasing all sorts of evil into the world but retaining hope as a means of addressing this evil. It seemed to fit. So why Lilith?"

"The story of Lilith is a complex one but I am not really concerned with all of its interpretations and ramifications. I will try to fit my answer to the needs of this situation. Lilith, as you may know, was created to be the first wife and helpmate of Adam. Because Adam wanted her to be subservient, and she saw herself as his equal, this arrangement didn't work. She managed to escape the Garden of Eden and settled herself in a cave by the Red Sea where she consorted with questionable angels and demons and gave birth to many demon children who brought all sorts of evil into the world. Hence the connection with Pandora. My affiliation with her relates to her rejection of male dominance and regulations. Before I moved here, I worked for many years at the Met, almost entirely male-dominated and almost entirely regulated according to political necessity. The persona of Lilith provided me an opportunity to escape that patriarchal system. I'm no demon Lilith. I'm more in line with the modern reinterpretation and reintegration of Lilith into a society where woman are gaining equality with men."

"So what would be Lilith's prediction and advice for the hypothetical client that you described earlier?"

"It would not be Cora's," replied Lilith, her expression enigmatic. Karen/Pandora's jaw dropped in astonishment at this disclosure and its implications.

A loud cough and a combination of scratching and knocking at the tent flap announced that someone was outside, wanting their attention. Lilith, closest to the door, opened the flap to reveal Reverend Nick. "May I come in?" he asked.

Lilith glanced at Pandora. "Yes, of course," Pandora replied.

"The most extraordinary thing has occurred," said the vicar. "James Anderson left a will giving his estate to the Barton family. They have all just met in your sitting room and discussed what to do with this legacy. They want to make an announcement and have asked everyone to come into the garden."

Lilith and Pandora looked at each other with combined shock and curiosity. Cora had learned of the will almost at the same time that Michael had, from the fax that had come in just as she had been about the leave her office. At first she had jumped on it as providing further motivation to kill James Anderson in order to gain the inheritance. But it had quickly become obvious, as she read through the document, that he had not informed the Barton family of his intentions. Karen, on the other hand, was completely baffled. "Let's go," she said.

Mary had cleared the buffet table of food and had set out two bottles of sherry, one medium and one dry, some shortbread, and pots of tea and coffee. Everyone in the Barton family was in the process of helping themselves to these refreshments and choosing a seat in the circle of chairs that Michael had set up with Rob's and Tom's assistance. It was evident that, once again, he would serve as spokesperson for the family.

Karen tried to read the faces of everyone in the circle. Betty looked worn, but her cheeks were flushed rather than pale. Rob, seated beside her and holding her hand, looked uncustomarily stormy. Willie was, as usual, inscrutable . Mabel looked more placid than she had for days. Dan stared down at his feet. Tom sat straight, tight-lipped, but eyes steady, hand clasped in Sue's, whose face was turned toward Tommy. Mary also was tight-lipped but her blue eyes were signalling some short of shared understanding with Karen that Karen was not yet able to appreciate. Reverend Potts had been invited to join the group, in addition to Karen and ... Lilith? or Cora? Karen had removed her mask. Lilith had not. Karen wondered whether to warn the group who this person really was but then decided that was not her place in this group to do so. On the other hand, she was very concerned that Michael might say something that would provide the hard evidence that Cora needed.

When Michael chose to sit rather than stand, the tension in the air seemed to relax somewhat. He cleared his throat and began. "This has been probably the most taxing week in our lives, barring that week five years ago when we lost and buried three beloved members of our family. We began the week with a marriage, undeniably the most pleasant aspect of these past seven days. That joy was cut short by the death and horrid dismemberment of James Anderson, the subsequent police investigation, the discovery that this new member of our community had been involved in the accident five years ago, and now his will." Rob and Sue, who had not yet been apprised of what had transpired in the sitting room, registered their shock and surprise at the mention of Anderson's identity and then of his will. Karen's mind was swirling. "We have spent the past hour discussing this will and its implications for us. While Karen and Lilith? – pardon me, but we haven't yet been introduced so I don't know your real name." Michael paused to provide Lilith an opportunity to reveal herself. She chose not to and simply nodded, acknowledging that, yes, they had not yet been introduced. Michael swallowed the snub and continued. "For Karen's and Reverend Nick's sister's benefit, as well as Rob and Sue, who have not had the opportunity yet to learn of our discussion, James Anderson's will states that Sparrow Cottage is to be left to all of us in the Barton family. We may dispose of it as we see fit and divide the profits amongst ourselves. He has also left a small landholding on Gilbert Farm to Willie for his use as he sees fit. Since what we have decided will affect everyone here, except possibly you, Lilith, although the vicar indicated that you likely would be very interested in the outcome of our discussion, we thought we would announce it here. We're excited about it," although Karen could see that most in the group were at this late stage of the afternoon more exhausted than excited, "and are eager to begin to talk about it." Almost as though on cue, backs straightened and spirits seemed to lift. It appeared as though this slightly more public sharing of their private deliberations was beginning to sluice away the tensions and pressures of the week.

"We spent the first half hour of the meeting coming to the agreement that we do not want to sell Sparrow Cottage. We decided that we would like it to be used for some good purpose by the people of Coombe Gilbert. At that point, we invited Reverend Nick to join us, as we thought he might provide some guidance. And he did. Reverend Nick, would you please take over now?"

"Gladly, Michael. Karen, we apologise for not having involved you in the decision that we came to, since Sparrow Cottage is right next to where you live, but we did consult with Mary and she was quite certain you would approve. It's really a wonderful opportunity that everyone has agreed upon. As many of you know, our church contributes heavily to the support of children and young people who have been abused within the foster care system. Some of the abuse is systemic, most notably what happens to foster children when they turn eighteen and are set out into the world with no family support or love. The shortage of housing in the village has prevented our providing any assistance whatsoever for these young people. The Bartons have agreed that they would like to turn Sparrow Cottage into a transitional home for eighteen year olds leaving the foster care system. There is, of course, a lot of work to be done before this can happen. Planning permission will be required and will depend largely upon the support of the neighbourhood, most strongly the two other cottages adjoining Sparrow Cottage -- Lark and Kestrel. Betty and Mary have both indicated their support. Betty would even like to take a course so that she can provide nurture and assistance for the young adults who come to live in the house. Some changes will be needed to make certain that it meets all health and safety regulations and Tom has agreed to donate his skills to ensuring the property meets all requirements. The home can accommodate 2-4 young adults plus a supervisor and Mabel has agreed to volunteer at least two days a week as a live-in supervisor. That's about as far as we have come in our deliberations.

And, of course, this is just a rough idea of what we would like to do. Social Services will likely advise us about the best way we can help and whether our ideas are even feasible. What do you think, Karen?"

Karen was thinking many things at that moment. Reverend Potts was talking about people who were planning to donate not only the potential money they might have received from the sale of Sparrow Cottage but also a considerable amount of their time and expertise. She saw all of her speculations falling into place. This was atonement as she had never before experienced it. The Bartons were seizing an opportunity to make amends for whatever fraud or abomination they had committed with whatever they had to offer just as James Anderson had, at the end of his life, tried to make amends. This was justice working itself out, not quickly, not easily, not according to restrictive or predictive algorithms but according to the clumsy and difficult balancing of human capabilities. She could not have wished for a better outcome. She looked across at Mary who smiled her encouragement. "I think it is a wonderful plan and an excellent use of this lovely old cottage. Along with Mary, I assure you that I will give my full support to your planning application when it is presented and we will provide whatever practical support we can to help your project get underway."

Lilith stood. "It's time for us to go. I'd like to thank you all for including me in your party and in your exciting announcement. I wish you all the best. May I make a prediction?" Tired and eager to get home, the group politely nodded.

"Please look at your hands," Lilith said, in her deep and exotic voice. "Hold them out, palms up, slightly cupped, just in front of you, not resting on anything. Feel the weight in your hands. Feel the weight of this week in your hands. Place all the troubles, tensions, stresses, concerns and problems into your hands. Feel them. Let them hold the full weight of the week." She stopped and waited, waited a full minute for everyone to fill their hands with all the anguish and stress they could fit into them. "Now turn them over and let it all fall to the ground. Feel the tension fall down, float away. Shake out your hands, and hold them out again. Now take each others' hands and feel the clean strength within them. This is the strength that will take you forward and help you to succeed with your plan."

Lilith looked at her brother. "C'mon, Nick. I've an early day tomorrow."

TEN: MONDAY

DI Cora Bodkin, trim and crisply beige, ginger hair under the strict control of a green scarf, called DC Johnson and DC Kendal into her office. "Jenny and Dave, I want to thank you both for the dedication you have shown on the Anderson case. I presented our evidence and hypotheses to the super first thing this morning. After consultation with the Chief Constable, he has concluded that we have insufficient evidence to press charges at this point. I agree. Everything is circumstantial and speculative. With a heavy backlog of child and domestic abuse cases in addition to last Thursday's homicide, our resources are too tightly stretched to maintain a dedicated team of three detectives on this investigation. I will continue to monitor our main suspects and also to explore an alternative possibility I uncovered over the weekend but priority has been moved to other cases. You have both been reassigned to the Gillespie homicide that came in last Thursday. The forensic report is already in and the notes of the officers who responded to the call are all in this file. Some preliminary witness statements have been taken by duty officers. DI Jones has been working the case and will brief you. I'll meet with you and DI Jones in the Gillespie incident room at 1:00 tomorrow. This afternoon, I have a funeral to attend.

***

Mary and Karen had slept in, exhausted after post-party clean-up. The warmth of the summer sun, already blazing high in the almost cloudless sky, had encouraged them to enjoy their breakfast on the patio. They had left the installation of the masks in the garden and had buried the sparrow right in the centre of the installation. It was a tiny grave easily covered with a divot of grass. Karen had brewed herself a huge pot of tea and Mary was indulging in a cafetiere of freshly ground and brewed coffee. Neither had said much to the other about the previous night's revelations but both had been absorbed with all that had transpired.

"I wonder if I'll need a hat," pondered Karen, placing her mug of tea on the circular Victorian wrought iron table and spreading some wild Moroccan orange marmalade on her toast. They had decided to forgo the usual fruit salad and poached eggs this morning.

"What?" Mary briefly stopped struggling with the lid on the peanut butter jar to turn her attention to Karen.

"Well, for the wedding we needed hats. Do we need hats for James Anderson's funeral?"

"I doubt it. There are going to be only a few of us at the crematorium, followed by drinks at the Trout and Salmon, where a hat would definitely be out of place."

"Here, let me help you with that lid. What do you think will happen to Michael and Sam and Mabel and Tom?"

"I think whatever was going to happen has already happened."

"You don't think DI Bodkin will bring charges?"

"She could and she might but I doubt it. After all, she doesn't know the entire story, does she? Nor do we, for certain. Although I think we can piece most of it together now, especially with the few nuggets that slipped out in the conversation after Reverend Potts and Bodkin left. Actually, Karen, I meant to tell you this last night, but I was too tired. I think you are truly amazing. You had it all figured out on your chart with your first possibility."

"I know," agreed Karen, not with any smugness or self-importance but just as a matter of fact. "I was staggered when I heard Michael and Mabel talking last night and realised that I really had put it all together. But surely if we've worked it out, Bodkin will have worked it out as well."

"That Bodkin is a strange character. I think she actually quite likes you. I don't mean she fancies you. I mean that I think she senses something in you that she often has to bury beneath her detective inspector persona. Looking back on it, I think she felt that right from the beginning whereas I didn't work it out until you both appeared as Lilith and Pandora. She had her reasons for behaving as she did that morning in the Grove, I'm sure, although I still haven't worked out what they are. They probably had more to do with her than with you."

"Nonetheless, similarities aside, she still has a job to do and her performance standards are based on arrests, aren't they?"

"That's true, particularly if the arrests result in convictions. If the charges cannot be proven sufficient to a judge or jury, then the arrest becomes essentially a waste of time and money and takes a heavy toll on police resources. I'm sure that many factors play a role in determining whether or not to press charges. Without any familial or political pressure for an arrest, it's quite probable that resources will play a significant role in the decision."

"I don't want any of them to be charged. And yet a man's life is gone, his body desecrated. Where's the justice?" asked Karen.

Mary thought. "There's a lot of talk these days about restorative justice, wherein criminals meet with their victims to learn how their actions have affected the lives of their victims. I think, from what I heard last evening, that there has been a considerable amount of restorative justice occurring over the past three weeks, ever since Willie and James Anderson met." Mary stopped to take a large bite of toast generously spread with peanut butter.

"Restorative justice," mused Karen, choosing Scottish heather honey, soft and runny in the hot morning sun, for her second piece of toast. "I think I see what you mean, primarily in relation to James Anderson's moving here and learning about those whose lives had been affected by the accident. I wonder if Mabel experienced any sense of restorative justice when she met with James in the Trout and Salmon. Last night, as Reverend Potts was explaining about the proposed use of Sparrow Cottage, I thought a lot about atonement. I kept thinking that the Barton family's decision to make Sparrow Cottage available to the council as a transitional home for foster children after they turned eighteen was to atone for the terrible acts they had inflicted on James Anderson's body." She considered a moment. "Well, I mean as much as it would be possible for such an act of desecration. But building on your notion of restorative justice, I suppose you could call their plans a kind of constructive justice, making something good come out of something bad."

Karen started clearing away the dishes, taking them into the kitchen for the washing up, while Mary sipped the last of her coffee and then came indoors with her mug. "What time is the service?" she asked.

"It's at 1:00. We'd better get ready. The Crematorium is in Torquay."

***

Michael and Willie were smartly dressed in black suits, both of which, sadly, had been worn to more than one funeral of family and friends over the past few years. Tom, Dan, Rob and Andy wore the same pale pastel suits they had worn to the wedding but without the colourful cummerbunds, frilled shirts and bow ties. Sam appeared in a beige linen suit, still rumpled from his suitcase, which he had barely had the time to unpack after having arrived back from France only an hour earlier. Adele, slightly breathless from rushing, wore the same dress she had worn a week earlier to the wedding, a bright floral sundress, subdued by a smart grey silk jacket she had just purchased in Paris. Mabel wore a serene blue dress draped softly around her sturdy frame. Betty looked fresh and lovely in a loosely fitted white summer frock flecked with very tiny strawberries. Karen and Mary completed the ensemble gathered together for James Anderson's funeral, Karen hopefully proper in a navy dress with white jacket and Mary more artistically swathed in a flowing silk purple and pink abstract print. All women were hatless. And then the hat walked in, a creamy beige fedora over the hennaed head of DI Cora Bodkin. She took a seat at the back, the recorded rendition of the Pachobel Canon came to an end and Reverend Nicholas Potts took his place in the Crematorium Chapel.

Eyebrows flicking constantly up and down, the vicar smiled and nodded individually to every person in attendance. He began the service traditionally. "'I am the resurrection and the life. He who believes in me will live, even though he dies,' says the Lord." Reverend Potts looked around the chapel. "James Anderson may have lived much of his life alone and died alone but in death he seems to have acquired quite a number of friends." That brought a little smile to the assembly as several pairs of shoulders hunched in stress or sorrow or fear or guilt relaxed. "As you know, we had very little time to plan this funeral. The police released the body to us early this morning and we had no family or friends or legal instructions through his lawyer in Florida or his solicitor in Exeter to consult. According to Willie, who came to know James Anderson better than any of us during the last three weeks of his life, James was a professed atheist. This service therefore will not follow the ordinary rituals of the Church of England. My role here today is primarily to provide dignity and honour to the departure of James Gilbert Anderson from life to this next phase of existence and comfort and solace to all of you."

Karen looked at Mary, as both recalled their conversation about rituals the day of the wedding. Was it really only nine days ago? Karen's mind moved quickly to what Mary had said about rituals providing hope and solace that day. And now Reverend Potts was talking about solace and comfort. But Karen was thinking that the source of that solace and comfort was hope. Hope was paramount in the minds of everyone here today. The Barton and Mason families had together agreed to organise and pay for this service rather than subject James Anderson to the sterile disposal of his remains that would otherwise have occurred. Were they seeking the comfort of hope and solace by going through this ritual? Solace for the wrongs they had committed? Hope that they might once again find some relief from the guilt that was tarnishing their lives? And hope for a more promising future for the young adults who might benefit from their plans for James Anderson's estate? Karen's musings were interrupted as Michael rose to speak.

"Friends and family, we are gathered here to pay our respects to a man whom none of us knew well. For the past five years, many of us had, in our minds, reviled this man as the cause of the death of our loved ones. We had no idea that his sorrow for his role in those deaths was even stronger than our unexpressed but deeply felt anger. We had no idea that he had been living among us for the past several months, getting to know us far better than any of us had tried to get to know him. We had no idea that he was intending to try to make restitution in his will for our great loss. And so each of us, according to our place in the community, met and interacted with James Anderson, ignorant and innocent of that knowledge. I looked after his banking needs, Mabel provided the meat for his table, Tom kept his cottage in good repair, and Betty and Adele provided his groceries. But Willie, you were the only one of us to see into James Anderson, the man. You were the only one of us to challenge his character and then to try to understand it. You were the only one of us who cried for his loss because he would be gone from your life. He had become important in your life. When the rest of us cried over his death, whether outwardly or inwardly, those tears were for the loss of something that we had valued in ourselves. When you cried, it was because a man whom you had grown to like and respect was gone.

We have all lost something important in ourselves with the death of James Anderson and each of us knows what that is without it being spoken. Yet, in a paradox hard to believe, James Anderson has left us the ability to recapture some of what we have lost. His death, we were informed this morning when we arranged to have his remains sent here, was apparently due to his illness and not his fall." Karen and Mary, not yet having learned of the full extent of his illness, glanced quickly at each other when they heard this. "Nevertheless, according to the final forensics report released late yesterday, while his death was not caused by the impact of a wrench or the resulting fall, it was most probably precipitated by the fall. His death was unintentionally but nonetheless undeniably hastened by our trying to help a young couple enjoy a productive and happy life in our village.

We all will have to live with that knowledge for the rest of our lives. But we do not need to allow that knowledge to weigh us down. Instead, as you know, James Anderson himself has provided us with the means to make amends. To make something positive out of the loss of the four lives that have been meaningful to us in so many different ways. Since the impetus for this most recent tragedy was our desire to help two young people in our community have a good start in their adult life, we all have agreed to use his bequest to help many more young people gain a productive foothold in our community. I won't go over all the details of that because most of them still have to be worked out and we have a long path ahead of us. We may have walked in here feeling that we have little idea about how to celebrate the life of James Anderson because we knew so little about him. I say we have much to celebrate because we will become the means of honouring his memory, increasing his humane gesture to us a hundredfold by investing in the future of vulnerable young adults. You know, Reverend Nick, I think that's actually downright biblical."

Taking his cue, Reverend Potts returned to the podium. "Thank you, Michael. Yes, you're quite right. The scriptures frequently implore us to use our resources to increase the bounty of others. And yes, going forward with your plan for Sparrow Cottage will be a truly wonderful way to celebrate the life of James Anderson, not just this afternoon, but for years to come. You will help many others and in so doing you will bring unexpected joy and fulfilment to yourselves." He paused, caught Cora's eye at the back and saw the affirmation he hoped he would see. "And now the time has come to say our farewell to James Anderson as we commit his body to the hereafter, ashes to ashes, dust to dust, in the sure and certain hope of the resurrection to eternal life."

"Amen," signalled the end of the service. The deep blue velvet draperies closed around the coffin as it moved inexorably toward its final phase, accompanied by the gentle lilt of Vaughn Williams' *The Lark Ascending,* so exquisitely rendered that Karen could visualise the lark's fluttering wings and graceful arcs.

"The lark ascends as the sparrow falls," Karen mused, as she and Mary walked to their car. "I think I have the title for my novel. I'm going to call it *Fall of a Sparrow*. So much hope is implied in that simple, elegant phrase, 'There is a special providence in the fall of a sparrow.' With the generosity of the Barton family and the Masons, and, of course, James Anderson, our fallen sparrow, that special providence has the potential for so much good to happen. I'm quite intrigued by the prospect of having young people living beside us who basically are abandoned by the foster care system when they become eighteen years old and have to try to succeed on their own."

"I'm sure you would be, having spent your own early years in the foster care system. But I agree with you. I also am very interested in seeing how our little community can help to nurture these young adults' transition to independence."

"I look forward to getting to know whoever moves in there. It will take some time for it all to happen but I imagine the people who live there will have some powerful stories to tell of their experiences."

"And I wouldn't be surprised," replied Mary, "if you find yet another mystery to write about in the lives of those young people."

***

Deep in Churston Woods, a carrion crow glimpsed a speck of glimmer in the dome of a magpie nest. He swooped down to investigate and tried to tug it free. Heavier than the twigs holding it in place, the glinting object easily slid out but the crow had difficulty balancing its length and weight in his beak. He spread his wings to fly away but could not hold his newfound treasure. The brass key to Sparrow Cottage slipped from his beak down through the branches of the tree, settling momentarily on a large limb, losing its equilibrium, and falling, falling, finally to nestle among the tiny white blooms of the enchanter's nightshade carpeting the woodland, unheard and unseen.

The End